Kathleen Irene Paterka

Royal Secrets

Copyright © 2013 by *Kathleen Irene Paterka*. All rights reserved.

First Print Edition: 2013

Editor: Anne Victory

Cover: Karen Duvall

Formatting: Streetlight Graphics

ISBN-10: 098928381X

ISBN-13: 978-0-9892838-1-6

Also by
Kathleen Irene Paterka

The James Bay Novels:
Fatty Patty
Home Fires
Lotto Lucy
For I Have Sinned

Non-Fiction:
For the Love of a Castle

Dedication

To Linda Mueller
Who shares my love for all things royal

Acknowledgments

To Jenna Mindel and Christine Elizabeth Johnson. Thank you for sharing the journey with me.

To Catherine Chant, for always being there. Always.

To Terri Winnell, Claudia Guerra, and Diane Russom Harrison, my team of beta readers. Thank you for putting up with my constant barrage of questions and answering yet *just one more thing*. Your feedback was more priceless than the royal tiara.

To my amazing editor, Anne Victory, who held my hand, talked me down from throwing myself off the top of the castle, and rescued me as I dealt with a royal mess.

To Karen Duvall, for her vision and skill in designing a stunning elegant cover.

To Bob Gorkiewicz, for sharing his expertise about physical rehabilitation and stroke victims.

To Janel Colquhoun, who shed considerable insight into the left-brained world of accounting.

To Alissa Post, who shared her savvy and skills in dealing with the ins and outs of social media.

To my Castle ladies: Sarah Hagen, Johanna Alexander,

Larissa Ulrich, Jessica Anderson, Alissa Post, and Anora O'Connor. The brides love each of you and so do I!

For Stacy Heath, my original beta reader. Stacy loved books, and she loved the opening chapters of this book in particular. Unfortunately, she passed away before I had finished writing the novel. But still, I draw comfort from the knowledge that Stacy knew before any of us (including me) exactly how the story would end. God bless you, Stacy, for your friendship, encouragement and support. Your words from that one night will remain with me forever: "*You are an author. Do you know how rare and wonderful that is? Everyone at one point in their life has wanted to write a book. You actually did it!*"

To my very own dear sweet girl, Abby Paterka Carter, who had the foresight to move to Las Vegas, and then suggest, "*Mom, you should write a book about a wedding chapel.*"

And last—but always first in my heart—to my husband Steve. Only a man who truly loves his wife would rise at 3 am and endure hours of continuous live television coverage of the Royal Wedding, while sporting a gold crown atop his head. Only a man who truly loves his wife would endure her daily updates about the comings and goings of the royal family without complaints. Only a man who truly loves his wife would suffer listening to the moans and groans emanating from the office of an author giving birth to a novel, occasionally daring to comment in a panicky voice, "*Are you okay in there?*" The book is finished, sweetheart, and to answer your question: Yes, I am okay. And as long as you are at my side, I will always be okay.

"Here is the stuff of which fairytales are made..."

~ Robert Runcie, Archbishop of Canterbury, at the July 29, 1981 wedding of Prince Charles and Lady Diana Spencer

Prologue

THERE'S A REASON THEY CALL this town *Sin City*, my mother told me long ago when I questioned her about something I'd heard at school that day. But when I asked about the *secrets* part, Mimi had refused to explain. "You're much too young to hear about such things, Lily," she said and left it at that.

I wandered away, a confused eight-year-old, my head filled with even more questions. How could Las Vegas be full of sin and secrets when it was filled with so much sunshine? Growing up in this town, in the ornate, spacious villa behind Mimi's Royal Wedding Chapel near the center of the Strip, I saw the glitz and glamour. It shimmered and sparkled like the beautiful brides in their wedding gowns gracing the aisles of the chapel. Peeking around the pews, I saw their glowing faces, heard the vows exchanged, witnessed the beginnings of so many happily-ever-afters.

And then I grew up.

It took a while—around the time Mimi's third marriage, the one to Jack's father, collapsed—for me to discover the truth. Las Vegas *is* full of sin and secrets. Most of them stay in Vegas, left behind to be cleaned up by maids and blackjack dealers who sweep away the debris. Others get carried home like guilty luggage, busting up marriages and businesses and causing bankruptcy.

I'm forty years old, and that naïve little girl I used to be disappeared long ago. She learned that happily ever after is merely an illusion and that sins and secrets can weigh just as heavy on your heart as our family's heirloom tiara can weigh on your head. The dazzling crown, in the special display case behind bulletproof glass in the lobby of the Royal Wedding Chapel, gleams like the fortune it is worth. But the antique combs pinch and the diamond diadem is a burden. How my grandmother managed to keep the jewel-encrusted crown on her head when presented to the Queen is the stuff of which family legends are made. With my grandfather descended from British nobility and in distant line for the throne, the tiara is a priceless treasure, proof of our family's heritage.

As far as I'm concerned, though, that tiara is exactly where it belongs: safely behind glass, viewed from a distance. It glitters and sparkles, but the pain isn't worth it. Dare to wear it, as I did once, and—just like the secrets hidden in Sin City—the pain and guilt will tear you down. I'm lucky I managed to yank it off in time.

And I refuse to allow that tiara to ruin my daughter's life the way it almost ruined mine.

Chapter One

"AS USUAL, LILY, YOU ARE overreacting. Tori is fine. She's here, and perfectly safe with us. Why do you see this as such a problem?"

I bite my tongue and count to five before saying something I'll only regret. My mother stockpiles emotions like a professional arms dealer. The less ammunition I provide, the better the chances we'll survive this war of words. "Tori needs to learn that she can't just run off whenever she feels like it."

"She didn't run off." Mimi's voice marches over the phone. "She drove."

My stomach twists. As usual, Mimi is twisting my words. We're supposed to love our mothers... and I do. It's just that sometimes—more often than not—she drives me crazy. I pace my living room, halting before the floor-to-ceiling windows, and stare out into the gathering dusk. The ocean is a calm, mirrored sea. Far off in the distance, the twinkling lights of San Diego dot the darkening landscape. For the life of me, I can't understand how Tori could turn her back on the beauty of the California coast for the harsh glare thrown off by the lights of Las Vegas.

I gather a deep breath and force myself to turn away from the view I've come to love. "Put yourself in my place. How would you feel if you got a call from your teenage daughter's school and discovered that she'd ditched her classes? That she'd taken off for Las Vegas? That she'd driven across the mountains and crossed the desert, alone in her car—which, by the way, I totally did not agree with Jack and Ed giving her in the first place."

Jack and his father had never even asked me before surprising her with that car. "For God's sake, Mimi, she doesn't even have a driver's license yet. Anything could have happened."

"But it didn't."

"But it could have." My voice shakes as my mind once again starts considering the possibilities. Tori running off the road and crashing down the mountainside. Having a flat tire in the middle of the desert. A group of guys out cruising for a good time and coming upon my daughter.

I shudder and push the thoughts away. "I'm sure if it had been me, you would feel the same."

"Don't be ridiculous. You, behind the wheel of a car? You hate driving. Besides, you grew up in Las Vegas. Why on earth would you drive somewhere you already lived? And for that matter, I will never understand why you decided to leave. Everything a person could want is here in this town."

Not true. I don't want Mimi breathing down my neck.

"It is time you faced facts, Lily. My granddaughter has moxie you'll never have, which she showed by walking out of class."

I tamp down my frustration. Much as I hate to admit it, Mimi is right. Tori and I are nothing alike. Never in a million years would I have dreamed of cutting school or taking off alone in a car before I had my license. Even then, I never would have climbed behind the wheel to drive those mountain curves, let alone cross the long dry stretch of desert highway before hitting the outskirts of Las Vegas.

"She didn't walk out. She never showed up."

"That is beside the point," she brushes off my protest. "Tori has a soul for adventure. Celebrate her for the free spirit she is and give the child a little credit."

Which is exactly what Tori is... *a child*. At least for another four months, until she turns eighteen. A vision from late last night flashes to mind. Tori, sprawled on her bed, iPod buds dangling from her ears, texting madly as I stopped in to say good night. Her bedroom is a scattered mess of clothes, shoes, and jewelry. She is just a child; a seventeen-year-old-woman-in-waiting who believes she's all grown up.

Hands off. That's been her motto the past few years. But it's hard for any mother—especially a single mom—to maintain a distance. Sometimes, not often, I find myself wondering if things would have been easier with her dad at my side. Then I push away the thought. I don't need a man. Especially not *that* man. And for now, Tori is still underage and still my responsibility, regardless whether she—or Mimi—likes it or not.

"Put her on the phone. I want to talk to her. She hasn't been answering her cell, and she hasn't responded to my texts."

Mimi hesitates. "I think she might have gone to bed," she finally says.

And I think not. Tori's always been a nighttime person. Plus, she's in Las Vegas, the city that never sleeps.

"She isn't there, is she?" I take a wild guess, though I don't need my suspicions confirmed. I have a very good idea exactly where my daughter is.

"Are you calling me a liar?"

Choose your battles wisely, Ed always told me, and I know I've lost this one. Mimi will lie, steal, and cheat when it comes to protecting those she loves. Tori shot to the top of her grandmother's list the day she was born.

"Never mind," I say. "I already booked my flight. It arrives at eleven tonight. Could you have someone pick me up at the airport?"

"You're determined to spoil her little vacation, aren't you?" Mimi's voice bristles.

"She isn't on vacation, she's in summer school. Tori signed up for those courses—"

"Under protest. Don't try to pretend you didn't force her into it. She told me all about it."

I push away the frustration and heaviness of two generations conspiring against me. "Will someone be there at the airport for me or should I call a cab?"

"I'll send Jaabir with the car. But you are making a big mistake, Lily. Don't say I didn't warn you. You are much too hard on that child. Tori is a smart young woman, and I don't understand why you insist she sit through classes in the summertime. Chemistry and physics have nothing to do with the real world."

"Tori needs those courses to get into college. A good

college." That will be her ticket out, just like it was mine.

"Maybe she doesn't want to go to college. Have you considered that? Not everyone is college material."

"She is going to college." But not in California or Nevada, either. I didn't have the courage to put up a fight when Mimi insisted I stay home and attend the University of Nevada in Las Vegas. But I am determined that will not happen to my daughter. I want Tori in a college someplace far from here and far away from Mimi. My daughter is vivacious, charming, and exceedingly bright, but she's also stubborn and headstrong, exactly like her grandmother. A college out East would be best. Her SAT and ACT scores this spring were high. Enrolling her in summer school for advanced placement courses gives her a heads up on her senior year. She can do it if she tries. Tori could have the world, if she'd only make the effort.

But after the little escapade she pulled today, I have a sinking feeling she won't be inclined to apply herself.

I know what Tori wants. I've always known. She fell in love with all things royal—the family tiara and the family business—on her second birthday. That was the day Mimi plucked our family's treasured tiara from its velvet pillow behind glass in the Royal Wedding Chapel and placed it on my daughter's blond curls. I should have stopped her. I should have yanked the tiara off her head before it was too late. But just like my grandmother Lillian when presented to the Queen, Tori managed to keep it on her head.

That day was the beginning. Her happy cooing and delighted clapping left Mimi thrilled and me appalled. I should have known being pronounced a real-life princess, descended from British royalty, would inspire her dreams.

But the last thing I want is Tori's life ruined by Mimi's world of happily-ever-after nonsense. Mimi would have her believe that life can be perfect, that weddings are the end-all-and-be-all, and the Royal Wedding Chapel is the only game in town.

But while Tori is nearly an adult, she still has a little girl's dreams. And what my daughter doesn't realize is that her dreams aren't her own.

They belong to Mimi.

Half an hour later, I stumble out the door, lugging my suitcase and laptop. The air is sweet with the scent of flowers hanging in the night breeze and the tangy ocean air blowing in across the beaches of Del Mar, not more than a half mile from our cozy two-bedroom house. It's Friday night, and rush-hour traffic is against me as I wind my way down the highway into downtown San Diego and the airport.

Parking at Lindbergh Field is crowded with people headed out for the weekend. Travelers snake their way through the maze of ropes cordoning off different areas. I make my way through security and pop two Dramamine as I board the jet. My nerves are already jangled from me thinking about Tori. How could she have left? Why did she do it? What am I going to say to her? I dread another Mother-when-are-you-going-to-learn-that-I'm-growing-up conversation. The jet rumbles down the runway with me white-knuckling it as we lift off and head out over the Pacific, due west. Finally the jet makes a hard bank and we make the turn. My Dramamine kicks in as we climb through the night, high above the mountains. Somewhere due east, in the vast arid nothingness below, Las Vegas awaits.

The flight doesn't take long. I straighten in my seat as the jet begins its final approach. The glow from the Vegas Strip lights up the night sky, and I catch a glimpse of the famous landscape, punctuated by Luxor's sky beam and the shimmering green of the MGM Grand, the gaudy Rio, the palatial Bellagio. My stomach sinks as I spot the sprawling brilliance of Caesar's Palace, where one night long ago, a dream danced with decadence and nearly destroyed my life.

My fingers grip the armrests as we drop from the sky. I wait in my seat as the jet quickly empties out. Flying into Vegas is always the same. Everyone looks forward to hitting the town, hitting the casinos, hitting it big. But unlike everyone else, I'm in no rush. I am not looking forward to confronting Tori, arguing with Mimi, or seeing Jack.

Damn it. I am going to wring that man's neck if I find out Tori let him know she was on her way. The least he could have done was call and tell me. I've texted him twice and he's not responding.

The noisy chime of slot machines greets me as I head across the half-empty baggage claim area toward the luggage carousel, only to just miss my suitcase. Too tired to chase it, I watch it make another lazy foray around the track, circling its way back to me.

A man pushes forward and makes an easy grab for it.

"That's my..." I sputter to a stop as I catch sight of muscular arms, flashing black eyes, and a swarthy face heavy with a ten o'clock stubble. A familiar face. A friendly face.

Jaabir grins. "Hitting the Dramamine again, Lily?"

Laughing lightly, I give him a quick hug. "What can I say? I hate flying."

"You're on the ground now, girl. Here, I'll take that." He points to my laptop, which I willingly surrender. Mimi's chauffeur and chapel handyman has strong arms, beautiful olive skin, and one of the biggest hearts I know. Born and raised in Detroit by parents who emigrated from Iran, Jaabir is a first-generation American who thrives on capitalism as well as sunshine. Five years ago, he decided he'd had enough with the snow and headed for Las Vegas. As far as I'm concerned, one of the smartest business decisions Mimi ever made was to hire him on the spot when he showed up at the Royal Wedding Chapel in search of a job.

Jaabir scans the luggage carousel. "Just the one suitcase?"

"Traveling light," I say. "Have you been waiting long?"

"I just finished my last run when Mimi called and said that you were flying in and I should pick you up. I decided to head over here to the airport rather than go back and face the Queen Mum's wrath."

"Is she that upset?" I know convincing Tori to come back home won't be easy, but Mimi can be a fierce adversary. If the two of them have joined forces, I'll need every resource I can muster.

Jaabir's face spreads in an easy smile. "Come on, the car's just outside the door."

"You left the limo in the parking lane? What about security?" I struggle to keep up as he strides through the baggage area and heads for the exit. "Aren't you afraid they'll tow it?"

"Do you actually believe anyone would dare tow Mimi's car?" He throws back his head with a deep throaty laugh and points out the chapel's gleaming white limo waiting at the curb behind a long line of taxis.

The wind and heat hit my face as the door whooshes shut behind us. It feels like walking into a hair dryer turned on full blast. It's nearly midnight, but the temperature must still be hovering in the nineties. By noon tomorrow, it could well be 115. Las Vegas, especially in the summer, isn't any place a sane person would choose to live. Then again, I've always wondered about Mimi's mental health.

My luggage safely stowed in the back and me riding shotgun, Jaabir pulls away from the curb. Palm trees line the road as we head for the Strip.

"It's good to have you back home. We miss you, Lily."

I throw him a fast smile. "I miss you all, too." Just a little white lie. I don't miss Mimi's nagging.

"How long are you staying?"

"Just for the weekend. Tori and I will drive back Sunday. I have work, and she has school."

"Ah, yes." He inches the limo out of heavy traffic and pulls onto a side street, picking up speed as he drives parallel to the Strip, headed in the direction of downtown. "The little teenage renegade."

"She knows better than to pull a stunt like she did today." I settle back in my seat. The lights of Las Vegas fly by in a blur as the traffic lightens. "Tori agreed to sign up for summer classes. She needs to finish what she starts. She needs to learn that you can't run away from things."

"School is important." Jaabir nods, scratches his chin. "You're a good mom, Lily. The two of you will work things out."

"I hope so." I've never been good at confrontations, and I'm not looking forward to the one looming with my daughter—especially if she's enlisted Mimi in the fight. I glance at Jaabir; his hands are steady on the wheel, eyes focused on the road. He's been taking night courses toward his college degree and he understands the importance of a good education. Maybe he could help me talk some sense into Tori. She loves Jaabir. He's always treated her like one of his little sisters, and she gobbles up his attention the way I would have if he'd worked at the chapel while I was growing up.

"Maybe you could talk to her," I suggest. "Tori always listens to what you say."

"And face the wrath of Mimi?" He flashes me a quick grin. "Thanks, but no thanks. I don't have my degree yet. I need this job."

The limo rounds a corner, flies across an intersection, and swings through the chapel's gates into the cobblestone entrance of the place I called home for so many years.

I climb out and glance around as Jaabir unloads my luggage. As usual, the chapel's entrance is lit brighter than Buckingham Palace. Behind the Queen Victoria Chapel Court Garden with its outdoor wedding gazebo, Mimi's villa is ablaze with lights. Everything looks the same... but not. The back of my neck prickles, and I lift my hair, knotting it in a high ponytail. Something doesn't feel right. But it isn't the heat or the wind blowing off Sahara Avenue that touches off the eerie sense inside me that something is wrong.

Why is the courtyard separating the chapel from the house so dark and quiet?

And why is Francesca hurrying across the cobblestones, wringing her hands?

"Thank God you're home." She envelopes me in a tight hug. A plump little woman who's served Mimi forever as cohort, colleague, and confidant, Francesca seems strangely unhinged. "I thought you would never get here."

Jaabir rolls my suitcase around the car. "What's wrong?"

"It's Mimi." Francesca pulls away. Her eyes are puffy and red, as if she's been crying. "She tripped and fell on the steps going into the courtyard."

"She fell?" My pulse quickens as I glance toward the villa. Mimi's bedroom window is glowing. "Is she all right? Is Tori with her?"

Francesca's hands flutter around her neck, like butterflies adrift in the desert breeze. "No, Tori is with Jack and Ed. And Mimi is gone. They took her away."

"Who took her? Jack and Ed?" I ask.

"No, the ambulance crew."

"Ambulance?" Jaabir stumbles on the cobblestone and catches himself on the hood of the limo. "Mimi's in the hospital?"

Francesca nods. Her nose is red and her thinning auburn hair, in its usual bun, has started to unravel. Wisps of hair fly around her head like tiny red wasps. "They left about fifteen minutes ago. At first I thought I would go with her, but then I decided I should wait for you."

Fresh tears well in her eyes. "I think she broke her hip. It all happened so fast. Mimi was in terrible pain. She kept moaning and trying to get back on her feet, but she couldn't, even with my help. When I told her I was going to call 911, she started swearing. I knew she was furious with me, but I didn't have a choice. I ran back to the house and made the call."

"You did the right thing, Francesca." I manage to choke out the words, though my mouth feels like it's full of cardboard and my heart is pounding in my chest. "You couldn't just let her lay there on the sidewalk."

She shakes her head. "No, you don't understand. Mimi wanted me to fetch her some clothes and fix her hair before I called 911. But I told her that she looked very pretty, and that the doctors would understand. She was wearing the bathrobe you gave her for Christmas. So elegant, and such a beautiful rich silk."

Suddenly I am furious. Even during a crisis, Mimi is her normal pretentious, arrogant self. The woman never gives a thought to anyone save herself. And I am immensely sorry for Francesca, standing before me in a mismatched pair of slacks and top. Any other evening, she would be immaculately dressed. She always takes her cues from Mimi. The two of them have been together for nearly forty years, working to build the Royal Wedding Chapel into the elegant bridal business it is today. Mimi even invited Francesca to live in the villa after Husband Number Two died, granting her a small private wing just behind the chapel's courtyard. Francesca is like one of the family. Thank God she was here tonight when Mimi needed help.

I push away the growing guilt that I wasn't.

Jaabir guides Francesca into the back of the limo. I climb in beside her, sinking down into rich white leather, smooth and soft as buttercream frosting on a wedding cake.

"All day, I had the strangest feeling that something was going to happen," Francesca says. "Mimi was acting odd even before she fell." She hesitates, then smiles for the first time. "Though she did calm down when the ambulance crew arrived."

No doubt. Either they gave her some nice narcotics to dull the pain, or the emergency crew consisted of attractive young men. Mimi's appreciation for the sight of a good-looking man hasn't dimmed in the least just because she's a grandmother and eligible for Social Security benefits.

"It all started with that man who showed up this morning without a bride and without an appointment," Francesca continues as Jaabir guides the limo out of the parking lot. "He and Mimi were shut up in her office for more than an hour. He threw off our entire schedule. Then Tori unexpectedly showed up in the middle of a ceremony. Then you called, Lily," she says, turning to me, "to announce you're flying in tonight and taking Tori home. Oh, I've never seen Mimi so mad. All hell broke loose after your phone call."

I sit in silence, my thoughts whirling. It's not difficult to imagine Mimi ranting and raving about anything—or anyone—who dares to counter her well-laid plans. The Queen Mum expects *noblesse oblige* from her entire entourage of family and friends. Those who do not curry the royal favor face the threat of losing the Queen's approval and being banished from court. I'm familiar with the position. I've held it for years.

"And she had the most horrendous headache after dinner," Francesca adds. "I remember thinking how odd it was. Mimi never has headaches." She draws a deep breath. "But she couldn't calm down, even after she had a nice warm bath and dressed for bed. Then I made us both a cup of tea, a nice Earl Grey, her favorite. That seemed to revive her spirits. We were in the kitchen, drinking tea, waiting for Jaabir to bring you home from the airport, and we started chatting about the weddings scheduled for tomorrow. That's when Mimi decided to run over to her office for one last check.

"I tried to talk her out of it, but you know your mother. She never listens. Not that I blame her. One of the brides has been phoning for weeks. I tell you, Lily, that girl has been a nightmare. First she switched rooms, then she switched flowers. But with Tori here and you on your way, Mimi wanted to make sure everything was in place. She wouldn't even finish her tea. I could tell she was in one of those moods, so I told her to go and that I would tidy up. But just as I reached the sink, I heard a sound like a muffled cry, and then a crash.

"Oh, Lily, it was horrible." She cringes, remembering. "I didn't know what to think. I thought maybe someone had been hiding in the courtyard and Mimi had been attacked. But when I got to the door, I found her lying at the bottom of the steps with the flower pot smashed in pieces around her. She was very groggy. She couldn't tell me what had happened. The only thing I can think is that she missed the first step. But I still don't understand why she didn't flip the floodlights. The courtyard is dark, even during a full moon. Then again, electricity costs money and lately Mimi keeps harping on how we need to be more conservative and trim costs. Maybe that's why she didn't use the floodlights."

"She didn't because she couldn't," Jaabir says from behind the wheel, his face darkening in a deep scowl. "I cut the power in the courtyard this afternoon. She asked me to switch out the lights for energy-efficient ones, but I didn't have time to finish."

He smacks the palm of his hand against the steering wheel. "Why is she always in such a hurry? She knew the courtyard would be dark. Why couldn't she wait?"

"You know Mimi," I say. "The word *wait* isn't in her vocabulary."

"I know it's her hip," Francesca frets. "By the time the ambulance got here, she was in such pain she couldn't even talk. My cousin fell and broke her hip last spring. She spent nearly three months doing rehab in a nursing home. What if that's what happened to Mimi? Neither of us is getting any younger. I'll be seventy next spring and Mimi isn't far behind me."

My heart sinks. As if I need a reminder. Time marches on, even for the Queen Mum. Is tonight the beginning of a future filled with fragile bones, cataracts, hearing aids, and liver spots? Mimi has always been all business, but I cannot visualize her as one of those women who successfully manages to embrace the business of aging gracefully.

"I bet when we get to the hospital, we'll find her sitting up in bed, swearing up a storm, and driving the nurses crazy," I say. "You know how dramatic Mimi is. She's never been one to suffer in silence. This could simply be a sprained ankle."

"No, it's more than that," Francesca says, fingering away some fresh tears. "The EMTs wouldn't say much, but I know they were concerned. Why else would they be in such a hurry?"

"This is my fault," Jaabir mumbles from behind the wheel. "I should have known she'd do something like this. I should have flipped the power back on."

"Quit blaming yourself. This is *not* your fault. Both of you need to calm down."

Keep calm and carry on. That's what the English people were told during World War II. Too bad Mimi never embraced that as her motto. Perhaps if she had, she would have stayed in the kitchen with Francesca, finished her tea, and none of this would have happened. Plus, Mimi wasn't even born until after WWII. She didn't visit London until the late 60s while on a whirlwind backpacking trip through Europe. It was during the height of flower power and free love that she met my father, Lawrence Lavender, Husband Number One. He swept her off her feet and within a matter of days convinced her to marry him. Always one to do exactly as she pleased, she quickly accepted and lived in England for nearly a year... until the fatal car accident that robbed a pregnant Mimi of her husband and me of the father I would never know. Then, in true Mimi fashion, she picked up the pieces and left the country that is half my heritage, never looking back, never to return.

"And what about tomorrow?" Francesca says. "We have two weddings booked."

"Only two? But tomorrow is Saturday." When I was growing up, Saturdays meant a whirlwind of weddings. The chapel is open throughout the week, but Saturday still remains the day most brides choose to be married.

"Things have been slow lately," she says. "I've told

Mimi we should advertise more, maybe update our website. But she refuses. She says the chapel is doing fine and that we will carry on with business as usual." Her voice drops. "But I think she's wrong. Things aren't fine."

Only two brides on a Saturday in June? I don't think things are fine, either.

"The other chapels in town don't seem to have a problem," she continues. "Then again, their websites are nicer than ours. Or maybe it's because they have a younger staff. Of course, we still have our reputation, which brings in some business, and we still get phone calls. But so many of the brides I talk to on the phone end up not booking. And some of those girls are so rude; they hang up without bothering to say thank you or good-bye." She bites her lip. "I try not to take it personally, but I feel bad for Mimi. The chapel is her life, and she's losing business. Girls are still getting married, but they're not getting married at Mimi's chapel."

The Royal Wedding Chapel has been a fixture in the Vegas community for decades, and its reputation for elegance and opulence has served Mimi and the business well. When I was in my mid-teens, she recruited me every weekend. Forced to man the reception desk, I answered the phones and worked with the walk-ins while she and Francesca handled the ceremonies. But once I started college, Ed stepped in and pled my case, and for whatever reason, Mimi listened. Thus ended my career in the family wedding business.

I'm still not sure why she allowed me to step aside. Even after Ed moved out and they divorced, she never pressed me back into service. Nowadays, Jaabir chauffeurs bridal couples to and from their hotels in the stretch limo while Francesca runs the music and Mimi officiates at each ceremony.

And if my mother gets her way, she'll have Tori behind the reception counter, working the phones, handling the appointments, and serving as a licensed minister as soon as she reaches legal age.

"What about Tori?" I ask as the limo speeds along the side streets. "Does she know about Mimi?"

Francesca nods. "I phoned after the ambulance left. She's probably already at the hospital."

Tori and who else? The mere thought of Jack being with her starts a slow burn simmering in my stomach. Hopefully Ed had the sense to accompany them or we could be facing fireworks in the waiting room. I love Ed, and I'm always glad to see him, but his son Jack is a different story.

"I suppose we'll have no choice but to call in a substitute minister." Francesca pauses, worry clouding her eyes. "I hope we'll be able to find someone. And what if Mimi isn't well enough to do the weddings next week?" Her face is in another free fall. "What if—"

"What if you quit worrying about things?" The last thing I need is Francesca worrying herself sick over minor details. "Everything will work out."

She tsks-tsks her way out of silence. "Mimi will hate paying the extra money for a substitute minister, but I suppose it can't be helped. This is an emergency."

"Mimi will understand." And if she doesn't, I'll make sure she does. When you're in the bridal business, the first rule of order is to make sure emergencies are covered by a backup plan. Las Vegas means brides—all kinds of brides.

Plain or gorgeous, sweet or demanding, drunk or sober, when a bride and her groom show up at the Royal Wedding Chapel, they expect a minister on site who will be able to marry them. The bridal business can be messy, but you don't mess with brides. A bride in meltdown-mode is not a pretty sight.

"Tomorrow's weddings will go smoothly," I assure her. "Wait and see."

She squeezes my hand. "I can't imagine what we would do without you. You are such a blessing."

Poor Francesca. She has no clue. Things are calm for now, but the *who-what-when-where-and-how* we'll get through tomorrow's weddings is beyond me. We can't cancel the bookings, and I'm not licensed to conduct the ceremonies. Mimi tried every trick in the book when I turned eighteen to get me to apply for a certified officiate's license. *Just in case*, she insisted, but I wouldn't budge.

I still don't think I would have had the courage to stand up to Mimi if it hadn't been for Ed. His advice to follow my heart and get out of the wedding business paid off with me graduating *summa cum laude* with a degree in finance. I was recruited straight out of university into their corporate training program by the international casket company I'm still with today.

Coffins? Funeral parlors? Mimi accuses me of mocking her happily-ever-after business by having allowed myself to be hired into the *death business*. But I'm happy where I am. I'm head of my department and successful at what I do. I've always preferred dealing with numbers; you can trust them. Unlike people, they don't cheat, steal or lie.

There's a good reason I've never been married. I'm

the last person who should stand before two people, urge them to join hands, and pronounce them husband and wife. Let someone else handle the happily-ever-after nonsense. As for the Royal Wedding Chapel, it's Mimi's passion, Francesca's paycheck, and—if Mimi gets her way—Tori's inheritance. But the last thing I want is Tori making the same mistakes I did. I love Ed bunches, but hanging around Mimi too long can break your heart.

So can hanging around Jack.

Chapter Two

THE HOSPITAL IS A BRICK oasis in the dark desert heat. A burly security guard stands sentry inside as Jaabir pushes his way through the crowded waiting room with Francesca and me close behind. There's a line at the counter, and the man in front of us reeks of sweat, urine, and stale booze. Las Vegas. Love it or leave it. Thank God I left.

Francesca edges close and I grab her hand, squeezing hard. When it's finally our turn, I step up to the counter and stoop toward the speaker embedded in the glass wall.

"We're looking for my mother, Mimi Alexander," I tell the woman behind the glass. "They brought her in by ambulance."

"At least an hour ago." Francesca nudges me.

"She fell at home," I add. "It might be her ankle."

"I still think it's her hip," Francesca hisses in my ear.

"What was that name again?" the woman asks, not bothering to glance up.

"Mimi Alexander." I rub away my growing headache with the palm of my hand. Today's events are beginning to catch up with me. The digital clock on the wall glows red, confirming my body clock's insistence that it is long past midnight. A brand new day, and I still haven't talked to Tori or located Mimi.

"There's no one here with that name," the woman finally says.

"I don't understand. This is the closest hospital to the villa," Jaabir mutters at my side. "Where would they take her?"

"I'm sure it was this hospital," Francesca says. "The EMS crew told me it would be this hospital."

"Try searching under the name *Elizabeth Alexander*," I tell the woman. Though her legal name is Elizabeth, my mother insisted we all address her by the nickname of Mimi when Tori was a toddler and babbled the word *Grandma*.

The woman checks her computer again, then finally glances up at me. "You said you're her daughter?"

Suddenly I wish she hadn't made eye contact. The odd look on her face has my heart pounding and my stomach beginning a slow uneasy slide into the world of *what-if*. What if Francesca was right? What if this is more than merely a sprained ankle? What if Mimi did break her hip?

"Yes, that's right." Somehow I manage to wrap my tongue around the words. "She's my mother."

"They brought her in a while ago. She's already upstairs."

"They must be doing x rays," Francesca guesses.

"Should we wait down here or go upstairs?" Personally, I would prefer escaping out the door into the hot night, but Francesca has a death grip on my arm, and Jaabir is blocking the way. I can't desert them. And even if I wanted to, my legs wouldn't cooperate. They feel like two spongy

36

rubber bands, and I don't trust them to obey me. I wouldn't make it past the first row of chairs.

"She's upstairs on the fifth floor. Take the elevator at the end of the hall." The woman stands and unlocks the window. Sliding it open, she grabs my wrist and affixes a plastic orange band. "Visiting hours ended at eight, so you'll need to wear this. It will allow you upstairs."

I blink at the gaudy wristband. "We'll need two more, please."

"Only family members are allowed upstairs after hours."

"You go upstairs, Lily. Francesca and I can wait down here." Jaabir's voice is calm and his words reassuring, but they only serve to strengthen my resolve. The three of us aren't related by blood, but that doesn't mean we aren't a family. And right now, there is no one I want more at my side than Francesca and Jaabir. They love Mimi, too.

"Two more wristbands," I tell the woman in a firm voice that sounds eerily like Mimi's own. "They *are* family."

Her eyebrow lift as she shifts her focus first to Jaabir's swarthy face, then back to me. Then, as if she decided it's better not to fight the inevitable, she nods and grabs two more wristbands. She hands them through the window. "I'll phone upstairs and let them know to expect you. Check in at the nurse's desk. The unit has a private waiting room."

Since when do orthopedic patients require private waiting rooms? "You said she's on the fifth floor. Is that where she's having x rays?"

For the first time since I stepped up to her window, the woman looks at me—truly looks at me—like I am a person with wants and needs, and perhaps what I am in need of most is some compassion. "The fifth floor," she repeats more slowly and gently. "That's where our Stroke Unit is located."

Mimi's had a stroke. The thought sinks to the bottom of my stomach as the elevator doors close. Jaabir's dark face is drained of color. Francesca weeps openly, but I'm too stunned to cry. The three of us hold hands, connected by our gaudy orange wristbands and unspoken fears.

"She'll be fine," I assure them, though my mouth is pronouncing truths I have no business uttering. What do I know about strokes? Nothing. For that matter, what do I know about what's happened? Or could happen? I sink back against the cold steel of the elevator wall, my brain running on automatic as I remember the story making the rounds in our company a few years ago about a man from another division who had suffered a stroke. Some years younger than me, he woke one morning only to have a blood vessel suddenly burst in his brain. They rushed him to the hospital, where he spent days recovering in the Stroke Unit as they waited for his body to heal enough for surgery. People who visited him came back telling hushed stories of how his face sagged, how he couldn't talk, how he drooled constantly.

I sag further against the elevator as my brain goes into overdrive with a mental image of Mimi, spit dribbling down the front of her silk dressing gown. God help her.

God help us all.

I push away the rest of the story and what happened to the man. How, a few weeks after the stroke, he had the corrective surgery to stop the flow of bleeding in his brain.

But he didn't make it through the surgery. Our company provided his family with a casket for his funeral. One of our best sellers, top of the line.

A shudder runs through me as the elevator doors open and I stare out at the looming reality of the hospital's Stroke Unit. For all I know, Mimi might already be dead. And while it's true that my mother and I have always had our issues, the thought of picking out her coffin nearly brings me to my knees. How could I do it? My ears are buzzing and my stomach does a lazy roll into nausea. I stagger backward against the cold metal wall.

"Whoa, there. Steady on your feet."

The words float toward me, emerging from out of a fog as someone slips an arm around me. "Deep breaths, Lily." Jaabir's eyes are dark and watchful. "Long, deep breaths."

My chest is tight and heavy and it's difficult to breathe. Am I having a panic attack, reacting to the news about Mimi, or could I be having a heart attack? The irony isn't lost on me. No matter what's wrong, at least I'm in the right place. The thought that I can make a joke out of something so morbid puts the hint of a smile on my face. Somehow I manage to drag in a slow breath, then another, and another.

"That's right," Jaabir encourages me. "You're doing fine, girl."

By the fifth breath, my head is clear and the ringing in my ears has nearly disappeared. I feel the color flooding back into my cheeks. "Thanks. I'm okay."

He watches me another moment, like he's trying to decide if he should believe me. Finally he nods and releases his hold on me. "All right, ladies. Follow me," he says, striding out of the elevator.

Linking arms with Francesca, we follow Jaabir through sterile, empty corridors. Finally we reach a long low counter where a lone nurse sits behind a bank of computers. I halt, holding Francesca back, as Jaabir approaches the counter. I'm not sure I'm ready to hear what the nurse has to say. Jaabir, however, has other ideas. He holds up his wrist and flashes the orange band as if it were an official pass into Buckingham Palace to see the queen. "Elizabeth Alexander. They told us she was up here."

The nurse eyes us for a moment. I'm sure we look a sight. Francesca, with her mismatched clothes and tear-stained face; Jaabir, with his swarthy features and no-nonsense tone; me, with what must be a *Stroke?-You-have-got-to-be-kidding-me-because-there's-no-way-in-hell-Mimi-would-ever-allow-this-to-happen-to-her* expression frozen on my face.

"We're her family." Stepping forward, I manage to croak the words. "I'm her daughter."

The nurse nods. "She'll be in Room 527 once they finish with her CT scan. It shouldn't be much longer. The waiting room is halfway down the hall to your left." She points with one hand. "The rest of your family is already down there."

An unpleasant tightness flutters in my chest. *The rest of our family?* They have every right to be here. They love Mimi, too. Well, maybe not Ed; he and Mimi have been divorced now for nearly twenty years. But his son Jack is a different story. Jack's always had a soft spot for Mimi. As for Tori, Mimi is her grandmother, and their love for each other is something fierce. Tori must be in agony over what's happened tonight. Hopefully she isn't blaming herself.

Hopefully she isn't blaming me.

Jaabir leads us down the hall and through the door of the waiting room. The lights are off, save for a dim lamp in one corner, which provides enough light for us to maneuver the room. For a hospital, it is spacious, and filled with all the comforts of home: flat screen TV; piles of magazines; big, cushy recliners. Ed lays prone in one of them, feet up, eyes closed, snoring softly. Off in the shadows next to his chair is a long, plush couch where two figures rest close together. One sits upright, his arm draped around the slumbering shadow at his side. He straightens as we enter the room. Our eyes lock in silent communication.

Is she okay?

She is. She will be.

Jack gently nudges the girl slumped against him. "Tori? Wake up, angel. Your mom is here."

Ed rouses, but before he is fully awake, Tori scrambles off the couch and into my arms. My heart clutches as I catch a glimpse of blond hair, blue eyes, and that familiar heart-shaped face. My daughter has always been a beauty, and most days I don't even notice. But tonight is different. Tonight, it's like holding a seventeen-year-old version of Mimi in my arms.

"Mimi had a stroke," she cries. "Oh, Mom, what if she—"

"Hush. Hush now." I stroke her hair and hold her tight, crushing the *what if* hanging between us, and all the other things that need to be said: Tori ditching school, taking off without permission, driving alone through the mountains

41

and desert. But now is not the time. "Mimi will be fine. She'll get through this. We'll get through this."

"Your mom is right." Jack joins us in the middle of the room and rubs Tori's back in long, comforting strokes. I mouth a silent *Thank You* over her head. Jack Alexander can be one of the most overbearing, inconsiderate, selfish men in the world, but for once, I'm glad he's around. Our fingers slide together, and a tangible snap of energy surges between us. I yank my hand away at the unexpected contact. Did he do it on purpose? Jack is a sharp attorney, excellent at searching out a person's vulnerable spots, but I learned my lesson long ago.

Fool me once, shame on you. Fool me twice, shame on me.

I'm not about to make that mistake again.

"Lily, sweetheart, how ya doing?" Ed wraps his arms around me and hugs me tight. His faded blue eyes hold kindness and compassion

I sink against him, breathe in the familiar scent of tobacco, bourbon whiskey, and the same aftershave he's worn since he and Mimi were married. Comforting smells from my childhood. Thank God some things never change. Of all Mimi's husbands, Ed is the closest I came to claiming a father-daughter connection. He was always there for me when I was growing up. He's always been there. And though he and Mimi have been divorced for years, he is here tonight.

How I love this man. Life would be so different if my mother still loved him, too.

"Any news?" I scan Ed's face, then turn to Jack. One of them must know something.

"I haven't been here long." Jack runs a hand across his jaw. Dark, heavy stubble covers his face. Thick, unruly brown curls tinged with gray brush the top of his crisp white shirt. Except for the fact he's not wearing a jacket or tie, he looks like he could have come straight from court. That, or a late-night rendezvous with some young woman from his current stable of girlfriends.

"Tori was over at our place. The two of us drove over here after Francesca called," Ed says.

"What did the doctor say?" I ask.

He shakes his head. "We haven't seen the doctor yet. The nurse told us to wait in here. She said someone would be in to talk to us after they finished the MRI."

Francesca sinks onto the couch, landing with a soft *oomph*. "A few days ago, Mimi complained about her vision being blurry. I told her she should call the doctor and have her eyes checked, but you know Mimi. Just the thought of wearing glasses was enough to set her off." Her face crumples in worry. "I should have insisted she call the doctor right away. I knew she was upset about her eyes, but it was more than that. She didn't look or sound right. Even her speech was slurred, though she only had one glass of wine that night. Then she went to bed early, and the next day she seemed fine.

"But it's not fine now." She dabs at fresh tears starting down her cheeks. "I should have known something was wrong. I should have known all this worrying would only make things worse. I should have—"

"Stop that." Jack hustles to her side and drapes an arm around her. "For now, let's stick with the facts. No matter what happens, remember one thing: you were the one who saved her life. You made the call to 911. You made sure she got to the hospital. So, no more of this *should have* business. You did what you could and this isn't your fault. It isn't Mimi's fault, either. Sometimes things just happen."

"And this is one of those times?" Francesca's voice wavers.

"That's right, dear." Jack thumbs her cheek dry, then plants a kiss on it. "And remember, you're not alone. We're all here with you: me, Pop, Tori, and Lily."

For the second time tonight, I find myself grateful that Jack is around. Just like his dad, he's the kind of man who takes charge and makes sure everything runs smoothly. I was only ten years old and Jack was already in college, planning on law school, when Ed and Mimi married. And though his father and my mother have been divorced for years, Jack remains devoted to some special ladies in his life. Francesca, I can understand; who wouldn't love Francesca? But the soft spot he carries for Mimi has always been a mystery to me. Mimi is the Queen when it comes to driving away those who love her. Even Ed keeps his distance, though they both live in Las Vegas, because they usually end up bickering whenever they're together. But when it comes to Mimi, Jack keeps coming back for more. He's earned a reputation as a ruthless litigator who isn't afraid to get down and rumble with the lowlifes in town, but he still treats Mimi like she's family or something. He even handled her recent divorce from Husband Number Four.

Mimi adores him, as does Francesca and all Jack's girlfriends. The man is a charmer, I'll grant him that. Then again, Jack's always been good at making people believe fairy tales can come true. Once upon a time, he actually had me believing. And Tori still does.

Then again, I suppose that's to be expected.

After all, she's his daughter.

Twenty minutes later, a long lean figure with a stethoscope around his neck strides into the room. Ed, on the couch beside me, grips my arm as we stand to meet him.

"I'm Dr. Nelson." He pumps my hand. His grip is cool and dry. "And you are Mrs. Alexander's...?"

"I'm her daughter. Lily Lavender," I say, trying not to stumble over the words. This young man is Mimi's doctor? In his wrinkled khaki pants, rumpled shirt, and running shoes, he wears a youthful weariness that makes me wonder what medical school he graduated from. The deep dark circles under his eyes aren't much reassurance. When was the last time he had any sleep? "How is she?"

"Doing great. If you have to have a stroke, she had the best kind."

"What does that mean?" Ed asks. "A stroke is a stroke."

"Not exactly. Heart attacks affect the heart; a stroke attacks the brain. There are two types of strokes: ischemic—the kind your mother had," he says with a nod for me, "or hemorrhagic. An ischemic occurs when a blood vessel bursts in the brain and causes bleeding. In this case, a blood clot formed on one side of her brain. It blocked a blood vessel and caused the stroke."

"A blood clot?" My stomach crawls at the casual way he throws out the term.

"An ischemic stroke is very common. We see them all

the time." He rocks back and forth in his running shoes as if he's done his duty by informing the family and now he's ready to sprint out the door. "She's a lucky woman."

"She had a stroke. You call that lucky?" Ed demands.

"Definitely lucky," he replies. "And it's a good thing she got here when she did. We were able to do some damage control. The longer people wait before coming in, the worse their chances of achieving some sort of recovery."

Thank God Francesca called and got her here in time. "Can you tell us anything else? What... what are her chances?"

"It's still early," he says. "But given her physical condition, plus after looking at the MRI and the other tests we've run, I'd say she has a good chance of recovery. Maybe fifty percent. Maybe more."

"Define fifty percent." There's a hard edge in Jack's voice.

"I understand your concerns. Believe me, I wish I could give you a better answer. Unfortunately, I can't. Every patient responds differently. The human body is like an intricate piece of machinery. It's composed of different systems, and each one operates separately to function as a whole. The brain is the heart of it all."

"Are you going to operate?" I ask.

He shakes his head. "She doesn't need surgery. We've already started her on an IV. We're giving her a drug designed to dissolve the clot."

"That's it?" Ed sounds bewildered. "That's all you're doing?"

"At this point, it's all we can do. That, plus keep her under close observation. Depending on how she responds to treatment, she might be out of bed as early as this afternoon."

"This afternoon?" I stutter. "Isn't that a little fast to have her on her feet?"

"Absolutely routine," he assures me. "We don't like to keep people lying around in bed. Believe it or not, that can create more problems than the stroke itself. If she can tolerate it, moving around would be the best thing for her. In fact, if physical therapy can work her in, I wouldn't be surprised to see her on her feet and using a walker by the end of the day."

His pager goes off and he glances down to check it. Meanwhile, my mind is cruising down the *what-if* highway. Mimi, a whirlwind of energy, reduced to using a walker? The Queen will not be amused when she hears the news. The Queen will not be amused about lots of things. Being stuck in this hospital. Taking orders from physical therapy. Mimi is accustomed to having control and issuing commands. When she speaks, people jump to do her bidding. All of that is about to change. From now on, Mimi will be the one taking the orders. And she won't be jumping... at least, not any time soon.

The doctor clips his pager back on his belt. "Sorry, I have to go. Physical therapy will be around later today. If everything goes well and she responds like I think she will, you should be able to take her home in a few days. Meanwhile, they've already taken her back to her room. You can visit, but not for long. She needs her rest. I'll check in on her later. If you have any questions, just ask one of the nurses." He starts for the door. "If they can't help you, have them page me. One of them can hunt me down."

He breezes out, leaving us to ponder his words in bewildered silence. I glance around the room, taking us all in. Tori's face is pale and stark under her summer tan. Ed, haggard and drawn, looks every one of his seventy-plus years. Francesca sits on the couch, struggling not to weep. Jaabir scowls and stalks the edges of the room like a caged black panther waiting to strike. Not one of them looks like they're capable of managing this. I wrap my arms around my body, trying to ward off the numbness as the chilling reality of the situation begins to sink in.

I won't be looking to them for answers. They'll be looking to me.

The thought is terrifying. How am I going to do this? How can I handle it on my own? I've never been able to handle Mimi in my life. What makes me think I can start now?

Jack stands not far away. His dark eyes narrow and lock on mine. I want to look away, but something keeps me from doing so. Could he? Would he? Am I crazy for daring to think he might help? Jack has no interest in rescuing me, but he's always loved Mimi and I know how much he loves Tori. He'd do anything to make life easier for the two of them. He did the whole *be-a-man-and-make-things-right* by offering to marry me when we found out about Tori. But I knew that wasn't what he wanted. Neither of us would have been happy. He would have felt trapped, I would have felt guilty, and both of us would have been miserable. Better that things ended as they did with me telling him *no* and raising Tori alone. I'm a strong, capable woman. I'm used to handling things. I've done it all my life.

But Mimi is a different matter. I don't think I can do

this alone. And if anyone can help, it's Jack. I hate myself for asking him. I've never asked him for anything in my life. But tonight, I'm desperate.

What are we going to do? How are we going to manage?

A long look passes between us.

I swallow down my pride. *Please?*

Then his eyes narrow and I blink, watching as he turns his back on me and strides to the window. He stares out into the night's blackness. His stance is straight. Unforgiving. Unbending. Unyielding.

His answer is clear. It won't be *we*. It will be *me*. I am Mimi's daughter and this is my problem. Jack doesn't have time to cope with the messy business of my mother's recovery.

My fists tighten and my heart hardens like the arid desert floor surrounding this horrible town. Stupid, to have thought he would help in the first place. What was I thinking? I don't need Jack Alexander holding my hand, telling me things will be all right. Things *will* be all right. Let him go ahead and turn his back on me. See if I care. Let him turn his back on us all. Taking care of himself has always been Jack's *modus operandi*. If it's in his best interests, you've got a deal; otherwise, forget it. Obviously, helping us with Mimi isn't in Jack's best interests.

And to think I actually slept with this man, once upon a time.

I shudder slightly, remembering that night more than eighteen years ago when he stumbled across me in one of the lounges at Caesar's Palace. I'll admit I was drunk, but damn it, I deserved it, after being deserted for a game of craps by that dreary date Mimi had hooked me up with. I'd

Kathleen Irene Paterka

sat there alone and celebrated with one drink followed by another. It was Christmastime, and the crew at Caesar's had done their part to contribute to the holiday atmosphere with swags of garland and festive decorations adorning every column and chandelier. Jack probably told me why he happened by that particular night, but the memory was lost once he sank down beside me and we started doing shots—top-shelf tequila, one after the other—to celebrate the season and our parents' recent divorce. Then things started getting hazy, way too hazy... Then it was the next morning, and I woke up in one of Caesar's best suites: naked, with a hideous hangover, and Jack Alexander sprawled in bed beside me, snoring in my ear, one arm draped across my breast.

Somehow I managed to wiggle out from under him, bolt from the bed and get the hell out of the room before he woke up and we had to face each other in the light of day. God, what was I thinking? Problem was, I hadn't been thinking, and neither was he. I was drunk and so was Jack. That night wasn't about us; it was all about sex. Pure, unadulterated, hedonistic sex. Mind-blowing sex. The best sex I ever experienced in my life.

Sex without condoms.

That much I deduced two months later when my period was late and the mere thought of food made me queasy. I should have paid more attention in biology class. One time is all it takes. Seventeen years later, I still can't drive down Las Vegas Boulevard and past Caesar's Palace without blushing. All the things we did with each other that night, the bruised lips, the tangled bed sheets... the best night of my life. It was the one and only time Jack and I ever connected on a physical basis, and we've never discussed it. We never even kissed again. He offered to marry me, to do the honorable thing, but I knew he didn't mean it. It never would have worked out. One more tragedy in our family saga. One more divorce. I couldn't do it. I couldn't let Jack do it.

But even if I had the chance to turn back time, I wouldn't change a thing. No matter how much Jack irks me, I would never take back that night.

That night gave us Tori.

I reach for her as she marches past me. "Where are you going?"

She wriggles from my touch. "The doctors said we could see Mimi. Maybe if she knows we're here, it will help her get better." Her fists are clutched in front of her and her eyes blaze, as if daring me to stop her. And suddenly, a tiny bit of hope leaps in my heart.

Maybe I'm not as alone as I thought.

Tori and Mimi. Mimi and Tori. Both of them are stubborn, selfish, and strong. When has Mimi ever given in? When has Mimi ever faltered? When has Mimi ever not been in control or not issued orders? None of us know what will happen with her recovery. But try as I might, I can't imagine her taking this lying down. Meanwhile, an unexpected source of strength is staring me right in the face. Someone who reminds me exactly of my mother.

I tuck Tori's arm in mine and hold on tight.

"All right. Let's go see her... together."

Chapter Three

HER EYES ARE CLOSED, HER figure frail and unmoving beneath the blankets. My stomach twists and my nose prickles at the stringent smell of antiseptic mingled with industrial-strength Lysol. Tori and I grip hands as we approach Mimi's hospital bed. An IV pole stands guard beside her. Two plastic bags drip meds through tubes inserted in her body. A cold fear drips through my own veins. Fragile is not a word anyone would associate with my mother, yet there is no other word for it. Seeing Mimi so vulnerable nearly brings me to my knees. How could this have happened?

"I didn't think she'd look so... so sick." Tori's voice holds an edge of fear.

"I know, sweetie." I give her a quick hug, one I need just as much as she does. "But remember what the doctor said. She's alive, and she's exactly where she needs to be. They're giving her the very best care."

I'm in automatic mom-mode, but my heart hammers with the echo of Tori's words. Will Mimi be okay? Will she recover? How could this have happened to her? Mimi has always been the strongest of us all.

It's three a.m. before we finally leave the hospital. The headache pounding beneath my eyes gains strength with each passing mile as the limo nears the villa. I can't shut out the questions pounding through my brain. How long will she be in the hospital? What happens when she comes home? I never planned on staying in Las Vegas, but Tori and I can't just desert her.

First thing tomorrow morning, I need to call Walt and make arrangements for someone to oversee my division until I'm ready to go back and run things myself.

I tumble into bed, but sleep is not an easy visitor. I lie in the darkness, mulling over the things that need to be done, that need my attention. If and when she recovers, the hospital will release Mimi. She'll come home to the villa. Home to us. Luckily, the villa is all on one level, large and spacious, with no stairs to maneuver. But what about the business? What about the weddings? How much of a recovery will Mimi make? Fifty percent, the doctor said.

But what if she doesn't make it that far?

What if she never recovers?

Throwing the pillow over my head, I try to smother the thought.

I wake to unforgiving sunlight streaming through the window of the bedroom that has been mine since Mimi married Big Mike, Husband Number Two, and we moved into the villa. I lie in bed a few minutes, allowing my thoughts to drift as I emerge from a lack-of-sleep fog. Bleary eyed, I stare at the bedside clock, then sit up with a start as all the horrors of last night come rushing back to mind. Less than four hours ago, I was at the hospital.

Now I'm back in town, back in Mimi's villa, sleeping in my old room.

Tori brought me here. Mimi will keep me here.

Eventually, I'll need to deal with Tori. Last night wasn't the time or the place. She left the hospital with Jack and Ed and I let her go, in no mood to protest. Mimi's villa is spacious and comfortable, but it can't compete with the luxurious penthouse apartment Jack and Ed share and the room they keep exclusively for Tori whenever she's in town. Her father and grandfather lavish money and gifts on her every chance they get, but I've always felt guilty about raising a protest. After all, I'm the one who swept her three hundred miles away. Jack could have made things unpleasant had he chosen to fight me. But he never insisted we go to court or have a formal agreement drawn up and signed by a judge. Tori carries his last name, but I have full custody and he's never disputed it. I suppose the fact that our parents were once married, that I love his father and he loves Mimi, played a big part in his decision. The loose, informal arrangement works for us all. And though I've argued with him that I'm financially capable of taking care of Tori on my own, Jack insists on contributing to her upkeep. A generous check shows up in the mail each month.

I have to give him credit. When he makes a mistake, he admits it and corrects it. What happened between Jack and me that night was definitely a mistake. The only good thing that came out of it was Tori.

I scramble out of bed, pull on my bathrobe, and stumble into the kitchen to the smell of Francesca's coffee. The rich aroma fills the room as I call the hospital to check on Mimi's status. For now the news is good. Mimi is alive and alert. Francesca urges breakfast on me. I choke down a piece of toast and chase it down with scalding-hot coffee. There's not much time to talk. With two back-to-back weddings scheduled for today, and as yet, no minister to officiate, both of us have plenty of work ahead. Back upstairs, I pull a simple black dress from the back of my closet and slide it over my head, wondering if Tori, Ed and Jack are already at the hospital. We agreed last night that the three of them would return in the morning while Francesca and I dealt with the chapel and the brides.

I grab Mimi's keys, head across the courtyard, and unlock the chapel door. Inside, I flip off the neon advertising sign on the Strip. Walk-ins are common, especially on weekends, but we're not accepting any today. Except for the two weddings already booked, the Royal Wedding Chapel is closed.

Francesca joins me at the chapel five minutes later. With the first ceremony scheduled for noon, she spends precious minutes on the phone trying to locate a substitute minister. She flips through Mimi's rolodex, begging her contacts for help. Eventually she hits the jackpot and he shows up ten minutes before the ceremony starts.

I haven't worked a chapel wedding in years, and for a few moments, I find myself caught up in the beautiful romantic dream unfolding around me. It's a large wedding party, and family and friends crowd the pews of our grandest room, the King Edward's Chapel. Francesca runs the music as I wait with the bride, who is radiant in a rhinestone-encrusted, strapless sweetheart gown with a floor-sweeping train. I stand just inside the chapel door, watching as she starts down the aisle to meet her groom. The ceremony runs a little longer than usual, but other than that, everything is perfect... until I hear raised voices and a din from outside. Opening the door a crack, I peek out and spot a second bride stalking the room.

"We've been waiting out here five minutes," she complains as I slip out to greet her wedding party.

"I'm very sorry," I say, remembering Francesca's warning that Bride Number Two would be a problem. Their ceremony is scheduled for early afternoon in the smaller, more intimate Queen Elizabeth's Chapel Royal. "We're a little understaffed today."

The scowl on her face deepens as the King Edward Chapel doors open and the first wedding party streams through the lobby. They crowd the room with noisy happiness as Francesca escorts them outside into the sunshine.

"These flowers are not what I ordered." Bride Number Two balks at the bouquet I remove from the cooler. "I ordered cream-colored roses. *Cream-colored.* These aren't cream, they're blush... and they're not even fresh." She shoves them back into my hands.

"Let me see what I can do." I slide behind the reception desk and scramble for her file. Not that it will make much difference. According to Francesca, the florist missed his regular delivery yesterday. Very few flowers are left in the cooler.

"Carlos, this is all your fault." She turns to her groom, seated on the bench behind her. "I told you we would have problems with this place."

I glance at Mimi's paperwork, praying everything else

is in order for their ceremony. At least this wedding party is smaller than the first: the bride and groom plus two witnesses and a toddler with wispy blond hair in a jewel-encrusted dress matching the bride's. I put the finishing touches on their contract and wait for the printer to churn out a copy while keeping an eye on the little one wandering the reception area. She can't keep her hands off anything. She leaves a trail of smeary smudges on the large glass cabinets showcasing the bridal jewelry, unity candles, and sand-pouring sets. She circles the room and yanks at the small potted trees lining the entrance. I cringe as she breaks off one of the branches, sniffs it, then tosses it on the floor. Finally she comes to a halt in front of Mimi's prized possession, the heirloom tiara. She sticks her nose against the bulletproof glass, fogging it with her breath. "I want that."

"Shania, you shut your mouth." The bride glowers at the little girl. "This is Mama and Daddy's wedding day. I don't need you making trouble."

The little girl starts to cry, and the groom grabs his daughter, hoists her in his arms. "Don't you worry, honey. We'll get you a crown of your very own once Mama and Daddy get married."

"But I want it now." She buries her head in his shoulder and wails even louder.

Bride Number Two rolls her eyes and turns back to me. "Like I said, these flowers are not what I want."

I take a deep breath. Dealing with this bride is not what I want. "I'm very sorry. Things are a little hectic around here today."

"That's not my problem." She shifts her hip and glares

at me.

"If you give me a moment, I'm sure we can make things right." Exactly how I'll accomplish that, I'm not sure. But I am convinced of the dire necessity.

"Damn right you will." She taps a glittering acrylic nail on the paperwork between us. "We paid good money to have our wedding here. That woman who booked us promised everything would be perfect. Well, guess what? It's not." Her eyes narrow. "Where is she? I want to talk to her."

Who booked their wedding? Francesca or Mimi? I suppose it makes no difference. Francesca is busy with Bride Number One. And as for Mimi...

"I'm sorry, but I'm afraid that isn't possible," I say, remembering Mimi's admonishment over the years. *Keep calm and carry on.* It worked with the English people in WWII. It works with brides.

"She said she was the owner. If that's true, she'd better own up to this mess and fix it now." She turns her head toward her groom. "I never should have let you talk me into this place," she mutters in a voice loud enough for me to overhear. "That bitch better show up and make things right or she'll be sorry."

"Excuse me?" My head snaps up and I eye her across the counter.

She turns back to me with a don't-play-dumb-you-heard-what-I-said smirk.

"I'll be glad to take care of things." I grant her a gracious smile, surprised to hear my voice so pleasant. A rush of cool calmness drapes me, and suddenly everything seems easy. "Why don't you have a seat while I make the arrangements." I point to the upholstered couch where Carolos, their daughter, and the witnesses wait. "This should only take a minute."

"About time," the bride mutters. She flounces across the room and wiggles her way onto the bench without spilling out of her mermaid gown. The groom's face is nearly as red as the plush velvet covering the seat. My heart goes out to him. Poor guy. He hasn't a voice, and he hasn't a clue. This marriage is doomed before it starts.

I scan their contract and verify the deposit they made last month. Mimi would kill me if she ever found out what I'm about to do. The chapel's policy is firm. Brides are never wrong. Brides pay the bills. But Mimi isn't here. She's confined to a hospital bed. And no matter how much Mimi might annoy and frustrate me, no one—NO ONE— calls my mother a bitch.

Picking up the phone, I punch in a number I could recite in my sleep. "Jaabir, please bring the limousine around."

Five uncomfortable minutes later, he strolls in the front door. Suave and debonair in a black suit, crisp white shirt, and stiff-brimmed hat crowning his head, Jaabir looks every bit capable of chauffeuring the royal couple at Buckingham Palace.

I nod toward Bride Number Two and her party. "These people need a ride."

"Is the wedding already over?" He glances at his watch. "I thought it wasn't until two o'clock."

"It's been rescheduled," I say. "They are getting married today. They just won't be getting married here."

"Now, you just wait a minute." Bride Number Two extricates herself from the bench and thunders across the room, a fiery storm on glittering five-inch heels. She slaps her rhinestone clutch on the counter. "We came to Las Vegas to get married."

I ring up the refund, print the receipt, and punch the button opening the cash register. "Congratulations."

"We drove all the way from Los Angeles to get married *here*... at the Royal Wedding Chapel."

"Las Vegas has plenty of wedding chapels. Our chauffeur will take you wherever you like."

"Forget this shit. We're not going anywhere." Bride Number Two scowls at me. "I want to talk to the manager."

"You're talking to her." I count out five crisp one-hundred-dollar bills and slide them across the counter. "Here's a full refund and your receipt."

"You can't do this," she sputters.

"I believe I just did."

She glares at me, looking as if she'd like nothing better than to spit in my face. For a moment, I wonder if she'll dare. Then Carlos intervenes, tugging at her shoulder.

"Come on, Marlene, we'll go someplace else. You said you didn't like it here anyway. At least we got our money back and they're giving us a ride in the limo."

Bride Number Two yanks away from his touch. She stares at me harder, and I steel myself, waiting for the gob of spit to hit me in the face. Then suddenly she scoops up the cash and jams it in her clutch.

"You're right, Carlos. Let's get out of here." She glances around with a sneer on her face. "The Royal Wedding Chapel? It's just as tacky and cheap as I thought it would be. And I'll bet that tiara isn't even real." She nods at the family heirloom showcased under discreet lights.

The display cabinet is grimy, courtesy of their daughter's hands, face, and nose.

"You messed with the wrong woman." The look in her eyes is lethal. "You might think you ruined my day, but you just wait. I'm going to smear you all over the Internet. I've got lots of friends. By the time I'm through, every one of them will know exactly what kind of an effing bitch you are."

"Good-bye and good riddance," I mutter as she and her entourage storms out. I grab the keys and head for the door, officially locking us down for the day. I don't care how dismal the chapel's finances might be. We don't need her kind of business. Who cares what she thinks? Who cares what she does? I'm glad she's gone.

And as for her threat to ruin our reputation? The chapel is a social media nonentity with no Facebook, Twitter, or Pinterest accounts. We don't even have a bridal blog. No real web presence, save for an outdated website.

Bride Number Two shouldn't be able to do much damage.

Once Jaabir's back from dropping off the bridal party from hell, the three of us return to the hospital. My nose prickles and my stomach lurches as I pick up a whiff of sterile antiseptic and cleaning fluids mingling in the air. We punch the elevator button for the fifth floor, which, as I learned last night, is entirely devoted to the Stroke Unit. Only two visitors at a time, the nurse warns us when we check in. Jaabir and Francesca volunteer to stay behind and head for the waiting room. I'm reluctant to let them go. I could use their support. Taking a deep breath, I head down the hall toward Mimi's room.

I hear Tori chattering away like a magpie even before I reach the door. It's partially open, and I stand there a moment, alone in the hallway, and peek inside. Tori is at Mimi's bedside. Her chair is pulled near the head of the bed, her hand curled around Mimi's. The other bed is empty. Is she here by herself? Where is Jack? Ed?

Rapping on the door, I slowly enter. "Mind some company?"

"Mimi, look who's here." Tori scoots from her chair and throws herself into my arms. I'm a little surprised. Normally she isn't so needy or affectionate. The last year or so, especially the past few months, the close relationship we once shared has disappeared. Just a typical teenager thing, I've reassured myself. Tori is growing up and it's normal for her to need time and space to assert her independence. But today is like old times. I give her a quick hug and kiss. While it feels wonderful to have my little girl back in my arms, I can't help wondering what gives.

Then Mimi turns her face to me and I suddenly understand what has Tori so unglued. Mimi was asleep last night and the damage wasn't readily apparent. A long pain slides along my ribs as I take in the sight of how the stroke has ravaged my mother. The entire right side of her face droops, as if it were being tugged downward by an invisible string. She struggles to lift her left arm in greeting, but it flops back on the blanket.

This woman isn't Mimi. This woman in the hospital bed isn't anyone I recognize. Mimi would say, "Enough with this nonsense," fling off the covers, and climb out of bed. Mimi would say, "For heaven's sake, Lily, what are you staring at?" and push me aside as she strolled out the door. Mimi would say, "What about today's weddings? Did you have any walk-ins?" And she'd give me holy hell to hear me admit I turned off the lights and sent them away.

But this woman's eyes are filled with pain and confusion, mingled with a hint of panic.

I grab Tori's hand, clinging to it like a lifeline as we approach the bed. A minute ago, she was leaning on me. Now I'm not sure which one of us is comforting the other.

"Hi, Mimi." I bend over and kiss her forehead, cool and dry beneath my lips. I catch a faint whiff of the rich floral perfume that is her signature fragrance, and a little lift of hope springs in my heart. I reach for her right hand, careful not to disturb the sterile tape holding the IV in place.

Her hand lays limp in mine. I squeeze her fingers, but there's no return response. It's as if her hand is dead.

"Mmph."

As she struggles to speak, the enormous reality of what has happened begins to seep into my brain. Mimi is partially paralyzed and she can't even talk.

Tori hurries to the opposite side of the bed. "Would you like some water?"

Mimi shakes her head and locks eyes with me.

The two of us have never been good at mother-daughter communication, but I pick up the question in her eyes. "Francesca is here," I say, guessing that might be what she wants to know. "Francesca, and Jaabir, too. They're in the waiting room. Would you like to see them?"

With effort, she raises her left hand and wiggles her

fingers. "Gruph."

Did she mean *Yes*? *No*?

"Gruph," she gurgles.

Is it the flowers? I glance around the room. For such a big city, Las Vegas is actually a small town. News of Mimi's illness has spread faster than a slot machine can spit out vouchers. Her hospital room is filled with flowers from people throughout the community. Business associates and friends. The largest arrangement is done up in Mimi's favorite—lush, fragrant roses in a deep, brilliant red. "The flowers are beautiful."

She slams her head against the pillow. "Mmph."

I raise my eyebrows and slide a glance across the bed at Tori.

"She wants to hear about the weddings," Tori says as she strokes Mimi's cheek. "Isn't that right? You want to know how the weddings went today."

Mimi gives Tori a droopy half smile.

The brides? That's what has Mimi so concerned? I should have known. She can't walk, she can't talk, yet all she cares about is that damn wedding chapel. My gaze shoots to the blood-pressure cuff loosely wrapped around her arm. They have the wrong woman hooked up to that machine. My own blood pressure is probably bouncing off the chart.

But I'm not the one who had a stroke, and I can't risk making things worse. I take a deep breath and count to five. "Everything went fine," I say, tossing Mimi a smile as bright as Bride Number One when she tossed the bouquet. "Francesca managed to find a substitute minister. She ran the music, and I ran the desk."

I also ran Bride Number Two out of the chapel, but that nugget of news I keep to myself.

"I was thinking it might be a good idea to close the chapel for a few days," I venture. "That will buy us some time until we see how good things are going."

Or how bad they truly are, I think to myself.

"Close the chapel?" Tori looks at me like I've suddenly morphed into a court jester reduced to babbling nonsense in front of the queen. "We can't do that. What about the brides? We can't ignore them. What about the weddings that are already booked? That would be a disaster." She looks to Mimi for backup. "We have to keep the chapel open. You want us to do that, right?"

Mimi barely moves her head, but the grim smile on her twisted face tells me that my mother and daughter are in complete agreement. "Bah," she spits for emphasis.

"I'll be there to help with the weddings next week." Tori runs a hand through long blond hair that looks like liquid gold. "I can answer the phone and run the reception desk. And if Francesca shows me how, I can handle the music, too."

I'm sure she can. A person can do anything if they have the desire. And when it comes to the Royal Wedding Chapel, Tori has the desire. One glimpse of the fierce look in her eyes, the firm set of her jaw, and anyone would know that.

The older my daughter gets, the more she reminds me of my mother.

Tori perches on the edge of the bed and smoothes her grandmother's hair with long, gentle strokes. "Don't worry, Mimi. We'll take care of the chapel for you." She nods at me. "At least we don't have to worry about tomorrow."

The chapel is closed on Sunday. But what about Monday? Tuesday? And all the days following? None of us has any idea how long it will be before Mimi is back up on her feet, or if that will even happen. And until we know, there's little doubt in my mind what we should do. Francesca can't handle things by herself, and I don't want to take over managing the chapel. We did it today, but we had no choice. It was an emergency.

And no matter what Tori thinks, I'm not about to let her take control. She has no business making promises to Mimi. She doesn't know the first thing about running a business. She hasn't the slightest clue what it takes or all the hard work that's involved. Tori is in love with all things royal, but the Royal Wedding Chapel is not hers.

And if I have any say in the matter, it never will be.

"We'll talk about this later," I say, closing the subject for now. Mimi is in the business of selling happily ever after. A bunch of nonsense, if you ask me; especially given the way her own life turned out. Two dead husbands. Two divorces.

Happily ever after? It doesn't exist, not in our family.

Correction. My own version of happily ever after will be seeing Mimi out of her hospital bed and back on her feet. And until that happens, I'm stuck in this town.

I find Ed in the waiting room with Francesca and Jaabir. "Hey, kiddo." He wraps me in a big hug and I hold on tight. Being around Ed has always made me feel safe and protected. In a city filled with crime and corruption, he is one of the good guys. In a world where Mimi rules supreme, he has always been my protector.

He's big and burly, and even though he and Mimi are no longer married, he still runs interference for me better than a football player. When I was younger, I used to pretend Ed was my dad. I used to pretend a lot of things while he and Mimi were still together. That the world was a happy place. That if my own father were still alive, he would love me just like Ed. That as the years wore on and their shouting increased, Mimi and Ed were still a happily married couple.

That Ed's son Jack, a handsome college jock on whom I nurtured a secret crush, would chance a look my way.

Even at the tender age of ten, I should have known better. Sometimes, no matter how hard you wish they would, things don't work out. Sometimes life gets messy. Sometimes, a father you never knew dies before you are born. Sometimes, the best of marriages end in divorce. I was already in college, but that didn't stop me from crying my eyes out the day I learned Ed and Mimi signed the papers ending their marriage. No more pretending Ed was my dad or that Jack—now a partner in his dad's law firm— would ever look in my direction. Ed moved out, leaving the villa behind the Royal Wedding Chapel inhabited by women: Mimi, Francesca, and me.

I moved out a few days following my college graduation. Recruited for their corporate training program, my company whisked me off to Chicago where I lived for a year, then sent me around the world to different locations where I could learn all aspects of the business. Eventually I settled in Del Mar, minutes from San Diego, where

I'm Director of Finance for the product-line division operating out of California. My boss, Walt Winchester, is our company's CFO. Walt has served as my mentor since I was hired, and our business relationship has deepened into a close friendship with both him and his wife. I trust and respect him, and he's a great sounding board when I'm tussling with a dilemma. As Walt often reminds me, I have more savvy than I give myself credit for. Part of me doubts him, but the other part yearns to believe he's telling the truth. I'm good at what I do, and it's paid off in being able to make a good life for myself and Tori all on my own.

Something Mimi warned I'd fail at. Something Francesca worried over. Something Ed encouraged.

Something Jack has never mentioned, one way or the other... even when he learned I was pregnant.

"Where's Jack?" I hate myself for asking the question, but the desire to know is greater than the desire to hide my feelings from my family.

"He had some work to finish up at the office," Ed says. "He's prepping for a witness we're interviewing tomorrow. We've got a big case we're working on, and we're headed to trial soon."

Why should I be surprised? Ed and Jack run a highly successful and respected law firm. In a city like Las Vegas, respect is like money in the bank. Jack's always made it clear that business comes first. Obviously today, business won out over family.

"How is Mimi?" Francesca asks. She appears to have gained a few more wrinkles and worry lines since last night. "Is she up to visitors?"

"Tori is still with her, but I'm sure it's fine for you

to go in." Seeing Francesca will probably do Mimi good. Plus, Francesca needs to see for herself how Mimi is doing. I sink down on the couch next to Ed as she heads out the door.

"I'll give you two some privacy." Jaabir smiles at me and follows Francesca out of the room.

"You doing okay?" Ed takes my hand, squeezes my fingers.

His question makes me feel like breaking out in tears and laughter at the same time. Twenty-four hours ago, I was at my desk when I took the call from Tori's school. Looking back, her skipping out on summer classes seems like the least of my problems.

"This all seems so... unbelievable." I twist to face him. Though the two of us are side by side in a hospital waiting room, the reality of the situation still seems a bit surreal. "I could understand if this had happened to Francesca. She's older than Mimi and always worrying about something."

"Don't let it get you down." Ed shakes my arm, rallying me like a prizefighter. "Mimi will get through this. Your mother is a strong woman."

"Don't I know it," I murmur, remembering how, moments ago, Mimi *mmphed* her insistence that the chapel remain open for business. Hopefully she'll channel some of that stubbornness into concentrating on a full recovery. "Have you seen her doctor today?"

"We got here about nine this morning, but he was already gone. The nurse said that he thought the medicine seemed to be working, which is a good sign. Then after lunch, two physical therapists showed up. They worked with her for about thirty minutes and did an evaluation.

They had Mimi sitting on the edge of the bed before they left."

"Really?" A tiny spark kindles inside me. If Mimi is already able to sit by herself, maybe things aren't as bad as I thought. A few minutes ago she looked so pathetic—crooked and helpless in her bed. Yet she was alert enough to follow my conversation with Tori... and stubborn enough to insist we keep the chapel open. Obviously, her brain hadn't suffered impairment. Thank God for that. The sooner she gets better, the sooner Tori and I can go home and all our lives can return to normal.

"The doctor mentioned a walker. What about that? Did that work?"

Ed falls silent. I think of Mimi's drooping face, her garbled *mmph*, her dead left arm, and my spirits flag. Who am I kidding? It will take time for Mimi to recover. There will be no miraculous intervention. Mimi doesn't go to church. She doesn't even pray. We can't expect her to get better in just a few days. She can't talk. She can't walk.

And I can't desert Francesca and Mimi. I'd never be able to forgive myself.

"Don't worry, kiddo. Everything will be okay." Ed wraps an arm around my shoulder, but the comforting gesture only pushes down the fog. It settles in a rumpled blanket of despair at my feet.

I bury my face in his shoulder and give in to the tears I've been holding back. I hate myself for being so weak. I'm the one who's used to being in control and making things work. But how can I? I hate hospitals. I hate being around sick people.

And though I don't want to admit it, I have to be honest.

She's my mother and I love her, but there are times I even hate Mimi.

Ed holds me for a few minutes, lets me cry it all out. Finally, a soft bump hits my arm. I open a bleary eye and peek at the box of tissues he offers.

"I know you probably feel overwhelmed," he says as I snatch a few tissues and swipe my tears away. "You feel bad. Hell, Lily, I feel bad, too. But do me a favor and remember one thing." He tucks a finger under my chin and lifts my face to meet his gaze. "You don't have to be Superwoman. You don't have to carry this load by yourself. You're surrounded by people who want to help."

"Who? In case you haven't noticed, Francesca is barely managing to keep herself together. And as for Jaabir, I don't think he has plans to drop out of night school. If the chapel shuts down, there's no reason for him to stick around."

"You're putting the—"

"And Tori?" I cut him off before he can go further. "She'd love to take over. She would take care of Mimi and the chapel, too. But I can't let her do it. She's so young, and she has no idea—"

He clamps a beefy hand across my mouth. "Lily, sweetheart, do me a favor and shut up. Because, in case you haven't noticed, you're forgetting some people."

"Such as?" I sputter through his fingers.

"Such as me." He pulls his hand away. "And Jack. We're both right here for you."

My face grows hotter. Ed, help Mimi? Like that's going to happen. The two of them squabble whenever they're together. I don't want her having another stroke. As for Jack, he might be Tori's dad, but he is not my husband. And no matter what Ed might think, Jack has no intention of helping us through this situation. He made that abundantly clear to me in this waiting room last night. Jack can be charming and persuasive, but he never does anything unless it's to his advantage. Tori is his daughter. He considers it his legal, moral, and ethical responsibility to take care of her. But taking care of Mimi? Why would he? Why should he? He owes her nothing.

"I wouldn't count on Jack," I say. "He's not even here."

Ed's eyebrows rise. "I told you he went back to the office. We're working on a case."

What a convenient excuse. Jack, running off to work. It's obvious to me. Too bad it's not obvious to Ed. "I'm sure it must be very important."

"He wanted to stay but I told him to go."

A hot blush sears my cheeks and for a moment, I'm ashamed of myself. Then I remember last night, the hardness in Jack's eyes, the way he turned his back on me, and I come to my senses. For all I know, Ed could be feeding me a lie. I know he loves me and wants to protect me. But Jack is his son. He loves Jack, too.

"Look, Lily, I know the two of you have your differences. Can't you at least try, for everyone's sake, to put your feelings aside and make this work?"

"I don't—"

"Do it for me?" he counters softly. "For Tori?"

I sputter into silence.

"Let me take care of Jack," he promises. "We'll get things straightened out."

Maybe Ed is right. After all, Jack was here this morning, I remind myself, and last night, too. Maybe I'm being too hard on him. Maybe I'm being too hard on myself. Maybe I need to loosen up, let go, let others help. At least give them a chance.

Ed waits, looking like the consummate attorney, hoping to obtain my signature on a release agreement absolving his client of all misdoing. But what's the use in arguing? He'll never understand. Never.

I muster up a smile. "Okay."

"That's my girl." He kisses my cheek. "Now, what say we go check in on Mimi?" Standing, he offers me a hand. "After that, maybe we can give Jack a call and all of us can go have dinner. My treat."

Nodding, I let him to pull me to my feet. Might as well indulge Ed's fantasies and allow him to believe I've bought into his rosy picture of togetherness. Ed might be a great attorney, but he's living in a fairy tale, not in reality. Fairy tales are magic that happens between the pages of a book. No matter what Ed says, I harbor no illusions.

When it comes to magical endings, Jack and Mimi are the King and Queen of *Happily Never After*.

Chapter Four

SOMEHOW WE MAKE IT THROUGH the next few days, shuttling back and forth between the villa and the hospital. Tori sticks close to Mimi while Francesca and I cover the chapel for the weddings already booked. I'm not sure which is worse: dealing with brides or facing the reality of Mimi's situation. The doctors have assured us that she is showing signs of improvement, which is a good thing. She's learned to manage a few shuffling steps with the help of a walker, but every time I see the clumsy way she uses her left hand to drag her right arm close, hear the garbled nonsense in her speech, or catch sight of her drooping face, my spirits sag.

Will Mimi recover?

"Things aren't looking good," I confide to Walt on the phone Tuesday afternoon. Just a quick bite to eat, I told Francesca before sneaking off to the villa. But instead of grabbing a sandwich, I got my cell phone and snuck into the dim, cavernous room down the hall off the kitchen. With built-in bookshelves and a safe in one wall, it was obviously meant as a den or office when the villa was first built, but Mimi has never used it. There wasn't even a piece of furniture in the room until last night when Jaabir helped me lug in a table and a few chairs. I set up my laptop and made the room into my own mini-office while I'm in town. I have to work somewhere and the room offers privacy, which is exactly what I need for my phone call with Walt. He's a good sounding board. He's a voice of reason. He's in San Diego.

I force down the lump in my throat. I feel horrible and guilty, longing for home and a return to normalcy, while Mimi is stuck in a hospital bed.

"What do the doctors say?"

"Not much." I rake my fingers through my hair. These past few days there have been plenty of moments when I've felt like pulling out every single strand. "*Each stroke victim's recovery is different* is all I keep hearing. It's like the doctors are playing some odd medical game of *wait-and-see*."

"Has she seen a physical therapist?"

"A physical therapist plus an occupational therapist and speech therapist." I think of the physical therapist who was working with Mimi today when I stopped by to visit. 'It's important you keep up these exercises at home, Mrs. Alexander. Do you understand?' she'd asked, but Mimi barely nodded. The grim, contorted look on her face was not a good sign.

"Recovery is based on a series of small gains." I repeat what the doctors tell us every day. "They build on the small gains, which hopefully add up to a lasting recovery. Once Mimi comes home, they'll work with her on an outpatient basis."

"Any idea when the hospital plans on letting her go?"

"Thursday or Friday." Two more days and the Queen will be back in residence. The mere thought terrifies me. How we'll manage is beyond me. Tori has been terrific at sticking close to her grandmother and helping out while she's in the hospital. But once Mimi comes home, things will have to change. Someone will have to help her attend to her personal needs, to bathe and dress. And from what the doctors tell me, Mimi doesn't have complete control of her bladder. Someone will have to help her in the bathroom. I can't ask Tori to do that.

"How's everything at work?" I quickly change the subject. "Are the second-quarter profits totaled? How did they compare to last year?"

"I expect we'll be up by five percent when we get the final figures at the end of the month," he says. A dead pause settles between us as we contemplate the company's growth. It's a sobering thought, knowing that our firm's financial success hinges on grieving families buying our line of products to bury their loved ones.

And if Francesca hadn't phoned 911 fast enough, if they hadn't gotten Mimi to the hospital in time, if she hadn't gotten that medicine that broke down the blood clot in her brain, it could have been our family picking out a coffin.

"Look, Lily, about work… I know we already discussed it, but I've been doing some thinking, and—"

"Quit thinking, Walt." The catch in his voice tightens the string of fear wrapped around my heart. "There's nothing I can't handle from here. I've thought it all through, and I know I can make this work. We talked about it last weekend, remember?"

"Yes, I know we did. In fact, that's all I've been thinking about since our conversation on Sunday. You, Tori, your mother... and how you intend to handle things. First of all, let me say that I think it's admirable what you're doing. You're stuck in a horrible situation, and you're trying to make the best of things. Other people might run, but not you. Can't say I'm surprised. It's exactly what I would expect from you. But frankly, I don't think—"

"Walt, please don't do this." He hasn't even said the words, but they're already roaring through my brain.

"It's for the best. You've got a lot on your plate right now. The last thing you need is more stress in your life. You put together a competent team at the office. Let them handle things. For once in your life, be good to yourself and concentrate on your family."

"But I know I can do this. All I need is for you to give me a chance—"

"No, Lily. You don't understand. There is no choice involved. I'm giving you an order. You're taking a leave of absence." His words march across the line. "We'll keep in touch via email. If things start to blow up and your division gets into a jam, I know how to reach you."

"So you're telling me that I'm supposed to walk away and simply forget about everything." My words are flat and they ring hollow in my ears. Inside I feel numb. How can I do it? I already miss Walt and my staff, my daily routine, my *boring life dealing with death*, as Mimi calls it. "Will I even have a job when I come back?"

"For God's sake, will you stop that nonsense? I'm not trying to replace you. I'm concerned about you.

Both Martha and I are concerned. She asked me to send her love." His voice softens. "Trust me, Lily. I'm only thinking of you. Right now your family needs you, and you need this time to be with them. A leave of absence is the best thing."

There's a catch in my voice and my heart is heavy as we say good-bye. I know Walt is only looking out for my best interests. He's not trying to replace me. My job will be waiting when this crisis is over. But even that knowledge doesn't lift my spirits. I didn't sign up for any of this. It's not as if Mimi and I exchanged wedding vows. I never promised to love and protect her, for richer or poorer, in sickness and in health, till death do us part. She may be my mother, but there is not a maternal bone in Mimi's body. Francesca was the one who watched over me while I was growing up. She was the one who made sure I ate my vegetables, who sat beside me at the kitchen table and drilled me on my multiplication tables, who fretted and fussed about where I was going and what time I would be home.

Mimi fretted and fussed, too. She was totally consumed with the chapel and the brides.

All my life, I was expected to obey Mimi's royal commands. *Do it and don't argue with me, Lily.* The only time I stood up for myself, it was with Ed's blessing. Mimi never forgave him for backing me up, and she never forgave me for running away from the business and leaving town. Now I'm back where I started, and I don't have a choice. I don't care about the chapel or fussing over brides. I don't know anything about running a wedding business. I especially don't know anything about caring for sick people.

What do I do now?

"This is totally unfair," Tori argues with me after we return from the hospital. Until now, she's been camping out in luxury at Ed and Jack's penthouse apartment, but she followed me home tonight when she learned about my plan.

"If you do this, you might as well shut down the chapel." She glares at me across the kitchen table like a petulant princess who's suddenly been stripped of her royal title. "It will ruin everything. Mimi will never forgive you. I'll never forgive you," she threatens.

I drag in a deep breath. I'd give anything not to be fighting with Tori. It's hard enough dealing with everyday life and normal mother-daughter teenager relationship issues. "Try to understand," I start again. "What I *want* and what we should *do* are two different things. I already said we're not canceling the weddings we have booked. We're not closing the business."

"You might as well," Tori mutters, "if you're not taking walk-ins."

"Your mother is only trying to help," Francesca says, glancing back and forth between us.

The worry in her eyes only adds to my guilt. Francesca doesn't deserve to be dragged through this. She's been involved with the business since before I was born. She, more than anyone, understands how difficult it will be to keep things running smoothly and to keep the chapel open.

"I can help," Tori insists. "I already told you that."

I struggle to hold back the sigh building inside me. "It's more complicated than that."

"No, it's not. Why do you insist on treating me as if I'm still a baby? Because I'm not." She crosses her arms against her chest. "You think I'm in the way. You think I can't help."

"I didn't say that."

"You didn't have to." A dark scowl crosses her face.

It's not as simple as Tori thinks. Mimi will be home soon. We need to muster our resources. Seeing to her needs will take considerable time and energy, even with a home-healthcare nurse and the three of us combined. Tori's idea to keep the chapel fully staffed and open normal hours is idealistic and naïve. Francesca and I can't handle things alone. And even if we went along with Tori's plan, we couldn't afford it for long. Our lopsided balance sheet won't support the expense of adding a full-time minister to the payroll.

"We don't even have a minister," I say. "Mimi did the weddings, remember?"

"You hired someone to fill in last Saturday," Tori says. "You could do it again."

"We can't—"

"You can't... or you won't? Which is it, Mom?"

I tamp down my growing frustration. "There are things about running a business you don't understand. Things like cash flow and expenses."

"For sure there won't be any cash flow if you don't take walk-ins," she grumbles.

I know she's upset. She's hurt, and she's scared that Mimi won't recover. How can I make her understand that

I feel exactly the same? I dig deep for another ounce or two of patience. "There's nothing I'd like more than Mimi back on her feet and our lives back to normal."

"Get real." She shoots me a look straight out of hell. "You'd like nothing better than to see the chapel shut its doors. You know it, I know it, and Mimi knows it, too. You've been waiting for years for something like this to happen."

"That's not fair."

"This could destroy Mimi's business. It could destroy everything. But if that's what you want, then go ahead. You're going to do it anyway. God, sometimes I hate you." She shoves her chair under the table and slams out the door. Francesca and I exchange glances over the sounds of a car engine catching. Tori roars out of the chapel's parking lot, headed back to Jack.

"*I hate you.*" Closing my eyes, I take in the hurt. Nothing weighs heavier on a mother's heart than to hear her child pronounce those dreaded words. But I deserve it, every word. Tori was only speaking the truth. She knows how much I hate the chapel. Just like I know how much it means to her.

The touch of a cool hand on mine brings my eyes open. "Don't give up hope, honey," Francesca says. "I'm here to help."

"Thanks, Francesca." I force a weak smile. She's sweet, but there's no way I can take her up on her offer. It wouldn't be fair. Francesca is nearly seventy, and she's already doing enough as it is. She doesn't need to take on the burden of more responsibilities. I doubt she has the energy. Sometimes I doubt I have the energy myself. I'm thirty years younger than she is, and the past few days have me feeling every bit my age. I can't imagine how hard all this has been on her. "You're a dear to offer, but I don't think so."

She squeezes my hand tighter. "You're in charge, and I respect that. But perhaps it would be best if you listened to me before saying *no*."

For once in my life, I take a good look at the plump little woman with the wrinkled face and fading auburn hair in desperate need of a touch-up. She was the one who tucked me into bed at night while Mimi worked late balancing the chapel's books. She was the one who made sure I ate my breakfast before heading to school, who helped me with my homework, who sat beside Ed and Mimi, her face flushed with pride, as I gave the Valedictorian address at my high school graduation.

Francesca kept her mouth shut whenever Mimi opened hers. But Mimi can't talk now. Suddenly I realize what a big part Francesca has played in my life. She's always been there, hovering in the background, stepping up when needed. While I've always treated her like a maiden aunt, she's always treated me like her very own daughter. More than that. Sometimes mothers don't listen to their daughters, just like sometimes I'm guilty of not taking Tori seriously. But Francesca has been there throughout the years, listening to whatever I had to say. Like a friend. She's treated me like a daughter, but also more.

Maybe it's time I quit thinking of her as a doddery old aunt and started treating her with the love and respect I'd show a friend.

She pats my hand. "There's no need to hire someone if

you decide to keep the chapel open. I'll help you through it. You manage the business and run the reception counter, and I'll teach Tori how to handle the music."

"What about the weddings? We need a licensed minister," I remind her.

"You already have one."

"No, we don't."

"Yes, you do," she says, nodding. "You have me. I've had my license nearly forty years."

"But... that doesn't make sense." My mind is spinning. "You never do weddings. *Never*. All this time, all these years..."

"Mimi insisted," she says, as if that explains everything. "I didn't want any part of it, but she wouldn't let it be. *Just in case*, she said, and she always made sure my license stayed current."

"But what about last Saturday?" I sputter. "You were so frantic, phoning around town trying to find a substitute minister. Why didn't you say something then? Why didn't you take over the weddings?"

She lifts one shoulder in a faint shrug. "I don't know, honey. Just because I'm licensed doesn't mean I've done it before. Besides, I was terribly worried about Mimi."

Forty years' worth of a license, and she's never stood before a bride and groom. "Why start now?" I ask.

"Because I think that's what Mimi would want." Her eyes slide away from mine, and she glances around the kitchen as if she's gathering her thoughts from the drawers and cupboards lining the room. "Remember the other night when I told you I thought the chapel was having financial problems? Well, I've been thinking about it. Now mind you, I haven't seen the books. But something tells me that if we close the chapel doors, they'll stay closed for good. That would kill Mimi. I can't let that happen, not if it's in my power to help. She's been so good to me. I don't want to officiate at the weddings. I never wanted it. But I think I need to do this. I need to do it for Mimi. When I think of all she's done for me, what she's given me..." Her eyes hold a plea. "I can't let her down."

My thoughts turn to all that has passed between the two women, of the story I've heard all my life. How Mimi inherited everything after Big Mike's unexpected death. How together, she and Francesca transformed his gaudy wedding chapel into the Royal Wedding Chapel and the elegant flourishing business it is today—or was while I was growing up. I think about what Francesca said. I think about how we're already losing business and what will likely happen if we close the doors. And I think about the phone call I took earlier today.

The man, calling for Mimi, introduced himself as an agent from the IRS. When I relayed the information about her stroke, he politely expressed his wishes for her recovery. But when I inquired as to the reason for his call, he firmly informed me that unless I was a principal in the business or had Mimi's power of attorney, he was not at liberty to discuss the details.

The phone call lasted less than a minute, but it left me bewildered, consuming my thoughts every minute of the day not taken up with brides. What does the IRS want with Mimi? I think about the agent's suggestion that I contact her attorney. Has Mimi already shared information with Jack? Does he know the IRS has come calling at the chapel?

"Francesca, has Mimi ever mentioned anything about the IRS?"

"The IRS?" A deep frown joins the furrows already etched across her forehead. "Heavens, no. Why?"

I hesitate to mention my conversation with the agent. Mimi has always played her cards close to her chest. If she'd told Francesca, I would be able to tell. Francesca has always been an easy read. Her face is empty, save for worry and concern. She doesn't know anything. I don't want to upset her more than I already have. "Never mind. It's not important."

"But the IRS? Lily, are you sure?"

"Absolutely," I reassure her. "Forget I said anything. And don't worry. If you're willing to take over officiating at the weddings, then I promise to figure out a way to keep the chapel open."

A faded smile blooms across her face like one of the wilting roses in the floral cooler. I make a mental note to call the florist tomorrow and make sure we're still on his regular delivery route.

"You're doing the right thing, Lily. You won't regret this."

"I hope so," I murmur. But Francesca is too late. The regrets have already begun. Me, run the Royal Wedding Chapel? What was I thinking? How did I get myself into this mess? "Two months," I add quickly. "Tori starts her senior year the end of August. We need to be home by then."

Francesca nods and slides off her seat. "That should give us enough time. Meanwhile, we'll still take walk-ins and book weddings?"

"Yes," I say, though I already have a nagging suspicion I've made the wrong decision. But guaranteed Tori won't think so. "Remember, it's only for two months. No bookings after the middle of August," I warn.

"Two months," she agrees.

Two months. It sounds like a prison sentence. Two months doing hard time in The Royal Wedding Chapel. *Two months.* Anyone can get through two months. I tuck the promise deep in my heart.

Francesca scoots around the table and catches me in a tight hug. "I'm proud of you, Lily," she whispers in my ear. "Mimi and Tori will be so happy when they hear the news. And I promise you won't be sorry."

My thoughts return again to the IRS agent. I hope she's right. God help us if she isn't.

Chapter Five

THE NEXT MORNING, STILL IN my bathrobe and sitting on my bed, I nurse a cup of coffee and make a few phone calls. The first one is to my housekeeper in Del Mar, a quiet lady who comes in once a week. Tori and I don't make much of a mess and she's paid to dust and vacuum, scrub down the kitchen, and tidy up the bathrooms. I let her know we'll be out of town for some weeks, tell her I'd like her to continue her regular routine, and ask for her home address so I can send her a check to cover the costs. She has her own key and can let herself in. Water the plants, I tell her, keep the dust at a minimum, and toss or take home any food in the refrigerator. It's bound to go bad before we return.

My next call is to our neighbor across the street. She's a stay-at-home mom with two small children whom Tori occasionally baby-sits on the rare occasions she and her husband go out. I share the news about Mimi and my neighbor murmurs little words of sympathy, promising to keep us in her prayers. I give her the phone number where we can be reached, tell her how long we'll be gone plus where I've hidden the spare key to the house, just in case. She assures me she'll contact me if a problem occurs. I hang up, feeling better than I have in days. So far, crime in our neighborhood is nonexistent, but knowing someone is watching over our house is a relief.

I stare at my open suitcase, a jumble of clothes on the stuffed chaise lounge. I'd never unpacked since I hadn't planned on being here longer than the weekend. I brought the essentials: laptop, clothes, and enough toiletries to last a few days. But two pair of panties, one bra, and a blow-dryer won't see me through eight weeks in this town. Either I make a quick trip home to Del Mar to replenish my wardrobe or I go shopping. Neither option is appealing, but I hate flying more than I do cruising the mall.

Three hours later, I'm back at the villa, loaded down with shopping bags. I sort through my new blouses, skirts, and dresses. Grabbing some hangers from the closet, I spy the shapeless black dress leftover from Saturday when I worked the two weddings. It's one of Mimi's unwritten rules: No one is allowed to outshine the brides... hence, the chapel staff wears black, a color guaranteed to fade into the background.

The guilt curves around my heart like the hook of the hanger gripping the closet pole. Bad enough I have to work at the chapel. Bad enough I look like a bleached-out stork in real life. Wearing a black dress will reduce me to feeling like an ugly old crow.

Then I remember my promise to Francesca. *You manage the business and run the front counter.* I think about the business. It's not mine, it's Mimi's. Her business, her rules. Do I have a choice? I shove aside the dress and peer into the dark recesses of my closet where similar shapeless black sheaths still hang, leftover from when I was a teenager and used to work the front desk.

I grab one of the dresses and struggle into it, zip up the back. I'm still as tall and skinny as I ever was and the dress still fits, though twenty years have passed and I've had a baby. I stand in front of the full-length mirror and take a good look at the somber figure staring back at me. The years have passed but the dress hasn't changed and neither have my feelings at seeing myself garbed in black. It's like being seventeen all over again. The dress is strangling me, holding me back from grabbing everything I want out of life.

But just because I've willingly sentenced myself to Wedding Purgatory for the next eight weeks doesn't mean I have to be a martyr and suffer wearing black sackcloth. I wiggle out of the offensive garment and toss it back on a hanger, shoving it deep in a corner.

Forget what Mimi thinks. Rules at the Royal Wedding Chapel are about to change.

I cut the tags from one of my new dresses, a sheer, sleeveless cornflower blue that matches my eyes. It shimmers in soft folds as I slide it over my head and down my body. Then, tucking my feet into a pair of strappy new heels, I head out the door, ready to take on the world... and the chapel.

What the hell?

I sit in front of Mimi's computer, watching it boot up, waiting for it to open, staring at the request flashing on the screen. User ID and Password? It's not as if the chapel has a bank of computers networked together; there are only two on site. The one in the reception lobby contains the wedding software program, and Mimi's computer is connected to that. But she's the only one who uses it. Why the concern about protecting her privacy? Francesca doesn't snoop, plus she's not exactly a computer wiz. More like, *Jaabir, can you tell me how to change the font on this document*?

Or perhaps it's not Francesca that Mimi was attempting to keep out. Maybe it's someone else. Someone who knows something about accounting. Someone who knows how to manage a business, forecast trends, spot financial downfalls.

Someone like me.

I hunch in the chair, cup my hand in my chin, and stare at the blank screen, racking my brain for a possible security code. *Chapel* is already typed into the User ID field, so I move on to the Password section. *Royal*. Error. *Weddings*. Denied. *Mimi*. Try again. *Brides*. Four failed attempts, and I'm no closer to getting into the computer than I was when I started.

What is that password? I slump back, stare at the screen. Mimi's never been one to sit at her desk wasting time on the computer. Whatever she chose, it has to be something simple; something she would never forget.

Then suddenly, a random thought flits across my mind. My fingers fly across the keyboard as I type in my guess. Like magic, the screen opens up. I can't help a little smile as Mimi's home page is displayed.

Tori. I should have known. It isn't something—but

someone—who is always on Mimi's mind. She's always treated Tori as if she was her very own.

"You had no right to name her Victoria. You knew I intended to call her Susan," I accused her that day seventeen years ago in the hospital's maternity ward. My stomach still sours when I remember how I felt, learning that Mimi had already filled out—and filed—the paperwork for Tori's birth certificate.

"Susan?" Mimi sniffed. "She might be your child, but she is my granddaughter, and I will not allow her to go through life with such a common name. Thousands of babies are named Susan, but there will only be one Victoria Elizabeth Margaret Alexander. She carries the names of queens." She straightens to an imperious height, enthroned on a plastic hospital chair. "Remember your heritage, Lily. You come from blue-blood stock, from British aristocracy. Victoria is a much more suitable name for this child."

I fold my arms across my chest, wincing at the unexpected pain. Moving makes my breasts ache and begin to fill with milk. No one warned me about the strange rush that happens when breast milk comes in and the sudden feeling of having two cement rocks strapped to your chest. "The least you could have done was consult with me," I mumble. "After all, she's my daughter."

"For heaven's sake, Lily, I simply do not understand why you are so upset. Victoria is a beautiful name." Mimi fusses over the Isolette crib next to my bedside, cooing as she picks Tori up and brushes a kiss against her forehead. "Victoria Elizabeth Margaret Alexander is a special baby and deserves a special name. That's why I named her for every one of us."

Precisely my point. I wanted my daughter to grow up being her own person. Instead, Tori is less than twenty-four hours old, and Mimi has already decided her chosen path in life.

"And you gave her Jack's last name," I accuse in a low tone. "I was thinking of naming her 'Lavender'."

"Ridiculous," Mimi scoffs. "She's Jack's child."

"She's my child, too. The name is good enough for me," I mumbled crossly as I watched Mimi stroll the hospital room with my daughter in her arms. Tired and sore from giving birth, I'm tempted to fling back the covers, snatch Tori from her, and make a break for it. Wouldn't that teach Mimi a lesson about mothers and daughters and the way things ought to be?

"Her name is Alexander, and I won't hear another word about it. Victoria Alexander... just like the rest of the family."

Not quite. While even Mimi had reverted back to using Ed's name after her recent divorce from Husband Number Four, I'm the lone holdout. Lily Lavender, never married. The only Lavender in the bunch.

"I might change it," I threaten. "I'm her mother. I have every right." But even as I test it on my tongue, I know the switch won't happen. Tori Lavender doesn't taste right.

"She is Jack's daughter, she is an Alexander, and that is that," Mimi orders. "And don't you dare call her Tori." She cuddles Tori close. "You don't want to grow up with some horrible common nickname, do you, my princess?"

Tori screws up her face in a scowl and starts to scream. Mimi turns back to me with a triumphant smile. "See? She doesn't like the name any more than I do."

My breasts leak milk at the sound of my baby's screams and I reach for her as the wailing intensifies. Tori is less than one day old, and she doesn't care one way or another what her name is. Right now, all she wants is to eat.

"Lily?" There's a knock on Mimi's office door, knocking me out of the maternity ward and back into the present. Francesca peeks inside, eyebrows lifting as she spots me at Mimi's computer. I feel like I'm ten years old and have been caught messing with things I've been told not to touch. I quash down the sudden impulse to run and hide or explain myself. But as her eyes widen and travel down my body, I realize it isn't the sight of me at Mimi's desk that has Francesca flabbergasted. It's my new dress... the cornflower-blue one I wore to work today.

Francesca, in her usual black garb, opens and closes her mouth several times like she thinks I've been away from the chapel so long, I've forgotten Mimi's rules. But when she finally speaks, she says something I never expected.

"Jack is here. He's in the lobby and wants to see you."

I straighten in Mimi's chair. Jack, at the chapel? As far as I know, he never visits except when Tori's in town and staying with Mimi. But Tori has been camped out at Ed and Jack's the past few nights. Surely he knows that she's spending every free minute at the hospital with Mimi.

"What should I tell him?" Francesca throws a glance over her shoulder. "Do you have time to see him?"

Not only do I not have time, I don't want to. I especially do not appreciate him showing up unannounced. "Did he say what he wanted?"

But before she can answer, he pushes through the door. He plants a quick kiss on Francesca's cheek with a quick nod for me. "Thanks, good-looking."

Francesca blushes and takes the compliment as her own. I'm glad to let her have it. God knows I don't need or want him starting up his little tricks with me. He strides across the room, slings his jacket over one of the chairs, and throws himself into the chair across from me. "Glad you had time to see me."

"Yes, well, I am rather busy." It's not like he gave me time to agree to see him. I glance out the bank of windows overlooking the courtyard and spot Jack's silver Porsche parked askew. He took up two entire parking slots. Damn the man, barging in like this. Silently I curse Ed under my breath. He promised that if I took care of Mimi, he would see to Jack.

"How's your dad?" I ask, blinking innocently.

"Pop?" Jack shrugs. "Fine, I guess. He was at his desk eating lunch when I headed off to court. I haven't gone back to the office yet." He slouches in his chair, loosens his tie. For some reason, the gesture irritates the hell out of me. Jack looks like he's settling in, but I'm in no mood for a nice long chat with anyone... especially if it happens to be Jack Alexander. The man has a way of messing with my head.

"Same old Lily." He chuckles, casually hitches one leg across his knee. "What has you in such a prickly mood today?"

My stomach does a slow simmer as I try to think up a stinging retort. Maybe it's the fact that he showed up without being asked. Barged his way into my office. Or maybe it's simply Jack being his normal, irritating, sexy-as-hell self. I stare at him a moment, take in the dark stubble brushing his chin, the firm jawline, flat stomach, the ripple of muscles playing under his crisp white shirt. Even with his fiftieth birthday coming up next month, Jack still has what it takes to make a woman sit up and take notice.

"Tori isn't here if that's why you came." I shift in my chair. "She's at the hospital."

"Yep, she told me this morning. She also said that you and Francesca plan on keeping the business open while Mimi recovers. I have to tell you, Lily, I'm glad to hear it. I know how you feel about the chapel, but someone has to oversee things. Obviously you're in the best position to do it." He glances around Mimi's office, then back at me. "I see you've already started making some changes."

"What are you talking about? I haven't made any changes."

"No?" He nods as his eyes travel the length of my body. A slow approving smile plays on his face. "Nice dress. That blue brings out the color of your eyes."

I blush despite every effort to calm myself. When I was younger, one compliment from Jack would have had my head spinning, my heart bursting, and me fantasizing about him all night long. I nursed that stupid dream all the way through high school. Talk about a fool. Graduation, and there he was, wrapping me in a bear hug. "Good job, kid," he whispered in my ear. "But I'm not a kid," I wanted to tell him, his words erasing the joy from the day. "I'm headed to college. I'm all grown up." But I knew it didn't matter. Jack always saw me as a kid. That's all I ever was to him. A kid, hanging around the edges of his life.

"Since you're making some changes, you might want

to consider a few more."

"Excuse me?"

"Come on, Lily, don't go playing dumb on me. Look at the place." He glances around the room. "You and I both know it needs an overhaul. I've been telling Mimi that for years. Same goes for your website. It needs some fresh material and new photos. It's outdated and starting to look its age."

I chew the inside of my lip rather than chew him out. Knowing he's right irks me to no end. Still, haven't I been thinking the exact same thing? Everything about the chapel—and the villa, built by Big Mike in the early sixties—could use an update. It's hard not to notice. I doubt anything has been done to the place since Big Mike died and Mimi remodeled. She built the business and established the Royal Wedding Chapel, carving out its reputation as one of Las Vegas's premiere wedding venues. But even Buckingham Palace needs refurbishing every now and then. Tattered elegance? The Royal Wedding Chapel looks every bit its age and more than a little frayed around the edges.

"Face it, Lily, you're up against some stiff competition. The big casinos have some major financial backing behind them. If I was running this chapel, I'd throw some money into fixing the place up. Brides coming here are buying into an idea of elegance, not shabbiness. You can't afford to lose your reputation."

I squirm in my chair. Reputation? He's a fine one to talk about losing a reputation. He ruined mine.

Jack shakes his head. "Mimi laughs and tells me to mind my own business. God knows I love her, but your mother has a stubborn streak that can drive a man crazy. Hopefully you have enough sense in that pretty head of yours to take my advice."

Exactly who does he think he is, shooting off about Mimi's stubborn streak? True, she used to be his stepmother, but they're no longer related. Jack knows squat about brides, let alone the wedding business. He's never even been married. Meanwhile, I grew up in the shadow of the chapel. I am imminently more qualified to figure things out.

"I see you haven't changed much," I say, throwing him a sweet smile. "You're still your usual arrogant self, telling me how to run my business."

"*Your* business?" One eyebrow lifts and I know he's amused. "Last I heard, Mimi is still alive."

"Fine... Mimi's business." I grind out the words through clenched teeth. "Let's cut to the chase, Jack. Why are you here? Don't tell me you're thinking about tying the knot with some doe-eyed beauty who's lured you into buying her a ring and going for the happily-ever-after?" I try to keep a handle on my emotions and remember that I'm an adult and not some ten-year-old kid with a crush on her handsome older stepbrother. A man who is no longer my stepbrother. A man who happens to be the father of my child. A man who, after all these years and all our history, still has the ability—with a quirk of his eyebrow and a tilt of his head—to make every inch of me melt with desire. And with one flip remark he can still bring my temper roaring to the surface.

Slap his face or surrender to his arms? We probably would have killed each other if we'd ended up together, despite the fact that Jack was—and remains—the best lover I ever had in my life. Not that there have been many. Not that I would tell him, either. There's a good reason I put three hundred miles between us after Tori was born, even though he begged me to stay.

"It must be a girl," I add. "Somehow, I can't imagine you're here just to see me."

"Lily, love, I'm always here to see you." A slow grin spreads across his face. "I take it you're not interested in discussing renovation plans?"

"Not particularly," I say, alternately cursing myself for noticing the dimple again and disgusted with myself at the surge of pleasure I feel at hearing he's not here because of a woman. Still, he must have better things to do than sit around and lecture me on how to run the business. Tori told me once that his billing rate is four hundred dollars per hour. With that kind of money at stake, he hasn't got time to waste. For that matter, neither do I.

"Perhaps," I say, "you'd rather discuss the IRS."

A shock of surprise lights his face. "What are you talking about?"

"They phoned the other day. The agent wanted to talk to Mimi."

He sits forward. "Did he mention what it was about?"

"Come on, Jack, let's not play games. I'm sure you know exactly why he was phoning."

A frown pinches his forehead. "Sweetheart, honestly, I have no clue."

I feel the anger simmering inside me. "When I told the agent about Mimi's stroke, he refused to discuss the matter with me and suggested I contact her attorney." I eye him across the desk. "And that, Mr. Alexander, would be you. Since I'm sure Mimi shares all her secrets with you, I assume you would know all the details."

Jack clenches his hands in a tight knot. "I don't know anything about the IRS and that's the truth," he says. "I'm not at liberty to tell you more than that. I can't breach an attorney-client privilege unless I have express permission from my client. And Mimi is my client."

Another stall tactic. Why am I not surprised? It's only what I would have expected from him.

"Whatever, Jack," I say. "Forget I said anything. I'll handle it myself. Now, I'm a busy woman. If you won't tell me about the IRS, tell me why you're here."

He looks a little surprised and frankly, so am I. Neither of us is used to me being so blunt, but that's the way things are going to be from now on. Jack had his chance in the hospital waiting room the other night. He turned away when I turned to him. All I needed was one word. One look, one caring gesture, and I would have abandoned the rules I've forced myself to live by. I would have thrown myself at his feet or thrown myself in his arms. But that won't happen now. Jack's coldness and callousness hurt. With everything I have going on in my life, I don't dare let down my guard. I did that at the hospital the other night, but it won't happen again.

"Actually, I'm here because of Tori."

"What about her?" My eyes narrow. "Did she send you over to plead her case?"

Tori and I still haven't had it out over her taking off that day in her car. She might think she's all grown up, but in many ways she's still a child. She has no idea how frantic or furious I was when I took the call from her school, then discovered she'd disappeared. As soon as this medical situation with Mimi calms down, I intend to sit Tori down for a nice long chat. We'll discuss life, her future, and how things are going to work from now on.

"She doesn't even know I'm here." Jack rubs his forehead like he's trying to rub away the problem or figure out the solution. "Look, Lily, I came over today because I'm worried about her. This whole thing with Mimi has her really messed up. When we got home from the hospital last night, she locked herself in her bedroom and wouldn't stop crying. I tried talking to her and so did Pop, but she refused to open the door. She cried all night."

"You should have called me," I admonish, chewing my bottom lip. But even as I chide him, I know my being there wouldn't have made any difference. Tori never would have opened the door for me, either, except to shout, "Leave me alone! Go away!"

"I'm at a loss, Lily. I don't know what to do." He rubs his chin, his eyes muddy pools of concern. "Pop's worried about her and so am I."

For once, Jack and I are on the same page. Tori's at a vulnerable age. She loves joking about my career in the death business, but until now, she's never had to deal with tragedy on a personal level. How would she react if anything were to happen to Mimi...

He leans forward, knots his hands together. "Driving into the office this morning, I came up with a plan."

"What kind of a plan?" I ask warily. Jack's ideas don't always work out according to Hoyle.

"Just hear me out before you go off the deep end. I

haven't even discussed this with Tori. I wanted to talk it over with you first. I think it could work."

I take a deep breath. Jack talked me into what he thought was a good idea once before, and look where it got us. At least this time there's a desk between us—and no tequila. "I'm listening."

"Mimi comes home from the hospital tomorrow, right?" He doesn't even wait for me to confirm his assertion. "But none of us, including the doctors, have any idea how fast she'll recover or *if* she'll recover."

"Of course she's going to recover," I say, tamping down the chill shooting up my spine. Mimi simply *has* to recover, that's all there is to it. I refuse to consider any other possibility. "The doctors say she's getting better every day."

"It's been five days, Lily, and she's still not talking," he softly reminds me. "And what about that walker they've got her using?"

He shakes his head and I can imagine what he's thinking: the same thought that's been doing cartwheels through my mind since this whole thing happened. What if Mimi never regains her balance? What if she never regains her speech? What if...

No. I push away the thought. We are not at that point, and no doctor, no therapist, has given us the slightest indication that we might have to face it. Jack can go off on all the tangents he wants, but he is not going to sucker me into playing his little game of *what-if.* It's a dangerous game; one I've played before, at great expense to my peace of mind.

"Tori says you plan to leave in August."

"That's right." I do my best to ignore the firm hint of disapproval in both his voice and eyes. "I've made arrangements so that we can stay through the end of August. That gives us two months. The entire summer. Mimi will be much better by then."

"Your mother is recovering from a major stroke. You mean to sit there and tell me that you believe she's going to be up, marching through the chapel and barking orders like she used to in merely eight weeks?"

My chin juts high. "Yes, I believe there's a very good chance that she'll be back at the chapel and it will be business as usual." But will it? The thought of Mimi *barking orders* is difficult to imagine. Right now all she can do is grunt.

"Maybe in six months," he concedes, "but not in eight weeks. Come on, Lily, think about it. Aren't you being overly optimistic? You can't leave."

Suddenly I am livid. It is absolutely none of Jack's business what I do or don't do. "Two months," I repeat firmly. "By then, we'll be in a much better position to know how everything has worked out. Besides, we have to go home. Tori starts school at the end of August."

Jack clears his throat. "That's what I wanted to talk to you about. If the two of you stayed longer, Tori could go to school in Las Vegas."

His words freeze my building anger into a thick wall of ice that slams up between us in the air-conditioned office. "Don't be insane. Tori is in one of the best schools in California."

"Las Vegas has good schools."

"We are not staying," I repeat coldly, words sharp as

a pickax. "Besides, it's Tori's senior year. She loves her school and her friends. I refuse to pull her out."

He rolls his eyes. "You and I both know she doesn't care squat about that school. She wants to be here, in Las Vegas, with us. That's all she's ever wanted."

"That's not true," I shoot back, though both of us know that I'm talking nonsense. Everything Tori wants is in this town. I never should have allowed Mimi to carry on that silly tradition of crowning Tori with the family tiara each year on her birthday. The vintage diamonds and antique combs have carved a place in my daughter's heart and head, convincing her that Las Vegas and the Royal Wedding Chapel are the crown jewels of the world.

How can I hope to compete with the royal tiara? How do I convince Tori that she's wrong? How can I make her understand that this business and this town will only break her heart?

"This conversation is finished, Jack. We're staying for two months and then we leave. Tori will spend her senior year in Del Mar."

"I wonder what Tori might have to say about that." His eyes narrow. "Maybe we should ask her."

"Don't you dare," I hiss. Jack mentioned he hadn't told her about his idea, but what if he isn't telling me the truth? He's a very sharp attorney and accustomed to talking his way through anything to achieve the verdict he wants. For all I know, the three of them—Jack, Ed and Tori—have already discussed this and have a plan in place.

Jack blows out a sigh. "I didn't come here to fight with you. I know you have Tori's best interests at heart. You're a good mom, Lily. A great mom. I've always thought that."

I suck in a soft breath. All these years and he's never said a word about the way I've raised our daughter. His contribution to child-rearing is to smother Tori with gifts she doesn't need and to pepper my bank account with monthly child-support checks. That and the huge bouquet of flowers that arrives every year on Tori's birthday. Flowers for me.

"We have to go back, Jack," I say. "I have a job, remember? I've taken a leave of absence through the end of August."

"Then you go back. But why not let Tori stay here? She can finish out high school in Las Vegas. Take some time and think about it, Lily," he urges. "It makes sense. She could live with Pop and me and see Mimi all she wants. Plus, she could work weekends at the chapel if she wants."

If she *wants*? Is he crazy? Tori would jump at the chance. It's all she's ever wanted, and he and I know it. If I give in to his request and let Tori stay, she'll never leave.

And to think that I was actually beginning to believe him. I'll bet he's had this whole scenario planned all along. He's probably already talked to Tori. Who knows? They might have even picked out a school. I can't believe, after all these years of me being in charge, he could think he has the right to make decisions about—

"And if Mimi still needs help once you're back in San Diego, we'll hire somebody to fill in during the week."

"We?" I sputter. "Exactly when did *we* get involved in this?" I should have known he was up to something, especially once he started in with the flattery. "This isn't any of your business, Jack. And what goes on in this house is none of your business, either."

"I'm only trying to help." He raises his hands high, spreading his fingers in a *You-win* gesture. "But what happens after you leave? What about Mimi?"

"If need be, I'll hire a private nurse."

His eyebrows shoot up. "That sounds expensive."

"It's none of your concern. I have money." But the truth is, the more we talk, the more nervous I'm feeling. I've worked hard for the past twenty years, intent on making a decent life for myself and Tori. Until now, I've managed quite well. Tori goes to a private school and I have a great job, a nice house, and despite the crappy economy, a sizeable 401K safe and secure in government bonds. But I've also taken an unpaid leave of absence for the next couple of months. No money coming in will make a serious dent in the six-month emergency fund I have stashed away. It will cover the mortgage, car payment, and utility bills. But will it cover the cost of a private nurse for Mimi?

I force the fear from my mind and a fierce smile to my face. I don't dare let him see that I'm running scared. If he senses hesitation, he'll take advantage of it. "I can handle this. We'll be fine."

"I don't doubt that," he says. "You've always been very good at handling things, Lily. In fact, that's part of your problem. You're so good at it, you never let anyone help. Even when you were a kid, you were always like that. Always wanting to do things by yourself. Always on your own. Like you had something to prove."

"I appreciate you pointing out my faults. I'll be sure to work on them." I don't recall asking his opinion about my personal failings. And much as I would love the opportunity to point out his own characters defects—cocky, stubborn, arrogant—I will have to forego the pleasure. Mimi will be home tomorrow and I have things to do.

"As far as I'm concerned, our little chat is finished," I say. "Tori is my daughter. I know what's best for her."

The smile melts from his face. "She's my daughter, too. Remember this, Lily: she'll be eighteen at the end of September. What happens then? What do you think Tori will decide when she's a legal adult and able to make her own decisions? What choice will she make when it's no longer up to you?"

Our eyes lock and we stare each other down.

"Think about it," he says quietly. "That's all I'm asking."

He's asking too much. I've sacrificed everything—career, home, friends—to stick around in this city I've always hated, to work this business I've always hated, to care for Mimi, who doesn't exactly deserve the crown for *Mother of the Year*. Now he's asking me to give up my daughter, too? I am not about to let that happen. "Get out."

Jack blinks. "Come on, Lily, you don't mean—"

"You heard me. Get out." The words burn my tongue like bitter acid. "I don't need you messing with my life or my head. You've already done enough of that."

His hands grip the arms of his chair. His eyes blaze, but he doesn't move. I wait for him to lash out, wait for the torrent of words, wait for him to remind me that he is Tori's father and has every right to speak up on matters concerning her welfare. How can I argue with that kind of logic? Until now, we've never argued about the way I've raised her. Jack knows how much I love her. To be honest,

I know how much he loves her, too. But I refuse to take back what I said. Not a single word. Tori belongs with me. And the sooner Jack Alexander gets that through his thick skull, the better off we'll all be.

"If you don't like it, take me to court," I growl. My hands knot into tight fists at the thought of doing battle with him. "Go ahead and try it. News flash, Jack. I'm her mother. I'll win."

His eyes narrow and he stares at me a long moment. Then, to my surprise, he abruptly shrugs and stands. "Fine. If that's the way you want it." Turning his back, he strolls out the door.

My heart slams against my chest as I watch him walk away. I don't know if he bought into the little act I just put on. All bluster and bravado. It doesn't matter. Nothing matters except something he said. Something I never gave a thought to until he showed up today. And the more I think about it, the more it scares me that Jack might be right.

What if Tori refuses to leave? What if, in two months, she simply says *no*. As Jack pointed out, she's not a little girl anymore. There's no way I can force her to get in the car and return home with me. No matter how much I might want to, it would be physically impossible. Tori inherited my height and every ounce of Mimi's stubbornness.

I bury my face in my hands. What am I going to do? If Mimi isn't fully recovered in two months, I could very well have a fight on my hands. But it's not the fight with Jack that scares me.

It's the prospect that if I'm not careful, I'll lose Tori.

Chapter Six

"MY DRESS IS RUINED." THE bride, a slim gorgeous redhead who looks barely older than Tori rustles through the reception area in a gown of satin and lace with elegant ruching... and an ugly red smear staining the side. "I dropped my lipstick," she wails as the tears start to flow.

"Don't worry, it will be okay." Reaching under the counter, I pull out a bit of modern-day magic. "Stand still." I blot the dress with the little white pen stain remover we keep handy for emergencies. Two minutes later, the lipstick has disappeared and the bride is as radiant as every girl deserves to be on her wedding day.

"Thank you so much," she gushes before heading back to the bridal suite. Smiling, I head back around the counter. If only all life's problems could be wiped away as easily as the mess on her dress. I wish someone would invent a magic eraser for physical ailments and emotional gloom. Mimi has the ailments, but I'm the one suffering from gloom and doom.

The Queen Mum is back in residence. Mimi has only been home one day, and though she still can't talk, she's doing a magnificent job of making her royal presence known. *Thump, thump, thump* is her new method of issuing commands to anyone within hearing distance inside the villa. Jack probably thought he was doing us all a favor when he bought her the elegant carved cane to use once she graduates from the walker. But I'm sick of hearing her pounding the floor. The next time Jack shows up, I just might grab that cane and do a little pounding of my own. *Thwack!* Right across his head.

As if Mimi's condition weren't enough of a headache, her balance sheet is giving me nightmares. Despite numerous attempts, I've failed in my quest to balance the books. The numbers don't add up, and I can't figure out how she's been able to keep the place open. The two bridal couples we hosted today—including the current bride resplendent with lipstick stain—purchased full wedding packages: corsages, bouquets, photography, plus limo service to and from their hotels. If every bridal couple bought the complete package, it would produce a nice healthy income. But the chapel needs to host five weddings daily to remain solvent, and my short forays through the wedding software Mimi uses to book and track brides shows that isn't the case. I scan the upcoming ceremonies scheduled for this summer. It doesn't make sense. The money coming in doesn't begin to cover the bills. I searched the database last night and ran a comparison of last year's financials against present day. The numbers were dismal.

No wonder the Royal Wedding Chapel looks shabby. Mimi's balance sheet is covered in blood. She's been operating in the red for at least two years. From what I can determine, there is no money left over for repairs or renovations. It's a miracle she's been able to keep the doors open as long as she has.

I wait while Jaabir escorts the last bridal couple into the limo and Tori scoots across the courtyard to check on Mimi. Finally my chance comes and I hunt down Francesca. I find her in the Queen's Chapel. "Do you have a minute? I'd like to talk with you."

"As long as we do it sitting down. My feet hurt." She follows me into Mimi's office and drops into a chair with a heavy pouf. Slipping off her shoes, she wiggles her toes with a sigh of pleasure. "Ah, much better. What's on your mind, honey?"

I sink into the other chair and scoot it close beside her. "I'm worried."

"Is it Mimi?" Her eyes widen and she clutches at her throat, looking as scared as I must have when I glimpsed this year's expenses on Mimi's balance sheet. "Has something happened?"

"No, she's fine," I assure her. Where do I begin? "It's about the chapel finances. I've been going over the books and things don't look good."

"Is that all?" She pats my cheek affectionately, the way she used to when I was a little girl. "For a minute, you had me scared. I thought something had happened to Mimi."

I think of Mimi, safely ensconced in the villa. She's still weak and needs help with everything. Simply getting out of bed is a major task. But it won't be long before she's strong enough to navigate the walk from the villa to the chapel. I have no illusions about what will happen then. I'll be banished from my seat on the throne—and Mimi's computer.

"I need your help. From the little I've seen, I can tell things aren't fine. In fact, they're downright terrible." I share with her what I've been able to discover. "Frankly, I don't understand how she's managed to keep the chapel open."

She draws a deep breath. "Are things really that bad?"

"I'm afraid so." No wonder the IRS came calling. The few financials I managed to pull together don't make sense. There are plenty of disbursements, with payroll obviously the number one expense, but the chapel's bridal income has dwindled throughout the fiscal year. Less brides equals less business. Less business equals less money. With June thirtieth and year-end looming, the chapel will once again end up in the red and could finally be forced to shut its doors. Given Mimi's medical bills, she might not have a choice.

"I can't imagine how Mimi would survive without the chapel. It's her business. It's her life. It's her home." Francesca's eyes fill with a quiet terror. "It's *my* home."

"We'll figure out something," I assure her, though I haven't a clue as to how we're going to manage.

"Lily, what would we do without you? I'm so glad you're home."

Her words are meant to soothe, but they've done anything but. I have no idea how to solve this problem.

More important, do I even want to try?

"This could be just the thing we've been waiting for." Francesca eyes me with a hopeful smile. "Maybe if we make the chapel more attractive, the brides would come. We could do some repairs. Make it a little more contemporary. More upbeat."

"There's no money for that," I remind her.

She pauses, thinking for a moment. "What about the Internet? That doesn't cost money."

The Internet. Las Vegas and the wedding business isn't the way it used to be. The Royal Wedding Chapel is in direct competition with huge hotels with elegant chapels, plus dozens of other wedding chapels springing up around town. It's a sure bet each of them has elaborate websites plus an active web presence.

"Before she got sick, Mimi was talking about replacing the carpeting."

My heart sinks deeper than stepping barefoot into the thickest cushiony pile. Carpeting is the least of our problems.

"Maybe we should hire someone to sit outside the County building," Francesca muses. "Some of the other chapels do that. It might stir up more business."

"No, I don't think so." The sidewalk outside the Clark County building is littered with people desperate for jobs and crumpled pamphlets from chapels desperate for business. Mimi's chapel might be floundering, but it has a reputation to uphold. Hiring someone to stand on a crowded street corner and push literature about the chapel on couples arriving for a marriage license screams of desperation. Things might be dire, but it's not that bad. Plus, I can just imagine what would happen if Mimi found out I'd sanctioned something like that. *"Off with her head!"* she'd scream.

"We have to do something to breathe new life into this place. It looks and feels old and stale, like King George and Queen Mary are still on the throne." I glance around

Mimi's office. "We need to toss out the old and bring in the new. Think about it, Francesca. If the royal family did it, why can't we? Look at all the changes the royals have been through. Charles and Diana, Andrew and Fergie."

"Don't talk to me about that woman." Francesca clucks her tongue. "I don't blame the Queen one bit for booting her out of the family. Such a disgusting thing to do, letting that man publicly suck her toes."

I bite back a laugh. "I agree that what Fergie did was horrible. The royals didn't deserve the publicity. But that's exactly my point. Things went downhill for a while, but then they rebounded. Think about William and Kate. The Royal Wedding breathed new life into the family. And now, with their baby, the whole world is interested."

"What a wonderful idea. We could model ourselves after William and Kate." She brightens. "We could even rename the chapel rooms."

Her suggestion catches me by surprise. Definitely not a bad idea. Definitely worth considering. "I like it," I say, nodding. "Let me think about it. Meanwhile, let's talk about something else you said. Do you realize how many brides find their wedding venue through an Internet search? Our website is pathetic. It needs to be updated."

"I could take new pictures," she quickly offers. "We could post them on our site."

"We need more than photos. I've been checking out some of the other wedding websites. You wouldn't believe how many of them post videos of recent weddings. There's no reason we can't do the same. Plus, we need links. And a wedding blog. We need a social presence. Facebook. Trip Advisor. Twitter. Pinterest."

I chatter on, pushing away the image of that *told-you-so* grin I'd surely see on Jack's face if he could hear me now. "The chapel is stuck in a time warp. We need to fast-forward into the future of today."

"Do you know how to do all this? Because I don't. And neither does Mimi."

My face falls as reality hits. I'm comfortable in the world of finance and could come up with a decent marketing strategy for the chapel in a pinch. But website design, hyperlinks, live streaming video, and social media connections are foreign territory. "I'm afraid not," I admit.

"Then we'll have to hire someone."

"Maybe," I agree, though I already know we can't afford it. The check I cut yesterday for Jaabir's weekly salary nearly drained the chapel's checking account. Francesca hasn't been paid since before Mimi's stroke.

"Just thinking about the possibility that the chapel might go under... well, it's horrible. And closing the chapel would just about kill Mimi. It's all she knows. It's all I know." She pulls some crumpled tissues from her pocket. "I don't know what I'd do if I didn't have the chapel. I've never felt so old and useless in my life."

How can I let her down? Francesca has worked at the chapel for nearly fifty years, even before Big Mike married my mother. His unexpected death several months later could have spelled disaster, but together the two of them had rescued the chapel. The business means as much to Francesca as it does to Mimi—maybe even more. I can't just sit here and do nothing. Maybe it's salvageable. Maybe I can figure something out. I lean across the space between us and plant a kiss on her forehead. "Don't give up yet. I might have a plan."

"You do?" She pulls in a slight breath. "What kind of plan?"

The small lick of hope flaring in her eyes sparks a huge heap of guilt searing my soul. What am I doing? I have no business lying to her, leading her on into thinking I know what I'm doing when I haven't the slightest clue. I've always hated the chapel. Why am I making promises I might not be able to keep? Wouldn't it be simpler to let things go? All my problems solved in one fell swoop. "Leave it to me."

"It's good to know we can always count on you," Francesca says.

I give her a weak smile, allowing myself the luxury of pretending that what I told her is true. How I'm going to come up with a plan to salvage this business is beyond me. But if my words gave Francesca some peace of mind, it was totally worth it.

When you're already stuck in hell, what's one more lie?

Tori has made elaborate efforts to celebrate Mimi's first dinner back home. Fine china is laid out on the immense mahogany table in the Mediterranean-style dining room. But rather than being a merry occasion, the whole thing seems odd, beginning with this room. Dramatic vaulted ceiling, tapestry wall hangings, and rich Persian carpet, it's rarely used. Oddest of all is Mimi, sitting at the table, walker parked close behind her, wearing one of her nicer dresses... and a bib.

Tori chatters nonstop as she dices Mimi's chicken

breast and broccoli florets into tiny pieces. I'm across from Mimi, my eyes on my own plate, making a valiant attempt to force down my dinner. It's painful watching Mimi as she struggles to eat. She can't use her right hand as the right side of her body was affected by the stroke. She needs help. The handle of her fork is wrapped with cushy red foam, a device the hospital's occupational therapist advised would be helpful in assisting during recovery. Mimi fought like hell tonight before she finally gave in and allowed me to slip the foam over the fork. But I didn't give her a choice. It was that or let her pick at her food with her fingers.

Don't baby her, the therapist warned yesterday before we left the hospital. She'll find her own limits. The human mind is fascinating in itself, capable of much more than we expect. Mimi will learn what she can do for herself if we give her the time and space. Meanwhile, strange as it may sound, this ordeal has already produced some major blessings, the most important being that Mimi is home. The doctors never would have released her if they hadn't felt she was making progress. No more daily trips to the hospital except for rehabilitation therapy. She's also regained control of most of her bodily functions, including her bladder. No need for adult diapers. No need to assist her. No need for Mimi to lose more of her dignity. And she's beginning to look her normal self again. Her face no longer has that strange, droopy pull, like a sad clown who discovered he was left behind when the circus packed up and left town. Those are the good things. But her speech remains garbled, her hand and leg movements are jerky, and she can't maneuver without the use of her walker.

It's going to be a slow recovery.

A fork clinks against a plate, and I look up to witness Mimi struggling to stab a bite of chicken. Somehow she manages to lift the fork toward her mouth. Just as the chicken reaches her tongue, it slides off the fork, bounces off her bib and falls on the plate.

"Mmph," she grunts and throws the fork down with a fierce disgust.

"You have to eat." Tori scoots closer, picks up the fork. "Come on, I'll help you."

I stare at my daughter, then at my mother. Something shifts in my heart. *Baby steps.* That will be the only way we'll make it through this. But if someone constantly carries her, where is the incentive for Mimi to relearn how to do things on her own?

"Put the fork down, Tori."

Both my mother and daughter shoot me dagger looks, but I keep my chin up. I refuse to back down. I'm merely following what the hospital team suggested. "Let Mimi do it by herself," I say firmly. "She can do it."

Francesca's face reddens, but she doesn't say a word, bowing her head and focusing on her own dinner. Meanwhile, Tori throws down the fork and folds her arms across her chest. She glares at me like I am the devil personified. Mimi slumps back in her chair, a twisted, contorted version of the woman she was once, but the defiant frown frozen on her face is familiar. Oddly enough, it gives me some comfort. Mimi is lurking in there somewhere. Maybe if I push hard enough, she'll eventually emerge.

"Tori, this chicken is delicious," I say, though it tastes

like wet cardboard. I force another bite down my throat. "Don't you think so, Francesca?"

"It's very good," she agrees quietly.

Mimi purses her lips and glowers at me. I suffer through two more bites with a forced smile. At least if she can't talk, she can't criticize me for anything. A horrible guilt starts to seep through my spirit. I shouldn't be thinking such terrible thoughts. Then abruptly, to my surprise, she reaches for the fork and stabs a piece of chicken.

Just as quickly, the fork slips from her hand and clangs across the fragile china. The piece of meat drops to the floor.

"It's okay, Mimi. I'll clean it up later." Tori pats her grandmother's hand and leans over to pick up the fork. Righting herself, she shoots me a *go-ahead-I-dare-you-to-stop me* look and begins to feed Mimi small bites.

"Put the fork down, Tori," I say once again. "Let her do it by herself." The therapists warned that it wouldn't be easy, and I'm beginning to understand exactly what they meant. Everything looked so simple while she was in the hospital and professionals were caring for her. Now that Mimi is home, she only has us. We can cook her meals, do her laundry, shuttle her back and forth to the hospital for outpatient rehab. But Mimi's physical recovery will be up to her. She's the one who will have to dig deep and find the inner strength to push through the hard parts.

Mimi grunts and picks up her fork.

None of us breathe as she slowly maneuvers the silverware. This time, the chicken makes it into her mouth. She chews, eyes glittering, face hard, glaring at me over every new bite. I square my shoulders and continue eating the rest of my own meal, along with frustration and more than a little satisfaction. Who cares if Mimi is mad at me? It isn't the first time and it won't be the last. At least she's eating.

"You didn't have to be so mean," Tori accuses me half an hour later. The two of us are clearing the table as Francesca helps Mimi get ready for bed. "You hate her. You've always hated her."

"That's not true. I don't hate her." My face reddens. Tori's words sting like a slap. "She's my mother."

"I was trying to make things nice on her first night home, but you had to go and spoil it." Tori snatches silverware from the table. "You saw how hard this was for her. You could have been nicer. You could have tried to help her. Why didn't you help? And why wouldn't you let me help? You're not being fair, Mom. Mimi needs us. She needs us now more than ever."

"Do you think I don't know that?" I stare at the silverware jammed in her fist. Right now Tori probably hates me just as much as she believes I hate Mimi. She could easily attack me with one of the knives in her hand. But she doesn't need a knife to hurt me. Her words have carved a hole in my heart. Tori knows my weaknesses. Maybe it's because she's growing up. Maybe it comes from two women living together. Maybe it's because I'm her mother. She knows how much I love her. That alone gives her the upper hand. Love always puts you at a disadvantage.

"I understand that this is difficult for you," I say carefully like I'm tiptoeing through a verbal mine field. "Mimi just left the hospital. It's only natural to want to help. But we're all on the same team. This is difficult for all of us and we all want what's best for Mimi." Sinking to my knees, I push aside Mimi's chair and pluck stray bits of chicken and broccoli from the antique Persian rug.

"She wouldn't have made such a mess if you had let me help her," Tori mutters, watching as I crawl around and gather bits of food. "Why did you have to make such a big deal out of it? You're always doing that, Mom. Making a big deal out of things."

"She has to learn to do things by herself. Besides, she used a fork in the hospital, remember? And she did it all by herself." I struggle to my feet and lock eyes with my daughter. "I know you wanted tonight to be a celebration—"

Tori's face hardens. "Yes, and it was ruined, thanks to you."

The harsh judgment rings in my ears, but I hold my ground. "You're absolutely right. Everything would have been perfect if I had let you help her. No fuss, no mess. We would have shared a delicious meal, and she wouldn't have dropped anything on the floor." Opening my hand, I dump the remains of Mimi's chicken and broccoli on a plate. "But we have to let her learn how to do things for herself. It's the only way she's going to get better. The next few weeks are going to require a lot of patience— from all of us."

I think of the tub chair being delivered tomorrow. Mimi won't be able to manage bathing by herself. Francesca is too old to assist, and while Tori would do it in a heartbeat, it wouldn't be fair to put her through the stress of coping with the sight of her grandmother naked. Helping Mimi bathe will be my task.

The rooms of the villa are filled with rehab equipment brought home from the hospital. Mimi's walker, her reacher, the utensil sponges, the transfer board. All designed to help Mimi. But none of them will work unless she wants to help herself.

"What if she can't do it? What if she falls?" Tori demands.

"Then we'll help her up."

"But what if she needs something? She can't talk."

"We bought a bell, remember? She can ring it if she needs us." I think of Jack's cane, how Mimi pounds it against the floor. "And there's nothing wrong with her left hand. If she needs something, she can write it down."

The harshness on Tori's face slowly melts into a soft puddle, fear curdling around the edges. "What if she never gets better?" she finally whispers.

Is that what's been whirling inside her head? Suddenly I remember she's only seventeen. She's world-wise and tech-savvy, but when it comes to matters of the heart, she's still just a baby. I open my arms and Tori sinks into me. I wrap her close, embrace the welcome feel of my daughter in my arms. It's been a long time since she's allowed me to hold her, and I miss it. Her hair smells like apricot and spices, sexy and exotic. When did she quit using the regular shampoo I've used on her hair since she was a baby? When did she start buying her own? Why didn't I notice? How many things have I been too busy to pay attention to?

No wonder she loves Mimi so much. Mimi notices everything about her.

I hold Tori close and let her cry out all the hurt and

loss. For once, I'm grateful for the villa's thick adobe walls. Not only do they keep the place cool and quiet, but they're solid enough that no one will overhear her sobbing. I stroke her back and murmur comforting words, though I already know that nothing I say will take away the pain. Growing up is hard enough under normal circumstances. The circumstances surrounding Mimi's stroke are anything but normal. My little girl is being forced into adulthood.

"You okay?" I ask as her breathing finally slows and her sobs start to cease. She clings tight, doesn't respond. I pause, wait a few more seconds. The last thing I want is Jack charging in to save the day, but it wouldn't be right if I didn't ask. "Maybe it would help if you called your dad."

Tori finally pulls away, swipes the last few tears from her eyes. "No, that's okay. I'll call him later." She puts on a brave smile.

I smile back and swallow the dread clinging at the back of my throat. At least I won't have to deal with Jack. "Why don't you go say good night to Mimi, and I'll finish cleaning up."

She eyes me cautiously. "Are you sure?"

I nod. "Yes. I'll take care of things here."

She squares her shoulders. "Okay."

I busy myself gathering the remaining dishes as she scoots from the room. After what happened tonight, part of me feels like crying, too. Will I ever see that little girl again in her eyes?

"Mom?"

I look up and find Tori halted in the doorway. "Yes?"

"I was just thinking." She stares at me with wide, beautiful blue eyes so like Mimi's own. "Maybe tomorrow night, it might be better if we eat in the kitchen." Her mouth twists in a question mark. "The terra-cotta floor is easier to clean."

I bite my lip. This admission has cost her dearly. "That's a wonderful idea, sweetie."

Tori nods, smiles, and we leave it at that.

Chapter Seven

"DID FRANCESCA TELL YOU WHAT happened to the groom? He nearly passed out!" Tori drapes herself over the reception counter, face flushed and radiant. "Oh, Mom, you should have seen him. It was absolutely one of the most romantic things I've ever seen in my life."

I've been trying to assess the IRS situation, but suddenly I find myself wondering how anyone could consider a groom fainting to be the slightest bit romantic... and how my lovely, intelligent daughter could be caught up in such silliness.

Tori's eyes go dreamy. "I love watching the grooms and their reaction when they see their brides. And this one was so sweet. He was at the altar beside Francesca when I switched on the music and started the bridal march. Everything was fine until the bride started down the aisle. He started taking deep gulps and brushing away the tears when he saw her. Then she reached the altar and took his arm, and that's when he started getting wobbly. Suddenly his face went white—whiter than her wedding gown!—and Francesca grabbed a chair. She made him sit down right there at the altar with his head between his legs. "And his bride?" Tori swoons. "Oh, Mom, I wish you could have seen her. It was adorable. She dropped her flowers and put her arms around him." Tori is all smiles. "It took a couple of minutes before he finally managed to get back on his feet and insisted they continue. Francesca kept the chair at the altar, just in case. After the ceremony was finished, he told us that he'd felt fine until he saw his bride starting down the aisle. And when he realized she was about to be his, it literally took his breath away." Tori exhales a dreamy sigh. "Isn't that the most romantic thing you ever heard?"

"Absolutely," I lie through my teeth. No wonder the groom nearly fainted. The two of them are barely legal age, and now they're married. What do they know about life, let alone starting a family? I think about the groom, how he pumped his fist in the air as they emerged from Queen Elizabeth's Chapel and showered his bride with kisses. Childhood sweethearts, they confessed, exchanging secret smiles as we waited for Jaabir and the limo. They'd known each other all their lives, kindergarten through high school, the bride giddily informed me. His proposal the night they graduated came as no surprise, despite both sets of parents' misgivings.

No wonder their parents had objected. If it were Tori, I would have objected, too. What are the chances of this marriage succeeding? The groom already has wobbly feet. What's going to happen when they have their first fight? When their first baby is born? When they sign the mortgage payment on their first house? What if one of them loses their job? Suffers a serious illness? Has an affair? Marriage is a huge commitment, and the State of Nevada makes it way too easy. Simply show up at the county building with photo ID and cash in hand. No fuss, no counseling, no *do-I-really-know-what-the-hell-I'm-doing*? No one thinks about the statistics on happily ever after vs. divorce. The younger the couple, the less parental involvement and support, the worse the odds are stacked against them. What percentage of marriages performed at Mimi's chapel end up in divorce court?

"Do we have another wedding booked today?" Tori hangs over the counter, scanning the computer screen in front of me, looking over the week's schedule. I know she's torn between running over to the villa and checking in with Mimi versus staying at the chapel in case someone wanders in.

"That's it for today."

She cups her chin in hand. Those luminous blue eyes have already captured more than her fair share of boys' hearts. Someday a man will come along and claim her as his own. Where does the time go? How did I let it slip away? Somehow, the days have turned into years and my little girl has turned into an elegant woman, regal as the lineage from which she was born. With her long blond hair pulled tight in a chignon, she looks just like a princess. Her formfitting black dress hugs her in all the right places. It also looks vaguely familiar. I take a closer look and abruptly realize I'm staring at one of those hideous dresses from the back of my closet that Mimi forced me to wear when I was a teenager working at the chapel. On me, it looked like a death shroud. But it fits Tori perfectly, like she was born to wear it.

The wide wooden door cracks open, blowing in a blast of hot air and a young couple holding hands.

"Are you still open?" the man asks.

"We want to get married." The girl, in a tight floral sundress and strappy sandals, clenches his arm.

"Welcome to the Royal Wedding Chapel." Tori bounces over to greet them before I have a chance to move. She introduces herself, shakes their hands. "Are you planning a large ceremony, or is it just the two of you?"

"We're not sure." The girl shifts her gaze between Tori and me. "It all happened so fast."

"Did not," he counters with a kiss on her cheek.

"Did too," she insists and punches him playfully on the arm. "I didn't know you were going to ask me."

"Sounds like someone has their story mixed up," Tori teases. I step back and watch as my daughter takes control of the situation. She has this handled.

"Steve and I came to Vegas for a little vacation, but we never planned on getting married."

"Kathy didn't... but I did." He grins. "I had the ring in my pocket the whole time."

"He asked me last night." She gazes up at him like he's her knight in shining armor—wearing chinos and a golf shirt. "There we were, just before midnight, standing with the crowds in front of the Bellagio fountains. It was dark, the music was playing, the fountains were dancing... and all of a sudden, he took my hand and dropped to one knee.

"And he proposed! In front of all those people!" A blush of color floods her cheeks. "I swear, everyone was watching us instead of the fountains. Steve was on his knees with a jewelry box in his hand and a gorgeous diamond ring. The crowd was clapping and cheering, I could barely even hear him ask the question... but naturally, I said *yes*."

"That is so romantic," Tori breathes.

"What woman could say *no* to a man who plans something like that?" Kathy flashes the ring and the three of them admire the diamond solitaire as it glitters under the flood lights. "He is just the sweetest man in the world."

"Congratulations!" Tori catches both their hands in her own, completing the circle. "I'm so glad you came today. Let me show you a few things and you can decide what you want."

In one fluid movement, she reaches over the counter in front of me and grasps a clipboard with a setup sheet. "First of all, you absolutely have to see the Royal Tiara." She leads them to the glass display case. Stepping aside, she allows them a close-up view. "It's an heirloom, from my grandfather's family. They were members of the British aristocracy."

Kathy's eyes widen. "You're related to Kate?"

"No, not Kate... but certainly Prince William," Tori replies, "though obviously, many times removed."

The three of them ooh and aah over the royal tiara. Kathy's eyes are luminous as she finally breaks her gaze. "Oh, Steve, this is all so perfect. I can't believe we're in Las Vegas and actually getting married at the Royal Wedding Chapel!"

Tori's smile broadens as she leads them into each of the chapels on tour. Eventually they reappear in the lobby. She points out the enormous glass cooler with the fresh assortment of flowers delivered this morning. She shows them the unity candles, explains the sand-pouring ceremony, chats about the video and photography package. Their questions do not faze her as she up-sells the chapel like she's done it hundreds of times. Finally she secures their signatures on the contract.

I push aside the thought of the IRS agent's phone call. I have just witnessed Tori's first bridal booking. And from the contented smile curving around her face, I know it won't be her last.

Chapter Eight

MIMI HAS NEVER BEEN KNOWN for her patience or tolerance. Dealing with recovery hasn't changed her one bit. Smiling grimly, I duck to the floor and retrieve the pen she deliberately shoved from the kitchen table for the second time in less than two minutes. If she doesn't get with the program soon, I might start shoving a few things myself. There's a limit to how much a person can endure and I'm reaching mine, what with seeing to Mimi's personal needs, keeping Francesca calm, trying to decipher the chapel finances, plus worrying about my recent argument with Jack. I never should have thrown out that threat and dared him to take me to court.

"Remember what the therapist said? Try sounding out the words. If you can't do that, write them down."

Mimi's mouth twists and she glares at me. "Mmph."

"You don't know... or you don't want to tell me?" There's a big difference, and it might just be that she didn't like the question. And until a medical professional tells us that Mimi's finally reached a point where she's gained back as much of her regular life as we can hope for,

I refuse to baby her.

Enforcing the rules is paying off. She's made remarkable strides in her recovery. Jaabir and Tori take turns shuttling her back and forth in the Bentley to the hospital for daily rehab. While her speech is still garbled and her right side remains weak, she continues to gain strength every day. Meanwhile, there's nothing wrong with her mind. It's time the two of us had a little chat about the chapel.

"We need to talk about the business," I repeat for the third time. "I've been going over the numbers, and the income and expenses don't add up. How have you managed to keep the chapel open?" I ask, though I already know the answer.

A furtive smile slides across Mimi's face, as if she thinks I'm clueless when it comes to running a business. As if I don't know how to add two plus two. As if I don't know anything about those secret cash deposits she's been making.

The financial mess surrounding the chapel business account had me nursing a royal headache... until yesterday, when last month's bank statement arrived in the mail. I ripped it open and spied two fat cash deposits—one for five thousand dollars, the other for seven thousand— sitting boldly in the credit column, both of them dated and deposited in the week before Mimi's stroke. My heart pounded as I stared at the healthy sums listed on the bank statement. Deposits not listed on the chapel's financial spreadsheet. Deposits that don't show up on the balance sheet. Deposits that kept the chapel solvent this month.

One look at the bank statement was all it took and I was at Mimi's computer, trolling for answers. For ten frustrating minutes, I flipped through her monthly financial reports. Nothing. I slumped in her chair, mentally kicking myself for being so stupid. Why would I assume Mimi would make things easy? I yanked open her desk drawers, pawed through paperwork, searched high and low, and eventually found what I was looking for stashed deep in the bottom of one of the drawers. Ten months' worth of bank statements, each showing cash deposits of various sums—three thousand dollars here, five thousand there. Relatively small deposits, all of them less than ten thousand dollars, the magical threshold that would have flagged a bank report to the IRS. And all of them untraceable, according to the phone call I had with the bank manager once I recovered from the shock of what I had found.

Where did she get the money? Has Mimi been gambling? She visits the casinos once in a while, but not on a regular basis. People who live and work in Vegas learn early that the only way to keep your job, your house, and stay solvent in this town is to have a healthy respect for the income gambling produces for our state—and to keep a healthy distance from the gaming tables. It's hard to believe Mimi finagled her way out of the chapel's demise by playing the slots or hitting the blackjack table. But the money had to come from someplace. Is she on the take or involved in something illegal? That particular thought I immediately toss out. Mimi might be a lot of things, but a criminal isn't one of them.

She's the only one with the answers but so far, she's not telling. She's not doing much of anything except throwing her pen and fiddling with the enormous emerald and diamond ring flashing on her finger. Idly I wonder if she managed to cover the chapel payroll by selling off some of her jewelry. God knows she has plenty; gifts from Ed, plus the lavish pieces she's indulged herself with throughout the years. No, that's crazy thinking. Mimi loves glitz and glitter too much to part with her beloved jewelry. Obviously the money came from somewhere, but I'll bet my life it wasn't from a pawn shop.

"Numbers don't lie, Mimi. You have a real fiscal problem here. So tell me: how have you managed to keep the chapel open?"

Mimi lifts her good shoulder and shrugs off my concerns.

I tamp down my frustration. My mother can be a formidable foe, but I have a paper trail to back me up. "The bank statement came in yesterday's mail. I opened it up. I saw the deposits. I know that's how you're keeping the chapel afloat. So, that leaves me with one question: where did you get the cash?"

Her eyes narrow, and she raises her left arm, curling her fingers as if what she'd really like to do is wrap them around my throat. "Mmmph."

I figured things would eventually get ugly. My heart pounds and beads of sweat pop on my forehead, despite the room's air-conditioning. "Write it down," I suggest.

Mimi flails her arm, giving the pen and notebook a heavy swipe. They fly off the table and crash against the cupboard. The pen rolls across the floor, coming to a rest halfway across the room. She smacks her left hand against the table. "Naah!" Defiance, anger, and determination gleam in her eyes. Her lips twist as she struggles to wrap her tongue around more syllables. "Mah... money." Her voice is hoarse and throaty, but there is no mistaking the meaning of her words or the threatening undertone. "Mah money."

"I know it's your money and your business." I choose my words with care. The doctors warned us not to excite her. I can't tell her about the IRS. I don't dare tell her I know about the investigation. She's still on medication to prevent blockage, and the last thing I want to risk is her suffering another stroke. "I'm only trying to help. Unless we generate more income, the chapel won't stay solvent. From what I can determine, the only thing keeping it going up to this point are those cash deposits. Please tell me where they came from."

She glares at me, opens her mouth as if to speak, but the words won't come. Finally she lifts a wobbly finger and regally points to the pen and notebook on the floor.

I debate the desire to have my questions answered versus helping Mimi achieve her goals in recovery. Life would be so much easier if I simply picked them up. But at what cost? Didn't I warn Tori earlier this evening about this very thing?

Plus, at the moment, the reigning monarch of the villa is acting as if her treasury isn't depleted when we both know better.

"No." My mind is made up. "You threw them there. You pick them up." I grab her reacher, an aluminum stick with plastic jaws on one end and hooked to the walker directly behind her chair. "You can do it."

She ignores the reacher, pounds the table with her left hand. "Mah money."

My stomach twists at the horrible guttural sounds

coming from her mouth. I'm the one who's reduced her to this. But at least she's talking. "I know it's your money. But where did it come from? Why didn't you enter it on the books?"

She grunts, splays her hands on the table, and struggles to stand. I pull her walker close so she can grab it. Her moves are sharp and shaky, and the cold, dark fury on her face is as menacing as a sudden thunderstorm threatening the Vegas skies. She glares at me and I understand what it's like to be subjected to the full weight of royal authority. It's a good thing the chapel doesn't have a dungeon or I probably would find myself immediately dragged off and thrown into the dark nether regions for the rest of my life.

Mimi shuffles out of the kitchen as fast as she can move. Resentment churns in my stomach as I watch her go. All those hours wasted trying to figure things out while all along, she knew there was money to cover the bills. Why didn't she tell me? Damn her for keeping me in the dark. Damn the chapel, too. For that matter, damn this godforsaken town.

But if Mimi thinks I'll leave before I figure out exactly where that money came from, she has another think coming.

"We have a problem," Tori says.

I come up for air from my spot at Mimi's computer. At this point, anything—problem or not—is a welcome diversion. I've spent the entire morning and much of the afternoon analyzing and entering ten months' worth of banking statements into the accounts receivables columns. Problem is, I'm not sure under which income account the mysterious cash deposits should be applied. Bridal income? Miscellaneous?

"What's wrong? Do we have another bridal couple in the lobby?"

"Like, I wish." Tori looks as miserable as if she just lost her cell phone, iPod, and the MasterCard Jack gave her in case of emergency. "Have you seen Facebook today?"

"Sweetie, at this point, I haven't even had time for lunch." I reach for my coffee cup and discover it empty, save for some cold dregs.

"You need to see this, Mom," she says. "I think we should look at it together." Tori scoots around the desk, leans across me, and reaches for Mimi's keyboard. Her fingers fly across the keys. Logging on to her Facebook account, she does a search for an unfamiliar name. Up pops a contact screen and a woman's face. Tori steps back and eyes me. "Do you know who this is?"

I nudge closer to the screen, scan the photo. Something about the woman makes me uneasy, though I'm not sure why. "I don't think so. Why? Am I supposed to?"

"Obviously she knows you. She doesn't like you. In fact, she pretty much hates you. Whatever happened, you definitely pissed her off."

"Excuse me?" I didn't raise Tori to talk like that. "Since when do you use that kind of language?"

She rolls her eyes. "Do you want to waste time lecturing me about etiquette or do you want to know what she said?"

I turn back to the screen, peering at the woman's profile again. While I'm sure she's not anyone I could name, she does look familiar in some odd unsettling way. "I give up," I finally capitulate. "What did she do?"

"Smeared you," Tori says. "Well, not just you, but us. The chapel. She smeared us all over the Internet."

"Smeared?" I squint up at her. "What does that mean?"

"She definitely has it in for you, Mom. She says she was supposed to get married at the chapel, but you threw her out."

I slump back in my chair as Tori continues pointing and clicking. My stomach lurches as I stare at the profile photo of Bride Number Two. The bride I threw out of the chapel two weeks ago.

"She's posted reviews about the chapel all over the web. I can show you. They're easy to find. Just Google them and they pop right up. She posted on different wedding websites like The Knot, plus she has reviews up on Trip Advisor and Yelp. I'm assuming she posted something to her Facebook account, too, but I can't check since I'm not a friend."

My mouth is dry and my heart is a dead weight in the pit of my stomach. Somehow I manage to find a voice. "The things... she said. Are they really that bad?"

Tori hesitates, and I have my answer.

"It's true. Everything she said is probably true." There's no sense denying it. I might as well admit it before things get worse. "She showed up at the chapel a few weeks ago. It was the day after Mimi had her stroke. She was rude; I got mad and threw her out."

"You did *what*?" Tori sucks in a breath and stares at me like I just confessed to pawning the Royal Tiara. "Oh, Mom, you didn't."

"I'm afraid I did." I bow my head, embarrassed to meet her eyes. "It's a long story."

"How could you throw a bride out of the chapel? You know what Mimi always says." Tori's voice hangs low, like a chastising ribbon of rules tightening around my neck like a silk noose. *"No matter what, the bride is always right."*

"Not this bride," I mutter. I feel myself growing angry all over again as I remember how blithely Bride Number Two called Mimi a bitch.

"Does Mimi know what you did?"

My head snaps up. "No, and you are not to tell her about it, either. We can't afford to have her upset. She needs to concentrate on her recovery, not worry about things at the chapel."

Yet didn't I recently do that very thing myself? Didn't I purposely try to goad her into divulging how she came up with the cash deposits? *Keep her calm*, the doctors said, but she was anything but as she shoved her walker out of the kitchen. It's a wonder she didn't fall or—God forbid—suffer another stroke. If she gets sick again, it will be my fault.

Tori nods slowly. "I won't tell her."

"Okay. So, let's think about this. We know we have a problem. Any idea how we should handle it?"

"Seriously?" She stares at me, dumbfounded. "You're asking me?"

Oh, Tori. Have I been that inflexible and unavailable for so long that she thinks I don't trust her? How many problems could we have avoided in the past if I'd been there for her? "I've never been more serious in my life. I don't know the first thing about social networking, but I bet you do." I eye her with a frank, appraising look. "What do you suggest?"

Tori nibbles on her bottom lip, her mouth twisting like a string of licorice. "We need to do some damage control. Stuff on the Internet spreads like wildfire."

"Think you can you handle it?"

"Sure, it's not that hard."

"All right." I nod. "Do it."

"What exactly do you want me to do? Respond to her reviews? Yank the bad ones if I can?"

"Yes. No. Whatever it takes." Standing, I surrender Mimi's chair and push Tori into it. I swing her around so she's facing the monitor. "First, though, you probably should show me exactly what she posted."

"Are you sure?" Tori watches warily as I drag a chair around the desk and sink down beside her. "Some of it is nasty."

I close my eyes, dreading the thought of viewing for myself what Bride Number Two has posted for the world to see. She was livid as she flounced out of the chapel, her last words to me "*You effing bitch.*" Her tirade is now available for anyone's reading pleasure on the world-wide-web.

"I need to see it," I say softly.

Tori squirms. "I'm warning you, Mom, you might be offended."

I squeeze her shoulders, ruffle her hair. Poor kid. She's been through hell the past couple weeks, and now she's worried about me? "I'm sure I've seen worse."

"Okay." She squares her shoulders and turns back to the screen. I sit back, watching her fingers fly across the keyboard. I'm so proud of her, of all she's accomplished and how capable she is. If only Jack could see her now. It wasn't too long ago that he and I had sat here in this room as he presented me with a laundry list of all the things the chapel could be doing. Tapping into the social network. Presenting ourselves with an online social presence. Working to update the chapel's website. Tori is the one who found the bad reviews. No telling what else might have happened if it hadn't been for her.

"Would you like to be in charge?" I suddenly ask.

"In charge of what?" She pulls her attention away from the screen for a moment. "I haven't even pulled up one of her reviews."

"I'm not talking about the bride. I mean this. All of this." Swinging my arm, I make a wide circle, taking in Mimi's computer, the room. "The Internet, social media, everything."

"You mean the chapel website, too?" She stares at me like I've lost my mind.

"Yes," I state firmly, even as I wonder if Tori's right and if I've gone over the edge. But we need to do something and my options are limited. Jaabir is way too busy, Francesca and I don't have a clue, and we can't afford to hire anyone. "Everything," I repeat, "including the chapel website. Do you think you can do it?"

She grimaces and rolls her eyes. "Who set up your laptop? Your email? Your PayPal page?"

As if I need a reminder. Tori is my link to cyberspace. She's the one who taught me how to text and surf the net. She knows the ins and outs of the social network. Her generation *is* the social network. She was playing with computers while she was still in diapers, and she knows how the programs work. When she doesn't, she figures it out. She's smart, learns fast, and that's exactly what we need. Someone smart and savvy when it comes to the Internet. Someone who can figure it out.

Someone *not* me.

"Are you really putting me in charge?" she breathes. "Really?"

"Do your thing."

Tori stares at me a moment, as if waiting for me to renege. Then suddenly her face blossoms in a smile as rare and beautiful as the desert cactus in bloom. "Awesome! You won't be sorry, Mom. I'll fix things. I promise."

She's positively glowing as she attacks the keyboard. I haven't seen her look like that since I broke down and bought her that purse we argued about last winter; the one I told her cost more than an entire week's worth of groceries; the one I bought her for Christmas against my better judgment. I couldn't help it. I'd do anything for Tori. She loved the purse. I love Tori.

And Tori loves the chapel.

The chapel I just put her in charge of.

God help me. What have I done?

Chapter Nine

DEPENDING ON WHO'S CALLING, CALLER ID can be a blessing or a curse. Unfortunately, the digital display on the reception phone shows Alexander & Alexander, LLP. Which Alexander is it? Jack and I haven't spoken since I dared him to sue me, and I haven't seen or spoken with Ed since Mimi left the hospital. With a silent prayer that I'll hear the right Alexander man on the other end, I connect the call. "Hello?"

"Hey, kiddo. How's everything going?"

Hearing Ed's voice rumble across the line slows my heartbeat and returns the smile to my face. I sink back in Mimi's chair and swirl around to face the bank of windows overlooking the courtyard, watching as Jaabir pushes a broom, sweeping sand from the bricks. The winds in Vegas this week have been fierce. "How are you? I miss you."

"Miss you, too. How are things going? Everything okay?"

"We're doing fine."

"You don't sound okay. Come on, Lily, what's wrong?" His voice drops. "Is it Mimi?"

Do I break down and confess how bad things are? Ed's

offer is tempting. I could use some support. It's been a lonely few days with no one to share with. Francesca is already handling more than she should, and Tori is too young to take on these concerns. And while Jaabir makes a great sounding board, he has his own set of problems. He's busy working at the chapel all day, and then he has his night courses at UNLV. I swallow the sudden urge to spill everything. If only I could. Hearing that familiar fatherly tone, filled with compassion and concern, suddenly has me wishing I were a teenager again. Being seventeen like Tori would be wonderful. No responsibilities, no need to make life-altering decisions. Simply step back and let the adults take charge. Ed is good at leading and so is Mimi. Maybe that was part of the reason behind their breakup. But the two of them have been divorced for years. Mimi is no longer his concern.

Neither am I, I remind myself. I have big shoulders. I'll do the worrying. No need to bother Ed with the messy details of our lives.

"Mimi is slowly recovering," I say. "She's able to feed herself, and her strength is coming back." The rest, I leave out. Mimi still can't talk, and her gait and balance are wobbly enough that she needs the walker. *Slow and steady wins the race*, the physical therapist reminds us, not that it seems to be doing much good. Mimi is slow, but she's certainly not steady.

I watch Jaabir finish his sweeping, heft his broom, head for the maintenance shed directly behind the chapel Court Gazebo. Jaabir is a royal treasure, always busy, super productive. Mimi will have a problem replacing him when he finishes college and starts his own business.

"You sure everything is okay?" Ed asks. "Remember, kiddo, if you need help, all you have to do is ask."

And have Jack find out and throw it right back in my face? Thanks, but no thanks. Much as I'm tempted by Ed's offer, I don't dare take him up on it. I am perfectly capable of handling things on my own. "Thanks, Ed, I appreciate it, but we're doing great," I say, surprised at how easily the lie trips off my tongue.

"Good to hear." His voice carries relief. "I figured you were, but I wanted to make sure."

A rush of affection sweeps over me. "You're a sweetheart, Ed Alexander, no matter what Mimi says."

"She's talking again?" He sounds surprised and hopeful.

"Sorry, I was speaking figuratively." Things would be so much easier if Mimi was talking. I never thought I would be grateful just having her yell at me. At least that would show she's made some improvement, but her speech remains garbled. I thought things would improve after she got angry with me and spit words in my face. But if anything, that day only seemed to make her more resistant to communicating with me. She glares at me when we're together and refuses to speak, even when I help her with her personal needs. Mimi isn't ready to do certain things by herself, especially in the bathroom. It wouldn't be safe. No matter how much she dislikes it, she needs someone to tend to her personal care. She needs me and I need her.

I need her to tell me where those cash deposits came from.

"Just remember I'm here if you need me," he says, "and so is Jack. In fact, that's the other reason I called. To talk about Jack."

I groan. The last thing I need is Ed running interference for his son. "Did he put you up to this?"

"Why would he do that?" He pauses, sounding confused. "Wait a minute. Did he say something to you?" he demands. "Does he know about the party?"

"Party?" Now I'm the one who's confused. "What party?"

"The one I'm throwing for his birthday."

"Sorry, I don't know anything about a party," I say as I catch sight of Jaabir reemerging from the maintenance shed, lugging a large wooden plaque. What is he doing? I crane my neck, watching as he crosses the courtyard, heading for the front entrance and disappearing from view.

"That's a relief." Ed huffs a long sigh. "You had me worried for a minute. But if you don't know about the party, then Jack must not know, either."

Party? Suddenly I remember and smack my forehead with the palm of my hand. I should have guessed. Jack turns fifty in just a few weeks.

"Anyway, I've got this great surprise party planned. God, I can't believe my kid is turning fifty. Makes me feel like an old man."

"You are not old."

"And you, my dear, are a very bad liar," he says, chuckling, "but this old man thanks you. So, I'm planning a big bash for Jack on his birthday: dinner, a live band, all his friends... and his family." Ed halts. "Turning fifty is a big deal. I think it's important his family be there."

"I'll make sure Tori is there," I say, but I'm already regretting my words as I speak them. While I love Ed dearly, the kind of parties he and Mimi threw when I was growing up aren't exactly the type of events I want my daughter attending. The thought of Tori caught up in the middle of some huge boozy birthday bash, surrounded by Jack's current stable of girlfriends, makes my stomach lurch.

"I'm not just talking about Tori," he says. "You're all invited. You and Mimi, and Francesca, too. You're all Jack's family. Times like this, people want their family around them."

Has Ed lost his mind? He, better than anyone, knows exactly how I feel about his son. The last thing I want is to celebrate anything involving Jack Alexander. And I'm sure if someone asked him, Jack would say he feels the same about me. True, we share a daughter, but that's the only tie that binds us. We're not even a family anymore. Mimi shattered that connection when she divorced Ed.

"Look, Lily, I know you and Jack have your issues, and I respect that. But I'm asking nicely. Please, can't you put things aside, for everyone's sake, just for one night?"

"It's not that simple," I say uneasily. "Jack and I aren't exactly on the best of terms right now." My thoughts drift back to that night when Mimi suffered her stroke. Family and friends gathered at the hospital without being asked, providing comfort and support. Ed and Tori, Francesca and me. Jaabir... and Jack.

"You being at his party would mean a lot to this old man."

The minute he starts in with that soft tender lilt, I feel the fight slipping out of me. How can I refuse him? Ed has always been my champion, yet rarely asks for anything in return. He never even took sides when Tori was born. It would have been so easy for him to ally himself with Jack, fighting me to keep Tori in Las Vegas. If the two of them had gone to court, even Mimi would have been on their side and joined them in battle. She's always insisted I was wrong in spiriting Tori away. But there was no court fight. Ed remained quiet, allowing Jack and me to work out our own flexible custody arrangements. I owe him, big-time .

"All right," I say. Giving in is against my better judgment, but I don't have the heart to refuse him. "We'll be at the party."

"All of you?"

"All of us," I promise.

"Thanks, kiddo."

"You're welcome." The mere thought of attending a birthday party in honor of Jack makes me feel sick, but at least I've made Ed happy. We don't have to stay long, I promise myself. Long enough to join them for dinner. Long enough to watch Jack blow out the candles on his birthday cake. And if things get too wild or wicked, I hold a trump card. Tori is underage, and Mimi is still recovering. Already my mind is planning the scenario. We'll stay for dinner, wish the birthday boy all the best, and make our escape.

"The invitations went out in the mail today. You should get yours tomorrow."

"When's the big day?" I ask, scribbling myself a reminder even as Ed starts to speak. The date of Jack's birthday has been carved on my heart since I was ten years old. "And where is this party?"

"Where else? Caesar's, naturally."

"Naturally," I say, feeling sicker by the minute. Why should I be surprised? Caesar's Palace has always been

Jack's favorite hideout. Luxurious and opulent, Caesar's speaks of elegance and splendor. Everything that Jack Alexander isn't.

We hang up and the phone immediately rings. I scan caller ID and pick up with a laugh. "What did you forget?"

"Well, I'm not sure... probably quite a bit. But at least it's good to know you're talking to me. Frankly, Lily, I was worried you might still be mad."

The wrong Alexander man. Damn it, I should have known. "What do you want, Jack?"

"Just wanted to tell you that I caught the new look, and I think it's great. Glad to see you decided to take my advice."

"Advice about what?"

He chuckles. "Quit playing games, Lily. No need to go fishing for compliments. I'm talking about the chapel website. Nice update. Great photos. Good job."

Photos? What photos? And what's this about an update? Abruptly I remember last week's conversation with Tori, how I put her in charge. She's been slinking around the chapel with her digital camera in hand and a sly smile on her face that would put Catherine de' Medici to shame. I knew she was up to something, but there have been so many other things demanding my attention. Jaabir is upset about the limo brakes, plus he's turned to me for help with one of the business courses he's taking at UNLV. Francesca is constantly tweaking her ceremony scripts, then asking me to edit them. And the past forty-eight hours have been filled with emails from Walt and senior members of my division's team over a sudden business crisis. There's been no time for me to check in with Tori and see how things are going.

No time? My fault. I'm the mom. I should have made time.

"Thanks," I tell him, making a mental note to Google the chapel's website as soon as we're finished talking.

"I like those links to Facebook, Twitter, and Pinterest, too. About time the chapel got itself involved with the social network," Jack says. "Want to make a little bet on how fast business picks up?"

Four brides had phoned this morning to book for the upcoming weekend. Had they checked out our new website? I debate sharing the info but quickly decide against it. No need for Jack to know. It's none of his business and hearing it will only swell that big head of his. Besides, the new bookings could merely be a coincidence, and nothing one could term an upswing in business. That kind of info comes after months of tracking business trends. We don't have months. We're down to weeks.

"I don't think so, Jack," I reply. "I don't bet, remember?"

"Not true, Lily," he says softly. "You took a bet on me once."

As if I could forget. My fingers clench the phone. *August*, I remind myself. All I have to do is make it to the end of August... then Tori and I are out of here.

"What do you want, Jack? Why did you call?" I ask coolly. "I'm busy."

A slow chuckle rumbles across the line. "Just wanted to say that I saw the website and thought it looked good." His voice relaxes. In the distance, I hear a door banging, Ed talking, background noise crackling. Jack has me on speaker. He's probably sprawled out in his big leather chair, legs propped up on his desk, arms crossed behind his head. Damn the man. Is he so self-important that he won't even pick up the phone and keep a conversation private? The whole office can probably hear our conversation. I fight down the urge to hang up on him.

"Rubbing it in," I say loudly, hoping everyone in his vicinity hears me. "Isn't that what you mean?" I'll be happy to let his entire office know exactly what kind of man he is.

"Did I say that?"

"You didn't have to. It's obvious." What else could he mean? "Good-bye, Jack."

"Wait, Lily, don't hang up." Suddenly I hear a click as he takes us off speaker. He's grabbed the phone and jammed it against his ear. I'll bet his feet are off the desk, too.

"You want to know why I called? Okay, I phoned to say I'm sorry. I'm sorry as hell about what happened last week. I shouldn't have said what I did, and I hope you forgive me."

To say that I'm speechless would be an understatement. It's not often you get an apology out of Jack Alexander. "It's over and done with," I say after a minute. "In fact, until you called, I'd forgotten all about it."

"Is that so?" A bit of humor returns to his voice.

"Yes, really. Don't forget who you're talking to, Jack. This is Lily, remember?"

"Ahhh, sweetheart, no need to remind me. I know exactly who you are."

The smirk in his voice, the old Jack, returns, coming through loud and clear, goading me on like he always does. "Good for you, Jack. And while you're at it, here's something else you might want to remember. I am not one of those girls who hangs on your every word, who thinks about you day and night, who sits around waiting for you to call."

A deep laugh rumbles over the line.

"You don't believe me?" I demand.

"Lily, you kill me," he says, laughing louder than before. "Listen, I'm due in court. Give Tori a kiss for me, will you? Talk to you soon."

The line goes dead as he cuts the connection. I swear under my breath. As if I didn't have enough to do, now I've got Jack Alexander on my mind again. Plus that damn invitation from Ed.

Why me? Why now? Why Caesar's Palace? I've managed to avoid crossing Caesar's threshold for the past seventeen years. The last thing I need is a reminder of the night I spent in Jack's bed.

But it appears my hiatus from Caesar's is about to come to an end. A promise is a promise, and I gave Ed my word. We'll be there for dinner. We'll stay for cake.

But as soon as the birthday boy blows out his candles, we are out of there.

The bride pulls a scrap of paper from her clutch. "I have a coupon."

Mimi never gives discounts. "I'm sorry, we don't do coupons."

"But it was on Facebook. I printed it off." She gingerly places it on the counter between us and scoots it toward me. "See?"

I stare at the scrap of paper bearing the chapel logo and the bold type offering a twenty-five-percent discount on our Royal Wedding packages. Facebook. Discounts. I close my eyes, swallow a sigh. I definitely need to have a chat with Tori.

"Please don't tell me it expired. Matt and I were so excited when we saw the discount." The bride's face is whiter than her veil.

The groom steps forward and shoots me a shy look from underneath a wide-brimmed cowboy hat. "Look, ma'am, to be honest with you, Cindy and I are flat-out broke. The wedding rings took the last of our money. I've got enough in my wallet to pay for this wedding. But if you're saying the coupon isn't valid and you can't make it happen, I appreciate that. If we can't afford it, we can't afford it."

The bride's face falls and her lower lip trembles. "Oh, Matt, are you sure? I had my heart set on the Royal Wedding Chapel."

"Sorry, honey." He takes his bride's hand, squeezes it tight. "Sorry, ma'am, to take up your time." He gives me a simple nod.

They start for the door—the bride, crushed but compliant; the groom, defeated but dignified. And suddenly, out of nowhere, a deep longing to do the right thing surges through me. These two are obviously in love. There's simply no way I can let them leave this chapel without wedding rings on their fingers. Damn the cost.

"Wait," I call out as they reach the door. They turn and face me and I think fast. "That coupon you gave me? The reason it's not valid is because we're running a silent promotion today. And guess what? You're the lucky winners."

"We won?" Cindy claps her hands together. "Oh, Matt, we won!" She plants a kiss on his cheek. "We won!"

"What did we win?" Matt tilts back his cowboy hat, exposing a deep frown cutting across his forehead. "I never heard of a silent promotion."

I don't blame him for questioning me; promotion is all about getting the word out. But it's the best I could do on the spur of the moment. "I know it sounds strange, but it's true." I smile, beckon them to return.

"What did we win?" Cindy asks breathlessly, tugging Matt back to the counter.

"You're today's lucky winners of our Grand Royal Wedding package."

"Really?" she squeals. "The Grand Royal Wedding package in King Edward's Chapel? With flowers, photography, and complimentary limo service?"

"That's the one, swear to God." I raise my hand in solemn oath. "You won. Congratulations."

"Halleluiah to Jesus!" Matt whoops and smacks my hand in a high five just like out of a Saturday-night hoedown. "We sure do thank you, ma'am!"

"It's our pleasure," I tell them, though the pleasure is mine. The chapel can't afford to cover the expense of their wedding, but I can. I'll write a personal check and deposit it with the day-end receipts.

"I can't believe this is happening!" Cindy twirls, nearly hyperventilating in the reception room.

I point them toward the floral cooler "Why don't you

pick out your flowers while I make a few phone calls." Rapidly I tick off mental notes in my head. Call Francesca back pronto from the villa. Tell Jaabir to ready the limo. Pull Tori off the computer so she can cue the music. "Let's get the celebration started."

Two hours later, the newlyweds repeatedly gush their thanks in the chapel courtyard, as Jaabir pulls the limo around. Something tugs at my heart as we watch them depart and disappear down the road. Does happily ever after really exist? If it does, Matt and Cindy will be the ones to find it.

"Weren't they just adorable? Cindy was just so cute in her little veil and those kicky cowboy boots. And Matt?" Tori swoons. "Ohmigod, talk about a seriously handsome dude. Just watching the two of them saying their vows makes me want to—"

"Don't you dare," I warn. "You are only seventeen, young lady."

She rolls her eyes. "Relax, Mom. I'm not getting married anytime soon."

"It's nice to know you have your priorities straight," I say. "First, you need to get through college."

"No; first, I need to find a guy," she flips back at me with a smirk.

I shake my head as she flounces off toward the chapel. Francesca laughs and pats my arm. "You know teenagers. She's just teasing."

"You're right," I say after a moment. "No worries." But I'm plenty worried. What if Jack is right? What if, when August rolls around, Tori refuses to leave Las Vegas? What if she refuses to attend college? What if all she wants out of life is to settle down and work at the chapel? What if my bright, beautiful daughter decides to toss away all the hopes and dreams I have for her future, simply to chase a silly romantic dream?

How can I compete with happily ever after?

I can't. I'll never be able to stop her.

Damn the Queen Mum for stuffing Tori's head full of nonsense. The chapel is a business, nothing more—a business that will go under fast if things don't turn around soon. And damn that silly tiara for making my little girl grow up believing that fairy tales can come true. If it wasn't a treasured family heirloom, I'd snatch it from the display cabinet and toss it in the trash.

Chapter Ten

"GOODNESS, IT'S HOT OUT TODAY," Francesca says, puffing her way through the front door into the air-conditioned reception area.

I check the computer, note the temperature reading listed in one corner. "It's one hundred and ten degrees."

"No wonder I feel miserable. I hate the heat." She sinks with a heavy poof onto one of several gold-and-white-silk-brocade couches gracing the room. "Ever since I was a little girl, I dreamed that someday I would live in a little town where it snowed in winter. I would play in the snow, and I'd make a snowman."

She fans herself with one hand while tugging the collar of her black dress with the other. "I suppose you think it's silly. Me, at my age, living in this city full of rocks and heat, talking about wanting to make a snowman."

I cup my chin in my hand and stare at her across the counter. "Can I ask you a question?"

"Anything, honey. What is it?"

"Why do you stay?"

She frowns. "I'm not sure what you mean."

"Here in Las Vegas. You have options. You could leave."

Francesca blinks like I've just announced the Nevada legislature decided to outlaw marriage. "You mean, leave the chapel?"

"Right. You could move." What am I saying? I must be insane. Life without Francesca? "You could move someplace where it snows," I conclude lamely.

"Why, Lily, that's just... that's..." She shakes her head slowly, as if trying to sift through the silken threads of a leftover dream. "I couldn't. I wouldn't. I've lived in this city since I was a young girl. I could never live somewhere else. Mimi needs me."

Dear Francesca, loyal to a fault, like a faithful servant who attends the family until death. But what about her own family? Vaguely I recall her having a sister in Arizona, whom she visited occasionally when I was a child. But her sister died years ago and the visits stopped. So did Francesca's vacations. I try to envision a life without Francesca, but it's impossible. She's been here from the beginning. We would all be lost without her, especially Mimi. They've been together so long, friends and confidants, a team. Always working toward the same goals, always on the same page when it comes to the business... and Mimi's personal life.

But what about Francesca's personal life? She's nearly seventy and never been married. She attends church on Sunday and never misses her weekly Thursday-night visit to the Bingo parlor at one of the smaller casinos off the Strip. She works, she prays, she plays Bingo. What kind of life is that? Doesn't she want to travel? Maybe a trip to England? Francesca is a true aficionado when it comes to anything concerning the British royal family. You'd think it was her, rather than Mimi, who married into aristocracy.

"Why don't you take a vacation?" I suggest. "Maybe go to England. You could visit Buckingham Palace and Windsor Castle. You could tour Westminster Abbey and see the spot where so many kings and queens were crowned."

Francesca throws me an indulgent smile.

"I'm serious," I insist. How many more years does she think she can push herself like she's been doing? "You work too hard."

"And you worry too much," she says with a tender look that she's always reserved just for me. "Besides, even if I wanted to, now isn't the best time to leave. Mimi is sick. She needs me."

Mimi. My mouth twists in a grimace. Always Mimi.

"Maybe when she's better, I'll think about it," she says. 'But for now, my place is here. Besides, if I left, who would do the weddings?" She smiles suddenly. "Or have you decided to become an ordained minister?"

"God, no," I say, horrified at the thought. Francesca is right. She can't go anywhere. We need her. I need her.

"By the way, when did you decide to add the sign?"

"What sign?" I ask.

"The one out front. Surely you must have noticed. It's been there for two days." Her face shines with a faint hint of sweat and surprise, and she dabs her upper lip with a tissue. "Go out and look. I'll cover the phone."

I stroll out the front door and down the sidewalk where I take a stance on the sidewalk of Las Vegas Boulevard in front of our flashing neon sign advertising The Royal Wedding Chapel. Swinging from the bottom, attached by eyehooks, is an elegant, white wooden plaque. Gold letters etched in black proclaim: *Check us out on Facebook*!

Francesca's eyebrows rise as I march back inside. "I take it you didn't authorize the sign?"

"No, but I have a pretty good idea who did." I head for the Queen Elizabeth bridal suite where I find Tori in residence on a velvet tasseled divan, typing furiously on her laptop. "Young lady, you have some explaining to do."

She barely glances up. "Mother, do you have to be so dramatic? What's wrong now?"

I sink into one of the gold damask chairs. "Tell me about that sign out front."

"You finally noticed. Don't you love it? I asked Jaabir to put it up yesterday, but I didn't expect it to work so fast. We've already had twenty-five hits today."

"Twenty-five hits?"

"On Facebook." She points at her computer screen. "That's how many people have *liked* us today. See?"

"What are you talking about?"

"It's our Facebook page," she explains in a patient tone, like she's explaining something to a three-year-old. "You told me I could do whatever I wanted, remember?"

Parts of our earlier conversation drift to mind. While it's true I did put Tori in charge of the website, and I vaguely remember us chatting about Facebook, I don't remember any discussion about adding a sign on Las Vegas Boulevard. Clark County and the city of Las Vegas have numerous zoning codes and sign ordinances that have to be considered. We could be facing a stiff fine for not complying with regulations.

"After I updated our website, I started working on

Facebook. I created the page about a week ago. Look how many friends we already have."

Leaning over, I squint at the screen. "Four hundred and seven? Is that good?"

"In one week?" Tori beams brighter than if it was her birthday and the royal tiara was crowning her head. "That's excellent."

"But where did you find all those people? How did they find us?"

"I texted all my friends and asked them to *like* us," she says with a fast smile. "They took it from there, and it started to spread."

"That fast?"

She nods, laughing. "Isn't it awesome? And wait till you see what I put up last night. Remember when I told you about the links I wanted to add? Well, I did, and it's adorable. People just love it. It's getting lots of hits." She points at the screen. Next to the chapel's logo is a shot of a familiar-looking couple. Next to their photo, a scripted text reads: *Check out this recent video of Matt and Cindy's wedding.*

I gape at their image. "You can't put that on the Internet."

"Why not?"

"It's an invasion of privacy. You need their permission."

"But I have it," she trumps me. "I asked them to sign a media release before they left. It's in their file. Sweet, isn't it? Now anyone can watch. Plus, check this out. It links to our website."

She clicks the arrow, starting the video. I stare at the screen, watching the edited footage of our cute country couple.

"How did you know how to do that?" I ask as the video ends.

"It's not that hard, Mom. Anyone could do it."

Not true. I can't.

"Eventually I'll have a bridal blog, too," she rattles on, "but we're not ready for that. A blog is supposed to teach you something. At this point, I think my time would be better spent posting photos and stories of our brides."

"And you've already done that, right?" I say, though I can already guess the answer.

"Only two so far. I haven't had time to do more. I want to concentrate on Facebook. That will drive more traffic to the chapel's website. Now we're up and running, I'm trying to figure out how to keep the momentum going."

"More videos?" I ask weakly.

"Probably," she says. "People love watching the videos. I plan on linking them to Facebook whenever I can. But you have to be careful about what you post and how often you do it. I'm shooting for three or four things a week. I don't want things to backfire. I don't want people to start ignoring us."

"What kind of things are you posting?" I think of the numerous phone inquiries I've handled today and the five brides we have booked for Saturday. "Are you telling them to phone for an appointment?"

Tori treats me to an eye-roll more dramatic than her first. "That's not the type of thing they want to see on Facebook. They can check out the info when they visit our website. Facebook is more about engaging in conversations. Asking them questions. Stuff like *We're excited about all the new photos we've added to our website. Take a look and tell us which one is your favorite!* or *Should we start a bridal blog? Yes or no? We'd love to hear what you think!*"

She cocks her head, smiles at me like she's conversing with some high school dropout who's never seen a laptop. "Know what I mean? Just telling them about our hours and the rooms isn't enough. Why should they care? My goal is to get them actively involved in wanting to help promote the chapel, even though they have no clue they're doing it."

Forget Computer 101. This sounds like Marketing 425. Who taught her about all this? For a fast second, I consider Mimi, then just as quickly abandon the thought. How could she teach Tori when she hasn't even bothered updating the website?

"How did you get so smart about all of this?"

Tori shrugs, but the smile on her face is anything but blasé. "I guess it comes naturally. I'm doing exactly what I've wanted to do all my life."

All my life. I take a deep breath as reality washes over me. I glance once more at Tori's laptop and glimpse our adorable couple, Matt and Cindy, waving at me from the chapel's Facebook screen. Our Facebook fan page, posted compliments of my multi-talented *Wanna-be-a-wedding-coordinator-planner-Royal-Chapel-owner* Tori.

My God, what have I done? I feel like beating my head against the floral wall of the bridal suite. I thought I was doing both of us a favor by giving Tori something to do that would occupy her time while we're stuck in Las Vegas. Instead, my decision has backfired. I gave Tori permission to do what she wanted, and she took me at my word. What was I thinking? But that's the problem: I wasn't thinking.

I never should have handed her the keys to the chapel and given her the means to start the ball rolling, to try to bring the chapel back to the success it used to be once upon a time. It might actually be working. Tori's committed to making it work. She's deeply involved. She's promoting the chapel. She's working it. She's loving it.

And come August, she's not going to leave.

Suddenly, I have a good idea who's responsible for this. Jack has mentioned Facebook more than once. He must be the one helping Tori. It wouldn't surprise me to learn that he's been giving her advice all along. Jack knows how to advertise a business. He and Ed run a successful law firm. Jack knows what it takes to attract customers—or, in his case, clients—and keep them.

"Did your father help you with this?"

"With Facebook?" Tori dissolves in squeals of laughter. "Mom, you have got to be kidding. Dad is clueless when it comes to stuff like this. He didn't even know how to post a message on his wall until I created his Facebook page and then showed him how."

I feel my face tighten. Jack has a Facebook page? Why am I not surprised? I'll bet he's got plenty of friends and fans... especially the female variety.

"Look, Mom, I won't lie to you. It's true that Dad did help me out a little," she admits, "but not with Facebook. That much I did myself. But when I needed help with other stuff, I went to him. He gave me lots of advice about marketing. So did Grandpa Ed," she quickly adds, as if mentioning Ed might chip away some of the stony resentment I feel chiseled on my face and in my heart. "Dad was the one who suggested the discounts. He told me that discounts and coupons would probably bring in more business. And Dad was the one who came up with the idea about the sign. Cool, isn't it?"

That damned sign, swinging boldly out front on Las Vegas Boulevard. *Bring in more business.* I should have known. It's not difficult to imagine Jack shooting off his mouth, planting ideas in Tori's head.

"Why do you look so mad?" Tori sets her laptop aside on the embroidered chaise lounge and gives me her full attention. "You're the one who told me to go ahead, to do what I wanted. You told me I was in charge."

She's right. I did tell her that. And it's not fair to make Tori suffer for her father's sins. "I guess I'm just surprised by how fast this is happening. You've done a wonderful job with the website, with the coupons, and the whole Facebook thing." I refuse to mention the sign. We could be facing a stiff penalty in fines for not having filed the proper paperwork for the zoning ordinance. "I'm very proud of you," I add, swallowing hard. "And I'm sure your Dad is, too."

"He is." Tori nods, and her hair swishes in silken strands around her shoulders. "He sounded super excited this morning when I told him about the hits we were getting." Her face softens. "You know, Mom, I never thought about it, but you don't even have your own Facebook page. I'll be glad to start one for you. It's super easy. I can have you up and running by tonight if you want."

Do I want? Damn right I do.

And the first thing I intend to do is check out Jack's home page and see exactly what he's up to.

Chapter Eleven

I WAIT ON HOLD, DRUMMING MY fingers against Mimi's desk as Jack's secretary announces I'm on the phone. After the last time we talked, I'm definitely not looking forward to this conversation.

"Lily, what a nice surprise," he says.

"We need to talk." I make a concerted effort to keep my voice steady. He is not going to rattle me like he's done in the past. "Can we meet?"

"This sounds promising," he says in a voice rich and neat as the smooth, expensive Scotch he drinks. "Are we talking lunch? Better yet, how about dinner? Just name the place. I'll take you wherever you'd like to go."

I push down the frustration building inside me. Why does the man always need to make everything be about romance? "This isn't about us."

"Ah, Lily, what's the harm in a little dinner between friends?"

"Last I checked, we weren't exactly friends," I retort, knowing full well we were more than friends. How can I forget? Each time I glance at Tori, I'm reminded of that night.

"Know what your problem is, sweetheart? You need to learn to relax."

"And you need to focus." I swallow over my nerves, feeling my face heating up, my insides melting. Damn the man. I'm way too old and we've got way too much history between us for this to be happening. "I called about Tori."

"Is she okay?" His voice drops into paternal concern. "I just talked to her a couple of hours ago."

"We need to talk," I repeat. "The sooner, the better. Today."

"Sorry, no can do. I'm due downtown in court in less than an hour, and I expect to be tied up all day."

"Tonight then," I demand, though the last thing I want is to meet him like that. Jack and Lily alone after dark equaled disaster once upon a time, and it's definitely not a scene I wish to repeat. But I have to make sure things are settled between us before he goes any further with Tori. "Where do you want to meet?"

"I can't make it. I'm headed out of town overnight."

The man never lacks for company. Whoever he's taking, I'll bet she's young, gorgeous, and very good in bed. "I see," I say, trying to keep a neutral tone of voice even as I hear the simmering disapproval coming out of my mouth.

"Lily, you kill me." A deep chuckles rumbles across the line. "Why do you always think there's a girl involved?"

"Because there usually is?" I haven't forgotten all those girls he had hanging around him when I was growing up. Girls he was stringing along even when he was intimate with me.

"Well, sorry to disappoint you, but you're wrong. Pop and I are headed up to South Lake Tahoe for an attorney seminar. We're presenting a workshop on civil litigation."

"That sounds interesting," I stammer. If he's dragging Ed's name into this, then he must be telling the truth. Jack's not about to make a stupid mistake. It would be easy enough for me to check things out.

"You're welcome to come along, if you like," he offers. "Tahoe is gorgeous."

"I've been there."

"That's right. We used to spend Christmases up there together."

As if I could forget.

"You were how old then? About twelve?"

"Thirteen," I whisper, thawing out an icy memory from long ago. Jack was in law school, Ed and Mimi had rented a private chalet, and he flew in to spend the holidays with us. That Christmas was a special time, before all the fighting began. Snow, sleigh bells, Jack teaching me to ski. Nights spent together in front of the crackling fireplace, Ed and Mimi laughing over drinks, me sipping hot chocolate, the three of us playing blackjack.

The three of us. Jack had spent a lot of time hanging out at the bar, playing with the girls. The grown-up girls.

I shove the reminiscence back in my mind's deep freeze. "Thanks, but I'll pass. I haven't got time for fun and games right now."

"The offer's open, in case you change your mind," he says. "Ed would love to see you, and we'll only be gone overnight."

Out of the corner of my eye, I catch sight of something

moving in the courtyard. I swing around in Mimi's chair for a better angle and peer through the bank of windows to see the Queen Mum herself. She has a grim, determined smile on her face as she shuffles across the walkway, shoving her walker. Francesca hovers beside her. They are headed toward the chapel.

My day is about to get a lot worse.

"You and Ed have a good time in Lake Tahoe. We'll get together when you get back," I say, hanging up.

"I couldn't stop her," Francesca whispers as we trail Mimi's walker into the Royal Reception Room. "Tori told her about the sign, and she insisted on seeing for herself."

As long as it's only the sign. I eye my mother warily as she scans the room, moves through the area. She starts for the cooler with the floral arrangements and abruptly her walker catches on the Persian carpet. I lunge forward, grabbing her arm before she stumbles and falls, but Mimi steadies herself and shrugs me away. I step aside and let her be. So much for an attitude of gratitude. The Queen Mum is being her usual regal self. Some things never change.

"Why don't we sit down?" Francesca suggests. She helps Mimi get situated in one of the gold damask chairs, then sinks into the chair beside her. "Now, isn't that better? Goodness, it's hot out today." Francesca fans herself, smiling roundly first at me, then Mimi. "That was a nice workout, don't you think? The walk from the villa did us both some good."

Mimi ignores her, glancing hungrily around the room, giving it a once-over for cleanliness. Checking it out. Her gaze comes to land on me. Checking me out. Her eyes narrow and she lifts her left hand and points at me with a scowl.

"What is that?"

"You don't like it?" I glance down at the rose-colored sundress I donned this morning. Tori and Francesca still follow Mimi's rules when it comes to wearing *only black*, but as far as I'm concerned, the chapel's dress policy is dead and buried. "I think it makes a nice splash of color around here."

The Queen Mum is not amused. She leans on her good arm and grabs her walker, struggling to her feet. Francesca puffs to a stand, but Mimi shakes her off. "My office." She shuffles a few determined steps toward the office door.

"Why don't we put that off till another day," Francesca suggests. "Remember what your therapist said. It's important to pace yourself. We still have to walk back to the villa."

"Francesca is right. You're done enough for today." I step forward and block the doorway. If Mimi makes it through the door and reclaims her throne in front of her computer, there'll be hell to pay. She'll discover that I managed to break her password, and tallied the monthly figures for June. That I've added all the mysterious cash deposits for the past ten months, and put the balance sheets back into some semblance of manageability. The bridal income is starting to climb, but most of that shows up on July's receivables. The only thing that kept the chapel solvent through June was those random cash deposits, and there haven't been any since Mimi had her stroke.

"You should rest," I urge. "Don't you have therapy

this afternoon?"

Despite the comfortable, air-conditioned room, the look she shoots me is anything but cool—more like a fiery disgust that I'm the one making the rules, that I'm the one in charge. I'm the one who's now responsible for her precious chapel.

"Enhhhhh," she spits in a disgusted voice.

She shuffles out of the chapel, Francesca trailing close behind. I successfully stalled her from poking around any further, but oddly enough, I don't feel proud. How would I feel if the situation were reversed? What if this was my business, and Tori treated me the way I've treated Mimi? She knows how much I hate the place. But it's not so much hatred, as resentment. The chapel took up all her time and energy, her passion and love. Eventually it even took Ed. It robbed our family of a normal life.

Mimi has spent the past forty years building the chapel into what it is today. No wonder she's concerned about how I'm running things. I'm sure she thinks I'm running it into the ground. If Mimi wants to call the shots, I'll be glad to turn it over... but not until she's ready. And not until I solve the mystery that's been keeping me awake nights.

Maybe it's the skeptic in me that evolved from growing up in the shadow of the chapel. Or maybe it's because I'm an accountant and concerned about the bottom line. But until Mimi returns, I'm responsible for things at the chapel. And I'm determined to have things balanced and in fiscal order.

Starting with determining where those cash deposits came from.

"What did you say your name was again?" I rub the heel of my palm against my forehead as if by doing so, I could erase the pounding headache and all the day's frustrations. It's late afternoon, I'm tired, hungry, and wishing I hadn't picked up the call.

"Mitch Ryan, from the *Las Vegas Sun*." He sounds young, and he talks fast, like there's no time to waste. "I'm doing a feature article for the Sunday edition about the wedding chapel business in Vegas. I want to include the Royal Wedding Chapel."

"What kind of article?" Publicity without a price tag. I like the idea of free advertising. I put him on speaker and take advantage of the time by massaging the back of my neck with both hands. Too much stress. Too much tension. Jack always gave great back rubs.

"I'm going at it from an angle of old Las Vegas chapels and how they've adapted throughout the years. You get what I'm saying? From the whole Rat Pack thing back in the sixties, through the seventies and disco fever, the eighties and the town's phenomenal growth, yadda, yadda... which brings us to present day. It's a changing market out there. I'm concentrating on the chapel industry. How many have gone under, how the ones that managed to survive—like yours— are coping in a depressed economy and a changing world."

I don't know if it's the furious clip of his words or the way he presented the topic, but suddenly I'm feeling uneasy. "Could you tell me a little more about the article?"

"Like I said, it's an article on old Las Vegas chapels."

There's an edge to his voice that wasn't there before. "Look, I was in your place a couple months ago and I talked to the owner about the possibility of doing an article on the chapel. She was interested. She asked me to keep in touch and get back to her when I was ready to do the story."

"You spoke with my mother?"

I hear papers rustle, and I assume he's checking his notes. "Elizabeth Alexander. That her?"

"Yes." I can just imagine Mimi snapping at the free publicity. When it comes to money, she's got the purse strings tied tighter than at Buckingham Palace.

"I'd like to talk to her."

"I told you she's ill. I'm running things until she's fully recovered."

"Look, if you don't want to be included, that's your choice," he finally says. "But I got the impression that your mother thought differently. Frankly, if I were you, I'd jump at the opportunity. This will be the lead article in the Sunday feature section."

I drum my fingers against the counter. Free advertising in the Sunday edition. A big splashy article featuring the Royal Wedding Chapel. Guaranteed there will be photos, too. What would Mimi do? I already know the answer. She wouldn't hesitate at the opportunity to promote her beloved chapel.

"I'm on a deadline." His voice edges up a notch. "I've already got interviews lined up with some other chapels tomorrow. Any of them would be thrilled at the opportunity I'm offering you. The Royal Wedding Chapel is one of the oldest and well-known chapels on the Strip. But let's face it. Times have changed. The market has changed. You're got some stiff competition for all your brides from the big casinos. Places like Bellagio, Venetian, Cosmopolitan, and Caesar's. They have major money to carry them through this tough economy. As for the Royal Wedding Chapel? It's obvious you're struggling to survive."

"That's not true," I shoot back.

"No? Let me check my notes. *Dusty chandeliers, shabby carpeting, chipped tile in the reception area.*"

My gaze flies to the floor near the heavy front door and comes to rest on the tile he mentioned. It's only a small crack, and nothing that would put one of our brides in danger. But Mr. Ryan is right. It does diminish the mood of elegance and royal splendor. I've been meaning to call someone about having it fixed, but with everything else that's been going on, I haven't had time.

"Look, Ms. Alexander—"

"Lavender," I say firmly. "The name is Lily Lavender."

"Okay, Ms. Lavender, here's the way I see it. It's clear you're looking to promote your business. You've got a new sign up on the Strip. Why wouldn't you want to participate in this article? Free publicity."

Not if he intends to slant his story the way I think he does. Old Vegas wedding chapels, shabby and run-down, struggling to survive. Does the Royal Wedding Chapel need that kind of publicity? Do we really want to be part of a story that tears down the chapel rather than building it up? If I cooperate with him and the article runs, I'll have no control over the way he spins his content.

"So, do we set up an interview time for tomorrow?"

"You know, Mr. Ryan, I think we'll pass."

"Your loss," he says. I hear the shrug in his voice, like he's surprised that I turned him down, yet he couldn't care less. "But if you think you can compete in today's market simply by relying on your reputation, then all I can say is good luck."

Exactly what we're going to need. Good luck.

Chapter Twelve

THE QUEEN MUM IS NOT amused. In fact, she's downright furious. Mimi throws the Sunday feature section on the kitchen floor with a menacing scowl and raises her left hand to stab a finger at me over her empty orange-juice glass. The glare on her face says *off with her head!* "You... knew."

"Yes," I admit. "He contacted me the other day about setting up an interview, but I turned him down. There was just something about him I didn't like."

And after reading the article he wrote slamming the chapel, I really don't like him. In fact, I don't blame Mimi for being mad. "I had no idea he would go after us like that."

It's a weak excuse, but it's the only one I have. Despite my refusal to cooperate, Mitch Ryan decided to go ahead with his plan to feature the Royal Wedding Chapel as the lead in the *Las Vegas Sun* article. Rather than lauding us as a chapel that's struggling to reinvent itself, everything derogatory he quoted me from his notes is splashed across the front page... from the crack in the tile, the shabby interior, and the outdated wallpaper, right down to a burned-out bulb in a chandelier. He listed it all and ended his piece by deeming Mimi's business the Royal Chapel of Shoddiness.

Tori grabs the paper and quickly scans the article. The further she reads, the redder her face grows and the more her mouth drops. She fixes me with a wide-eyed stare. "This is horrible. You must have known he would mention us."

"I'm sorry." I glance around the table, cringing at the sight of Mimi's disgust, Tori's shock, Francesca's disbelief. "I don't know what else to say."

"You had... no right." Mimi's eyes narrow. "My... chapel," she spits out.

"I know." No matter my personal feelings, I should have consulted her. Now it's too late. The damage is done. *The Sun* has a readership of over a half million readers, and the article is being digested across breakfast tables all over Las Vegas even as we speak.

And there's not even a question of asking for a retraction or suing for slander. Mitch Ryan is an excellent journalist, I have to give him credit. He might have taken literary license with the chapel's overall ambiance, but every single fact and flaw about the chapel in his story is true, right down to the tiny stain on the chaise lounge in the Queen Elizabeth bridal suite. "I'm sorry," I say one more time, though *sorry* doesn't begin to cover it.

Mimi glares at me. "Why?"

"Why didn't I agree to the interview?" I nibble at my bottom lip. "I don't know. There was just something about him. He was so smug and arrogant."

The look in Mimi's eyes could melt the butter on Francesca's toast faster than the scorching mid-July 110-degree temperature outside. "Why... not ask me?" she finally says.

"I don't know. I wasn't thinking." Hindsight is always better, and I made a mistake not telling her about his phone call. This is still Mimi's business, not mine. The Royal Wedding Chapel is her livelihood, and my actions could have done it severe damage. But there's no going back, no way to reverse time and allow her to make the decision. The damage is done.

The air inside the kitchen hangs hot and heavy with tension. *If you can't stand the heat...* I slide from my chair, scoot it under the table. "I'm sorry," I say one last time and make a quick exit.

"It's horrible, Walt. She's furious with me, and I don't blame her." I pace the floor of my old bedroom, gnawing at a torn cuticle as I glance through the window. Craning my neck, I can just glimpse the garden separating the villa from the chapel. The top of the chapel's Court Gazebo is visible beyond. "It was a bad decision on my part."

"You did the best you could with the information you had."

"No, I didn't. I could tell the guy was a jerk, and I didn't trust him. That's why I said no." I clench my fist. "What a mess."

"He's the one who wrote the article, not you."

"But I'm the one who refused to sit for an interview. Maybe if I had, I could have protected the chapel. Maybe he wouldn't have printed all those dreadful things." I press my palm against my forehead, trying to rub away both the stress headache and the ugly memory of Mitch Ryan's story in the *Sun*. "I should have seen it coming."

"Quit beating yourself up. None of us is perfect."

But I want to be perfect. I want to do this right. Or do I? Do I even know what I want anymore? "Sometimes it feels like…"

"Like what?" he prompts softly.

"Like even though I'm busy doing all these things, I'm doing them wrong." I sigh. "It's a no-win situation. Mimi is getting better, but she's nowhere near ready to take control again. Meanwhile, she's upset about how I'm running the business." I think about our clash over the dress code, my refusal to book future weddings past August, my preventing Mimi from entering her own office. "What do you think? Do I try to gradually ease her back into things or keep her away until she's stronger? How would you handle this? Mimi doesn't seem to realize how much—"

"Lily, you're obsessing," he breaks in. "Listen to me. Do not doubt yourself. You're doing a great job. Remember, she's sick. She's not thinking properly."

"You have no idea how much I want to come home." I think of my cozy little house back in Del Mar, with its sweeping view of the Pacific. Right now I'd give anything to simply be puttering in the flower beds surrounding the tiny patio and the front entrance. "I miss my house. I miss my job. I miss my life."

I blink back hot tears that spring from nowhere. I am not a crier. I've never been a crier. But I've never felt so much like crying as I do right now. "You don't know what it's like, Walt. You have no idea how much I miss you all."

"We miss you, too." His voice softens. "But the house will still be there when you're ready to come back... and so will your job."

"Sometimes I feel like running away," I confess. "Like just saying screw it, and taking off. Being here was never my choice."

Leaving, though, would be.

"That's not like you, Lily. You've never been one to shirk your responsibilities." He pauses. "I understand there's tension between you and your mother. But whether you realize it or not, I think you love her very much."

But how can you love someone if they don't love you back? I think of how Mimi glared at me over breakfast, how she spit words in my face. She has always been disappointed in me. She's always regretted that I am who I am, that I didn't turn out the way she wanted, that her own daughter could profess such disdain in the business of happily ever after.

"If you didn't love her," he adds, "you never would have made the decision to stay in the first place."

His words stop me cold. Why did I stay? Why am I still here? Why am I beating myself up like this? I could walk away. Nothing is keeping me from leaving.

Nothing. Except Tori. And Francesca. And, like it or not, Mimi herself. She might treat me like a servant, but I'd never be able to live with myself if I allowed myself to leave like this. I can't do it to her. I can't do it to them.

Plus, there's that promise I made to myself, to solve the mystery. "Did I tell you about the secret money she was using to keep the chapel open?"

Kathleen Irene Paterka

"What money?"

Quickly I fill him in about the cash deposits I discovered. "None of them show up on the books," I add. "I don't know how long she's been doing it. I don't even know if she's reported the income to the IRS."

"Any idea where it came from?"

"Not yet," I say, "but I intend to find out."

"Maybe the bank extended her a line of credit. That would explain the random deposits."

"I don't think so. The deposits were cash, and a bank would issue checks," I remind him.

"What about a pawn shop? There are plenty in Vegas. That would give her easy access to cash, and no interest due. Have you noticed anything missing? Antiques? Jewelry?"

"No, Mimi would never hock her jewelry."

"Maybe she's been gambling," he suggests.

"Mimi's never had interest in hitting the tables. She'd rather work the room and chat people up." I halt as a random thought occurs to me. "Do you think someone could have loaned her the money?"

"She'd need collateral."

And without further thought, I suddenly realize the one way Mimi could have collected the cash. "Maybe she got it from someone who didn't require collateral," I suggest. "Someone with money plus an interest in making sure the chapel doors stay open."

"Makes sense," he agrees. "Any ideas as to who that someone might be?"

"Oh, I can think of someone," I say coolly. How could I have been so stupid? I should have thought of this in the first place.

"Let me know what you find out."

"Don't worry, Walt, you'll be the first to know," I promise.

We hang up, and my mind is already busy calculating how many days and hours until Jack Alexander is back in town.

Chapter Thirteen

"I NEED YOU AT THE CHAPEL." Tori's voice rushes over the phone.

"What's wrong?" Tori's been at the chapel since dinner, working on updating the website, while I shut myself up in the cavernous office off the kitchen. I glance at the unfinished business email I've been writing to Walt. "Can it wait?"

"No, it can't. Please, Mom? I need you right now." The line goes dead.

Whatever it is, it had better be good. I save a draft copy of Walt's email on my laptop, and head for the chapel.

Five minutes later, struggling through the pack of people crowding the Royal Reception Room, I realize Tori was right to call me... especially when I come face to face with Lee Roy Davison, a sports superstar. Lee Roy, only in his late twenties, is already a basketball legend. Lanky and graceful, with smooth ebony skin, he's more handsome in person than in his games or his television commercials pushing sports deodorants and healthy cereals. But he's most famous for his endless promo spots about the dangers of smoking cigarettes. Anyone with a TV knows his mother died of lung cancer just before Lee Roy made it big. His campaign ads warning young people *Don't smoke!* have made him unforgettable.

"I told Michelle she could get married anyplace she wanted," Lee Roy says in the soft familiar drawl everyone in America recognizes. "But she has her heart set on your chapel."

A stunning black woman in shimmering white who barely reaches the top of his shoulder leans into Lee Roy with an adoring smile. "My parents were married right here in this chapel thirty years ago," she says in a melodic voice. "Both of them are gone now. It would make me feel like they were part of things if we're able to say our vows in the same place they did."

A short heavy man in a shiny black suit barrels his way through the entourage to the counter. "I'm Lee Roy's manager," he barks. "The two of them want to get married tonight."

Tori and I exchange glances. Celebrity sightings are common in Las Vegas, but as far as I know, the chapel hasn't played host to a big-name ceremony in years. I face Lee Roy and Michelle. There are chapels in this town that would kill to have their business. They've been an item in the tabloids for years. Childhood sweethearts from Atlanta, they've stayed together even as Lee Roy's fame and legendary prowess at basketball grew. "You're eloping?"

She nods. "Just like Mama and Daddy did. They flew in from Atlanta and got married here at the chapel that night."

"Look, we got people waiting. You gonna make this happen, or do we need to go somewhere else?" Lee Roy's manager waves his hand toward the mash of supporters milling about.

"Back off, J.T. Give the lady a break." Lee Roy turns his attention to me with a sweet-as-honey smile that suddenly makes me understand why women of all ages adore him. "J.T. tends to get carried away sometimes."

"No problem." I return his smile. When it comes to dealing with people like J.T., I can relate. My personal J.T. is fast asleep with her walker parked close to her bed.

Lee Roy nods toward Tori. "She said you were closed. But I'd consider it a big favor if you would open back up and let us get married tonight. Michelle has waited long enough, and I'm ready to do this."

Tori and I trade rapid glances. A walk-in celebrity wedding? Tonight? Lee Roy Davison is a superstar, and I want to make him happy, but this wedding is certain to attract attention. With the recent negative publicity from the *Las Vegas Sun*, the chapel can't afford even the slightest thing going wrong. And this feels rushed.

"We are closed," I slowly say, "but that's not the problem. This is such a special day in your lives. We want to make sure you have the wedding of your dreams."

Michelle beams as I speak, and I trade on the courage. "Perhaps if you give us a little more time. Maybe tomorrow," I suggest. "We'd be able to—"

"No, it has to be tonight," Lee Roy insists. "If we wait until tomorrow, word might leak out and the press would be all over this. That's not what I want." His smile disappears. "This is our wedding. Michelle and I want to keep it private."

I glance at Lee Roy's entourage milling behind him.

The King Edward Chapel is the only room large enough to accommodate the crowd. Can we pull it off? It's already after ten, and Francesca is probably in bed by now. But maybe we could call her back, have her hurry over. Tori nods and I know we're on the same page. I glance over Lee Roy's shoulder at the flower cooler, grateful for the beautiful fresh blooms still available from this morning's delivery.

J.T. scowls, checks his big gold watch.

"Money is no object," Lee Roy softly adds. "Whatever we have to do to make sure this happens."

But this isn't about money. It's about making two people happy. I turn toward Tori. "I'll call Francesca and ask her to come over. Meanwhile, why don't you help Michelle and Lee Roy pick out the music and flowers."

"Thank you." Michelle catches my hand over the counter. Her eyes shine brighter than the lights on the Vegas Strip. "Thank you. You have no idea how much this means to me... to us."

But I do. It meant enough to her that they sought out the wedding chapel where her parents were married. It meant enough to him that Lee Roy came knocking on the door after hours, intent on keeping his bride protected from the press. A man and woman deeply in love. Not seeking publicity. Not seeking attention. Only seeking romance.

"It's our pleasure." It's something we say automatically to wedding couples, but this time, I really mean it.

And for a moment, I wonder. Maybe happily ever after does exist.

Despite the hasty arrangements, the wedding goes off as perfectly as if every detail had been planned for months by courtiers at Buckingham Palace. The bride was elegant and stunning in her simple satin gown. The groom choked up as he spoke his wedding vows. There was a lump in my throat as I watched Michelle lean over and wipe away Lee Roy's tears and kiss the knuckles of his right hand. I leaned against the chapel's back wall, and for the first time in years, found myself caught up in the whirlwind of romance.

The entourage in the pews breaks out in applause as the newlyweds depart the altar. Lee Roy flashes me a thumbs-up and a huge smile as they approach. He catches me in a hug as graceful as if he was cradling a basketball. "Thank you for making this happen. Michelle and I will always be grateful."

"Yes, thank you so much," she adds. "Everything was perfect. It felt like Mama and Daddy were here with us the whole time."

"You're very welcome," I say, watching the tears shimmer in her eyes. Oddly enough, I feel like crying myself. Then suddenly the crowd descends with hugs and handshakes all round. Men slap Lee Roy on the back, women surround Michelle, cooing over the wedding ring Lee Roy just slipped on her finger. The eternity band of diamonds flashes and sparkles under the shimmering chandeliers in the King Edward Chapel. Thank God Jaabir changed the burnt-out bulb. For tonight, the Royal Chapel of Shabbiness doesn't exist.

J.T. pulls me aside as the entourage winds its way into the Royal Reception Room. "Good job," he mutters and stuffs something into my hand.

I look down in my palm and see a fat wad of one-hundred-dollar bills. "This isn't necessary," I protest, pushing the money back at him. "We settled the bill before the wedding."

"Keep it," he growls and shoves it back at me. "You made Lee Roy happy. That's a little something to make you happy."

I'll split the tip between Tori and Francesca. I don't need it. I'm happy enough at what I've witnessed tonight. The chapel hosted a royal romance, a true love story. No amount of money could be better than that.

"Weren't they just the perfect couple?" Francesca says as the entourage precedes Lee Roy and Michelle through the massive front door and out into the courtyard. Tori joins us as we trail behind them into the hot desert night. It's nearly midnight, but the courtyard is flooded with lights. Four gleaming black stretch limousines, engines idling, stand ready.

Suddenly out of nowhere comes a flash of a strobe light, then another.

"What the hell?" Lee Roy's harsh voice rises in anger.

The photographer gets off another quick round of the bride and groom. An ugly frown covers Lee Roy's face. His entire body poses a threat as he charges toward the man, but J.T. grabs his arm and holds him back. "Calm down. He's with us."

"The hell he is," Lee Roy spits out. "I don't remember inviting him."

"I did," J.T. replies.

Lee Roy's jaw clenches. "I told you no publicity."

"And I kept my word. You and Michelle got married, nice and quiet, just like you wanted. No publicity."

"Then what the hell do you call this?" Lee Roy growls. He flings out his arm as the photographer snaps away. That's when I notice another man shooting film with a video camera. A large, expensive, professional-looking camera, the kind you see filming ringside at the PBR, the Daytona 500, or the NBA play-offs.

"Look, my man, when have I ever not looked out for you? It's my job, right?" J.T. slaps Lee Roy on the back. "But there's no way you can keep this marriage private. Things are going to leak. Better they get the footage from us than we let them have it for free. You know the game. That's how it's played. You gotta take control, take advantage of the situation."

Michelle steps forward, lays a hand on Lee Roy's arm. "Let it go, Lee," she says quietly. "J.T. is right. Everyone will find out soon enough."

The Lee Roy Davison I see glowering at J.T. is a different man than the one who stood at the altar next to Michelle less than thirty minutes ago. His legendary size-sixteen feet are planted firmly on the cobblestones and his immense hands are balled into tight fists. For a moment, I wonder if he's going to take a swing at his business manager. But the anger melts from Lee Roy's face as the camera continues to roll. He glances at Michelle. "You sure about this?"

"What else can we do? The press will be all over this sooner or later." She lifts one shoulder with a soft, helpless shrug. "This is the price you pay."

Lee Roy sighs. "Okay, then, let's give them what they

want." He takes her hand and tucks it in the crook of his elbow. They face the cameras and turn on their smiles. Suddenly it's like watching a superstar announced as he makes his way onto a glossy basketball court under a thousand brilliant lights and to thundering applause. This is the Lee Roy Davison I've read about, the man on TV, the handsome athlete who rocketed into superstar fame and glory. But this is not the man who just married his childhood sweetheart in the King Edward Chapel. That man was fiercely protective of his bride and wanted to keep things private. That man believes in love.

"All right, boys, that's enough." J.T. steps forward after a minute. "Let the newlyweds start their honeymoon."

The videographer quits filming, the photographer drops his camera, and Lee Roy and Michelle slide into one of the long stretch limos. Thirty seconds later, it glides across the cobblestones, under the courtyard entrance, and merges into traffic on Las Vegas Boulevard, disappearing into the night. J.T. and the others clamber into the remaining limos. Five minutes later, the chapel courtyard is empty save for Francesca, Tori and me, plus the photographer and the man with the video camera.

"I'm Mike." The cameraman, handsome and young, thrusts out a hand. "I'd like to get a couple shots of the chapel's interior. You mind?"

Tori steps up. "I'll show him, Mom."

I don't debate the issue for long. Lee Roy and Michelle already posed for photos. And after Mitch Ryan's article in the *Las Vegas Sun*, we could use some good publicity. "Go ahead."

"Great," he says, grinning at Tori. "Lead the

way, princess."

Francesca and I exchange meaningful glances. "I think I'll tag along," she offers.

"Thank you," I mouth silently. The three of them disappear inside the chapel.

The videographer steps forward. "Got time for a quick interview?"

"Me? But what would I have to say?" I look at him with surprise. He's not much older than his cohort, but with thinning hair and bloodshot eyes. Plus, he looks like he's been chasing the same story one too many times; like he already knows the type of footage he'll shoot, how he'll edit it, and how it will play on TV.

"Deep background," he clips out the words. "Look, if you don't want to do it, fine by me. I've already got shots of them coming out of the chapel. Still, this will probably end up on some of the major sports channels. Lee Roy Davison is a famous guy. Sure you don't want the coverage?"

Free publicity. I mull the offer. It wasn't long ago I turned down a similar request, only to have it backfire on me. Television advertising is expensive. If I agree, maybe it will pacify Mimi. "All right. Yes, I'll do it."

"Great." He shrugs, his blank expression doesn't change. "Let's start off with a shot of you standing at the door to the chapel and we'll go from there."

I back up and take directions from him, stand exactly where he wants me. With the camera rolling, he begins asking questions. "I'll edit them out later," he explains. So I continue answering, one side of my brain filtering facts about the chapel, the other part lamenting my tired-looking navy skirt and ivory blouse. If I end up on television, I'll come across looking more like a palace maid than a representative of the Royal Wedding Chapel. The interview is the longest five minutes of my life, and I'm grateful when Tori, Francesca, and the photographer reappear.

"Wasn't he awesome?" Tori breathes when the three of us are finally alone in the courtyard.

"Totally," I agree, even though I'm not sure if she's referring to Lee Roy the Superstar or the handsome young photographer.

Francesca stifles a yawn. "All this excitement. I'm going to bed."

"How can she sleep?" Tori chatters as she trails me back to the chapel. "I'm jumping on Facebook and posting the news."

"I don't know if that's a good idea."

"You heard J.T. The story will come out eventually. Plus, they already took photos," she says.

I can't stand the dejected look on her face. "Okay, go for it."

She throws her arms around me in a quick hug. "This is so exciting. We've got an exclusive!"

"Grab your laptop while I lock up."

"But why can't I work over here?" she wails. "Everything is already set up in the Queen's bridal suite and—"

"Tori, please, let's not argue about it." It's well after midnight, and even with the doors bolted, I don't want her alone in the chapel by herself. It's Las Vegas. It's the Strip. "The chapel doors are officially closed for the night."

Maybe it was Tori's post on Facebook. Maybe it was the photos splashed across the Internet, glossy tabloids, and front pages of major newspapers around the country. Or maybe it was the video footage I caught on CNN the very next evening. Whatever the source, the media hype focusing on the chapel following Lee Roy's wedding is immediate and totally annihilates any negative publicity lingering from the *Las Vegas Sun* feature article. One week after Lee Roy's wedding, the chapel phone hasn't quit ringing. We are now booked solid through the middle of August. We've even started turning away walk-ins.

Briefly I toy with the notion of discussing the extra business with Mimi and the possibility of hiring another minister to cover weddings in the chapel court garden gazebo or the Queen Elizabeth Chapel. But as it turns out, everyone wants to be married in the King Edward Chapel on the same altar where Lee Roy and Michelle exchanged vows. And just like Lee Roy and Michelle, everyone wants to be married by Francesca.

"How does it feel to be famous?" I ask as she wanders into the reception room. I've just turned down our fourth phone inquiry of the day about hosting a wedding this weekend.

She sinks into one of the chairs facing the reception desk and fans herself with one hand. "This is crazy, Lily. I've never seen anything like it."

"It *is* crazy," I agree. "How are you feeling?"

"Tired," she admits. "I'm doing my best to keep up."

"If it gets to be too much, let me know." Despite

what the brides want, it might be wise to call in an extra minister to relieve her of some of the stress. Francesca isn't getting any younger. But even though her faded face is lined with wrinkles, there's a perkiness about her that I haven't seen in years. She looks flushed and happy. Maybe all this busyness agrees with her.

"Don't worry about me, Lily," she says with an understanding smile. "I'll be fine."

"Am I that easy to read?"

She chuckles. "I've known you since you were a little girl, remember?"

How could I forget? Francesca was there when I started kindergarten, when I graduated from high school. She was with us through Mimi's years with Ed and their messy divorce. When I discovered I was pregnant with Tori, Francesca was the one I turned to. She was the one who handled things with Mimi. She was the one who always smoothed things over. She was the one who called 911 when Mimi had her stroke. Life without Francesca is unfathomable.

"Promise you'll let me know if you need a break," I urge her.

She nods. "I will."

"If business keeps up, we should probably hire someone to help Jaabir out with the maintenance work," I say. "It's not fair, expecting him to play chauffeur and shuttle these couples to their hotels, plus keep up with all the repairs. But first I want to see if this new business continues or if it's just a fluke."

The unexpected flood of income in the chapel's checking account has definitely made life easier. The cash register is stuffed with credit card slips, cash, and personal checks. I've been able to make payroll and finally reimburse Francesca the back pay she's owed. Professional cleaners visited two days ago and took care of all the furniture, including the stained chaise lounge. The entry's tiled floor is scheduled for repair on Sunday. The Queen Elizabeth Chapel carpet will be ripped up and replaced next week, and the King Edward Chapel walls repainted and carpet replaced the following two weekends. I knew it would be expensive, but I still cringed when I read the quote and the double-time pay for workers on Sundays. But I went ahead and signed off on the contract. It's a necessary expense. I haven't invested all this time and put in all this hard work for nothing. No way am I allowing us to slip back into the Royal Chapel of Shabbiness.

Not to mention, we can now afford it. Though I'm still curious about those mysterious cash deposits Mimi was making.

"I've always believed things happen for a reason," Francesca muses. "Lee Roy and Michelle showing up at the chapel came just when we needed it. Obviously someone was watching out for us."

"Do you mean fate, or are you talking about God?"

"I'm saying I think business will continue to pick up. So does Mimi. We were chatting about it this morning. She's very excited about what this could mean for the chapel."

Mimi, thrilled at the growing business? A slow shiver slides down my spine. In the busyness and melee of everyday affairs, I allowed myself to be sucked into the insanity of running the family business. When did I start caring about what happens to the chapel? I know better than anyone what goes into making the place sparkle, the chandeliers glimmer. And for what? The radiant glow on brides' faces as they walk down the aisle.

But the Royal Wedding Chapel has nothing to do with romance. It's all about business, about selling a product in the name of love, of conning gullible couples into opening up their wallets and purchasing a spectacular wedding package that will give them the perfect setting, the perfect flowers, photos, and memories... some of which will only last a year before the arguments start and the divorce papers are filed.

I need to make sure I keep my wits about me and my head screwed on straight. I can't afford to get sucked into the swirl of success. I need to remember what this place is all about.

"If business keeps up, we should talk to Mimi about hiring someone to help run things."

"But we don't need anyone," Francesca replies. "You're doing a wonderful job."

"Tori and I will be leaving in four more weeks."

For the first time in our conversation, Francesca's face falls. "I thought maybe you had changed your mind."

It's hard to meet her eyes. "You've always known that was never part of my plan."

She pauses a moment. "Do you really think leaving is the best thing to do?"

"I have a job, remember? I have a house and a life."

"I realize that." She falls silent.

"But...?"

"I was hoping you would stay. I was hoping you were getting comfortable with us."

But that's the problem. I am getting comfortable. A little too comfortable. "Francesca, you know how I feel. You know how I feel. You've always known. I never wanted any of this. I never wanted to live in Las Vegas or work at the chapel."

"I know, Lily, but I was hoping you had changed your mind." Her eyes sink with sadness. "When you were a little girl, you loved the chapel. You would come home from school, throw your backpack behind the counter, and scoot into one the chapels to watch a wedding. Don't you remember?"

Oh, I remember all right. I remember everything. Playing on the altar, pretending to be a minister, just like Mimi. Sneaking into a back pew during a real wedding, peeking over the wooden railing, caught up in the romance of a bride marrying the man she loved. Grabbing leftover flowers from the cooler and sashaying up the aisle, pretending I was on my father's arm as I waltzed toward a shadowy groom waiting and willing to give me his whole heart. A groom who looked uncannily like Jack.

I remember it all, down to every detail.

And I remember the day it fell apart. The day I quit believing in fairy tales and happy endings. The day the romance died. The day Ed walked out.

Why bother pinning all your hopes and dreams on a happily ever after when you know it doesn't exist? Why bother working in a business where fifty percent of the marriages fail? Why bother pouring your heart and soul into something that was never meant to be?

"I wish I understood what happened and why you chose not to be a part of this... of *us*, anymore," Francesca says.

"Please don't go, Lily. We'll miss you so much. We'll be heartbroken." She pauses. "Tori will be heartbroken."

But I don't want to hear any more. I can't.

"I'm going to check the chapel." I shut down the computer and stride out of the room without looking back.

Chapter Fourteen

THE MASSIVE DOOR SWINGS OPENS with a creak, announcing one last visitor of the day. I glance up from the reception desk and see a short, older woman hesitating in the doorway.

"May I help you?" It's late afternoon and the chapel is closed, though I haven't locked the doors yet. Jaabir drove off half an hour ago with the last newlywed couple of the day, and Tori is already at Caesar's Palace with Ed, helping with last-minute preparations for Jack's surprise birthday party tonight.

The woman looks lost, yet she still has a sense of purpose. Her face is flat and her features plain. Beautiful silver hair is her crowning glory. Clasping her purse tight, she abandons her post at the door and slowly walks the length of the room. "You must be Lily."

Something about the way she says my name, the way she tilts her head and studies me, makes the hair on the back of my neck prickle. "Yes, I'm Lily. How can I help you?"

She takes a few steps closer. "My son and daughter-in-law live in Henderson. We saw the wedding on TV."

"The wedding," I repeat, letting out a soft sigh. I hadn't realized I was holding my breath. "You mean Lee Roy Davison."

She nods, smiles, and suddenly things make sense. Funny, that someone her age would be a celebrity follower. I note the simple gold wedding band on her finger. Her husband, probably out parking the car, must be a sports fanatic. Just like so many others the past few days, they caught the wedding footage and my interview on TV and decided to renew their vows in the same chapel where Lee Roy and Michelle were married. Idly I wonder if Francesca has already left for the villa to help Mimi dress. I hate turning older couples away, especially those here for a vow renewal. Maybe there's still time before Jack's party to squeeze in one last ceremony.

"You were interviewed on TV after the wedding," the woman says. "You're Elizabeth's daughter."

"Yes," I confirm, even as I find myself wondering how she knows Mimi is my mother. I think back to that night: the cameras, the lights, the flurry of activity in the chapel courtyard. I only caught the TV interview once and I barely remember what I said or did, let alone if Mimi was mentioned. Was she?

"I often wondered what happened to Elizabeth. How is she?"

Something inside cautions me not to give out information I'm not sure she's entitled to. "I'm sorry, but how do you know my mother?

Her green eyes contain a mix of curiosity and concern. "Her name is Elizabeth, correct? Elizabeth Lavender."

"No, it's Alexander." It's merely a little white lie. Mimi

was Elizabeth Lavender, once upon a time. But for some reason, I don't want to admit the truth. Hearing Mimi's name cross the woman's lips has me on edge. Suddenly I wish I had locked the door an hour ago and that she hadn't come in. Who is she? I'm positive I've never seen her before. What has she got to do with Mimi?

"So, she changed names. I wondered if that was the case."

"You know my mother?" I repeat.

She nods. "My name is Rita. Your mother and I were friends many years ago. Then we lost track of each other. But when I saw the wedding coverage and your face on the screen, I knew I had to come."

I'm positive that I've never heard Mimi mention anyone named Rita. "My mother is ill. She recently had a stroke."

Rita's face falls. "I am sorry to hear that."

"She's getting stronger every day," I add. "But she is not up to having visitors." Even if she was, there is no way I'm allowing this woman to see Mimi.

"Actually, I didn't come here to see your mother. I came to see you." She studies me for a moment. "I knew who you were even before they flashed your name on the television. You look just like him."

"Like who?"

"Your father," she says. "Lawrence Lavender. You look exactly like him."

"You knew my father?" I barely manage to speak the words. My mouth is as rough and dry as the desert sand surrounding the city. Who is this woman? She is like a ghost, appearing like a fine mist out of my parents' past.

"Did you know him in England? Before he died?"

Rita frowns. "I'm not sure I understand. Why would you say your father is dead?"

"Because he is. He died before I was born." It's an easy Google search, one I spent plenty of time researching when I was younger. Lawrence Lavender, only son and only child of William and Lillian Lavender, minor aristocracy in the British peerage. Though hundreds of names were ranked before theirs, seeing my grandparents listed in line for the throne always made me catch my breath. I grew up in the shadow of the story of their noble lineage and of my father's untimely death. Supposedly the line died out with him... and yet, it didn't. His wife of only two months, Mimi, was already pregnant with me. She fled the country after his death.

"My father lived in England," I tell Rita. "He died in a car accident before I was born. He's dead. I've seen his grave."

I went there once after I finished college. Mimi never talked of my father when I was growing up. Eventually her dead silence taught me to quit asking about him, that my questions would remain unanswered. For years, I thought she was cold and heartless, but finally one day, after chatting with Francesca, I finally understood that Mimi acted the way she did in order to survive. She buried her feelings when she buried my father. His death had caused her so much suffering and grief, enough that she vowed never to go back.

Mimi is a tough woman, but some things in life can prove too heavy for even the strongest among us.

I never told her about my trip to London and my

pilgrimage to the village that my father and his family called home. It was before Tori's birth, back in the days when I did a lot of traveling for the firm. I'd been in Amsterdam on business when on impulse I hopped a flight to Heathrow. The next day, I caught the train and visited the small village fifty miles from London, which had been the family seat. It was easy enough to find the small church with its ancient cemetery. I strolled along the crooked rows, searching for familiar names. Finally I spotted them: two tombstones, side by side. Moss had nearly claimed them for its own. Crouching, I'd scraped away some of the damp green plant from the first, to see their names: William and Lillian Lavender, January 13, 1941. My grandfather and grandmother, killed during the war, victims of the blitz.

But it was the second headstone, next to theirs, that made my pulse quicken and my heart skip a beat. I read his name once, then twice: Lawrence Lavender, the year he was born and the year he died. The year of my birth.

I sank to my knees in front of his tombstone. The grass was wet and the smell of earth rich and pungent as I rested the flowers I'd brought from London before his headstone. My father had died never knowing Mimi was pregnant. How I wish he had known about me. How I wish I had known him. If he hadn't died, I probably would have grown up in England. Life as I know it would have been so different. There would have been no wedding chapel. There would have been no Jack, and there would have been no Tori. And with that thought, as I knelt there before my father's grave, I finally understood why Mimi left. With my father gone, there was nothing for her there... or for me, either. Just an empty graveyard, cold and damp. I whispered a prayer, touched my fingers to my lips for a final kiss, then touched them to his tombstone and bid him a good-bye. Brushing the dirt from my knees, I struggled to stand and caught the next train back to London.

And just like Mimi so long ago, I never looked back.

"I don't know what Elizabeth told you," Rita finally says, "but your father is very much alive. My husband, David, died in a car accident. It happened long ago, when we were all friends."

I feel myself go numb and slump into one of the soft pillowy chairs edging the reception room. "It can't be true. He was British. He died many years ago."

The soft look of pity in her eyes starts a shudder running through me. "I'm sorry, Lily. As far as I know, your father has never been to England, except for a brief time when he served in the military overseas. He's always lived in Detroit."

"Michigan?" I whisper. "Detroit, Michigan?"

Rita nods. "He still lives there today. He's in a nursing home."

My hands tremble and I clutch them together. "I don't believe you," I say, my voice shaking. "How would you know?"

"Because I put him there." She sinks into the chair beside me. "I was no longer able to care for him. He has Alzheimer's."

Something about the certainty in her voice and the dark look of pity in her eyes starts a shiver of dread snaking its way up my spine. I stare at her. "Who are you?" I stutter. "Are you his nurse?"

"No, Lily." She shakes her head. "My name is Rita... Rita Lavender. I'm his wife."

Chapter Fifteen

I T FEELS AS IF I'M trapped in a nightmare, yet how can I be asleep? Dreams do not make your stomach churn or your thoughts crumble. Dreams do not cause you to doubt everything you've believed all your life. Dreams are good things—and Rita's tale is anything but good. Discovering that she has been married to my father for the past thirty-five years has plunged me into my own personal nightmare.

"I'm sorry to be the one to tell you. I assumed you knew." She squeezes my hand. Sometime during the telling, she took my hand in her own. Despite everything she's said, I can't bring myself to pull away. Her touch is warm and alive, while I feel chilled to the bone, like I've just seen a ghost.

The spirit of my father, risen from the dead.

"It can't be true," I say, pushing against every instinct rising from deep within that insists Rita is telling the truth. "I would have known. My mother would have told me." I close my eyes, thinking back to the trip I made to England and my visit to the graveyard. I was there. I saw his tombstone. *Lawrence Lavender. Rest in peace.* "Why should I believe you?"

"I have no idea why Elizabeth chose not to tell you," she softly replies. "She was always very good at twisting the truth and making things the way she wanted them. When it didn't work out, if she didn't like it, she simply ignored it... or walked away."

Mimi had walked away from England. Or rather, she flew away and fled to Las Vegas. But what if she didn't? What if she walked away from Detroit, instead? I think about my childhood, how Mimi always turned a deaf ear to the times I asked about my father. I struggle to grasp the truth behind what Rita is saying. "How do you know my mother?"

"Our husbands worked together. David was a foreman on the assembly line at the Ford plant in River Rouge. Larry and Elizabeth were newlyweds. The four of us became good friends after Larry started working at the plant."

"Larry?" I whisper.

"Everyone always called him Larry... including your mother." Rita stares at me a long moment. "I still can't get over how much you look like him. The resemblance is amazing. The same thick, brown hair and long, straight nose. The way your mouth turns up in a little twist when you smile. And your eyes. There's a kindness in them, just like your father's." A wistful smile lights her face. "You're a beautiful woman, Lily. But then, I would expect no less from Larry's only daughter. He always was one of the most handsome men I'd ever met. He still is."

"How... how is he?" Somehow I manage to choke out the words over the sudden lump in my throat.

Her face softens into sadness. "Physically he's fine,

but his mind is gone. The Alzheimer's came on fast. After six months, I could no longer care for him at home."

Home. The two of them had shared a home and a life together for thirty-five years. "How... how did all this happen?"

She pauses a moment. "What has Elizabeth told you?"

"Nothing." I might as well admit the truth. What have I got to lose? Nothing else makes sense. Who do I believe? Mimi or Rita?

"Larry was years older than Elizabeth. He'd been around the world while serving in the military. Once he returned home, the two of them were married. Elizabeth was only eighteen, a newlywed just out of high school, when David and I first met her. She seemed happy enough at first, but things changed as the months passed. She grew quieter; not at all the vivacious young girl Larry had introduced us to. He never said a word about their marriage, but it was obvious something was wrong. Once, when the four of us went out for dinner, I came upon her crying in the ladies' room. She broke down and confessed how unhappy she was, that she'd thought life with Larry would be different and exciting, filled with travel and romance. Instead, she'd found herself married to a man who worked a factory job, who was content to put in his forty hours, then come home to her. She felt her life was over before it had begun. I tried to console her. She was so young. I thought all she needed was time, but obviously, I was wrong. She needed something much more than that. One night Larry showed up at our house. He was a wreck. He sat on our couch and broke down and cried. Elizabeth had disappeared."

My heart thuds to a stop. "What do you mean, *disappeared*?"

"Just that," Rita says. "When he got home from work, he found she was gone. She had packed her bags and left, with no forwarding address. Larry was nearly out of his mind. He couldn't understand why she was gone and what he had done to make her so upset. Two months later, he was served with divorce papers. Elizabeth had gone to Reno, established residency, and filed for divorce. There were no children and the divorce was final." She shakes her head. "The poor man. It nearly destroyed him."

"No children," I repeat dully. If Larry really is my father, then Mimi must have left Detroit shortly after she found out she was pregnant. She never told him. He never knew.

I never knew.

"I have pictures," she says. "Would you like to see them?"

I freeze. What if Rita's story is true? It would be the first time I've ever seen a photo of my father. Mimi had nothing to show me. She left everything behind when she left England.

Or left wherever.

Rita hunts through her purse and pulls out a fat wallet filled with money, credit cards, and a plastic sheath of photos. She flips through them and extracts three pictures, handing one to me. "This is a photo of Larry taken at work a few months after we met him."

I pinch the faded photo between my fingers and devour every detail. A young man lounges against the side of a brick building as he stares out across the years. Long and lanky, he's dressed in work clothes. A cigarette is pinched between two fingers and the other hand shades his eyes as he squints into the camera. His face is partially hidden.

Rita hands me another photo, this one of a tall man in a dark suit and a woman in a knee-length dress, wearing a corsage. His arm is around her waist. Both of them are smiling for the camera. "That was taken on our wedding day."

I study the black-and-white photo. There's no mistaking Rita as the woman and the man as the same fellow from the first shot. In this picture, his face is lit and his smile beams at me through time and space. While I don't see the family resemblance Rita mentioned, something about him does look vaguely familiar. I study the photo harder and finally realize what caught my attention is the thoughtful expression on his face. It's the same expression I often see on Tori's face.

She hands me a third photo, this one of a large happy group gathered around a fireplace. I stare at Rita and Larry, three younger couples, and small children of assorted ages sitting cross-legged in front of them. "This is our family."

I trace my finger over his face. He's much older in this shot, thin and haggard. His hair is white and a vacant smile lines his face. "When was this taken?"

"Two years ago. It was at Christmas, shortly before Larry got sick," she says. "I wish you could have known him the way he was then. He would have been thrilled to know he had a daughter."

I lift my head and glance at her. "He never knew about me?"

Rita shakes her head. "Larry lost all contact with

Elizabeth after he received the divorce papers. We never knew what happened to her. And we never knew about you."

I scan the faces of the younger couples in the photo, smiling for the camera. Do I have brothers and sisters? Nieces and nephews? "What about them?" I whisper.

"That's David Jr. and his wife." Rita points to one of the couples. "They live in Henderson, about eighteen miles from here. The two girls are our daughters, Kathy and Mary Lee, and their husbands and children. We had seven grandchildren when this picture was taken, but David's wife, Celia, just had a baby, so that makes eight. Celia had a C-section and I flew out to Las Vegas to help her out. Their little girl is such a sweet thing." She stares at me thoughtfully. "Guess what they named her?"

"I...I don't know."

"Lily," she says quietly. "They named her Lily, after Larry's mother. I thought that was very generous of Celia and David. But then, Larry's always treated my children as if they were his own."

My heart skips a beat. "You mean, they're not?"

"No, David and his sisters are my children. David Jr. was ten, and Mary Lee—she's our youngest—was just a baby when their father died. She was five years old when Larry and I married. She barely remembers the wedding, of course, but that's understandable. It was a very small ceremony. Just family and a few close friends. Larry was a wonderful father."

She quiets for a moment. "I wish you could have known him. Larry is a good man. We were blessed to have so many years together. I miss him."

I stare numbly at the photos in my hand. Rita's

revelations have destroyed much of the truth my life is centered around, and I don't want to believe her. Yet how can I not? The man I always assumed to be my father— Lawrence Lavender, of British nobility—is actually an American commoner named Larry. I think about the Royal Wedding Chapel and how Mimi built an elegant bridal business around my father's royal lineage.

Who do I believe? Mimi or Rita? Was it Lawrence and Lillian Lavender of England, or Lawrence and Lillian Lavender of Detroit? The odds must be a million to one. It's too much of a coincidence. In a world of seven billion people, naturally some people will share the same names. Yet how could Mimi have known? How could it be true? I stare harder at the images, and the man's face blurs into Tori's own. How can it not be true?

Rita pulls out a pen and scribbles something on the back of one of the photos, then hands it to me. "Here's my telephone number. If you ever decide you'd like to meet him, you're always welcome. I think he would like that, even though he wouldn't know you. Then again, perhaps if he saw your face..." Her voice lifts with hope. "It might stir something in his memory. Most days, he's lost in a shadowy world of his own. But sometimes something brings him back to us for a little while. Those are the sweet days, his good days. Maybe seeing you would help him." She eyes me quietly. "Maybe it would help you."

The air-conditioner hums in the background as we sit there together a long moment, staring at the photos. Neither of us says a word. Finally Rita stands.

"I should be going." She smoothes the wrinkles from her dress. "David and Celia will be wondering where I am." She squares her shoulders. "It was good meeting you, Lily. I know this must have been hard for you, but I hope you understand why I felt I had to come. I hope I haven't caused you too much pain."

Any doubts I have about whether Rita's story is true are erased by the grief I hear in her voice. She didn't come seeking reparation, redemption, or revenge against Mimi. She came because she wanted to meet me—a woman she believes to be her husband's only living child. She came in the slim hope of resurrecting the man she loves by knowing he lives on through me.

She starts for the door and I rise, the photos in my hand a burning reminder of everything Mimi withheld from me, of everything that might still be possible.

"Rita?"

She pauses and turns to face me.

"Thank you," I say. Simple words, but for now they are all I can manage. "Thank you for coming."

But what I really mean is thank you for the gift of my father.

Chapter Sixteen

HOW COULD SHE HAVE DONE it? My whole life has been built around a lie. How could Mimi have allowed me to grow up grieving for a father who never existed? Any doubts I had about what Rita told me are gone. There is no mistaking the face in the photos, her husband's eerie resemblance to Tori. I clutch the pictures tighter as I slam out of the chapel's front door and storm across the courtyard to Mimi's villa.

The Queen Mum has some explaining to do.

Francesca putters in the kitchen as I barge through the door. "There you are. I thought maybe you'd forgotten about the party." She halts, eyes me carefully. "Lily, are you all right? You look a little funny."

No wonder. After digesting Rita's revelations, my stomach is churning.

"You've been pushing yourself too hard. I hope you're not getting sick. Why don't I make you a nice cup of tea?" She opens a cabinet and reaches for a cup.

"I don't want any tea."

"Maybe some fruit?" She tilts her head, a pinched look

between her eyebrows. "Bananas are supposed to help with digestion."

"I'm not hungry." The only thing I'm hungry for are answers to the questions swirling through my mind. "Where's Mimi?"

"In her room." Francesca stares at me. "Is something wrong?"

"You could say that." I take another glance at the photos in my hand. Is Francesca in on the secret, too? It wouldn't surprise me. She and Mimi share everything. "I just had a very interesting conversation with a woman from Detroit," I say. "She came to visit me at the chapel. Maybe you've heard of her. She said her name was Rita... Rita Lavender."

Francesca's face reddens like she just gulped a cup of scalding hot tea.

Traitor.

"So it's true." I hear my voice shaking. I can barely contain my fury. "Everything Rita told me is true. How could you have kept that a secret?" I have never felt so betrayed in my life. I whirl and start for the door.

"Lily, wait." She hurries after me as I charge down the hallway toward Mimi's bedroom. "Please, stop."

I whirl and face her. "I think I deserve some answers."

What I deserve is the truth.

Francesca grabs my arm. "Please don't do this," she begs. "You have every right to feel the way you do, but... but Lily, you can't hurt her like this."

"What about me? What about all the lies she told me? What about how I feel?" I shake one of the photos of my father in her face. "Have you seen this? Do you know this man?"

Francesca scans the picture. "I never met him," she says after a moment.

"But you know who he is, don't you?" I demand.

She nods, her face ashen. "Yes."

I drag in a deep breath. The hurt is almost too much to bear. All my life I trusted Francesca. I trusted her with my hopes, my fears, my secrets. But this—the biggest secret of all—the one that would have made all the difference in the world, she chose to keep from me.

Someone should have told me. Francesca should have told me. Then again, why is this such a surprise? She and Mimi have always been close confidants. But this? This is beyond belief, beyond forgiveness. Together, they concealed the truth.

"It's my life," I say. "I deserved to know."

"I'm sorry, Lily. Mimi always said you were better off not knowing."

"Not knowing about my own father?" I feel the rage burning through me, boiling in my brain. All those years, all that wasted time. Time I could have known him. Time I could have spent with him. And now it's too late. He is ravaged by a horrible disease that has stripped him of his mind.

"What were you thinking? How could the two of you have done this? It's so unfair."

Her shoulders sag. "You're absolutely right. What we did was horrible. A child should never be kept from her father. You have no idea how many years I've lived with the guilt. I wouldn't blame you if you never forgive me. I deserve it."

There is no place to put my fury. She is an old woman, but this isn't her fault. Francesca kept the secret, but it wasn't hers to give away.

Someone else should have told me.

I fling open Mimi's bedroom door and barge into the room with Francesca fast on my heels. Mimi, in a brilliant, royal-blue suit that matches her eyes, sits at her dressing table, struggling to pull a comb through her hair. Her eyes narrow as she spots my reflection in the mirror.

I march to her side and toss Rita's photos on the dressing table. They scatter amid perfume bottles, brushes, and makeup.

"Recognize anyone?" I demand.

Mimi stares at the photos a long moment. Finally she reaches for the aged, black-and-white shot of Rita's husband in front of the auto plant. She traces a trembling finger across his face.

"It's him, isn't it?" I demand. "That man is my father."

She lifts her gaze to meet my reflection in the mirror. I wait, arms crossed against my chest, and we lock eyes for a long moment. Finally she nods. "Yes."

Hearing her confirm what I already suspected is like a fresh stab wound to my heart.

Francesca brushes past me and wraps her arms around Mimi's shoulders. "I think it's time Lily heard the truth. The whole truth," she urges softly. "She has a right to know."

The truth about what? What could be worse than knowing that they've kept my father from me all these years? The grief washes over me. Forty years wasted. Forty years of memories we could have made together.

Forty years too late.

"It was a different time back then," Francesca starts, but Mimi waves her away with an impatient hand.

"Tell her," she grunts. "Tell her... all."

For once I am in complete agreement with my mother. I stare at the two women who, for the past forty years, selfishly manipulated the facts surrounding my birth to suit Mimi's needs.

"Yes," I say. "I want to hear the truth. The *whole* truth," I add, remembering Francesca's words.

Francesca hesitates, glancing back and forth between the two of us. Mimi's face is grim. My spirit is unyielding. Finally, drawing in a ragged breath, she nods. "All right. I suppose you could say that it started with the murder."

Wait, what? For the first time since I charged into the room, my legs feel wobbly. "Murder? Rita told me that my father is still alive."

"No, not him. Oh, it's all so complicated." Francesca clucks her tongue and sinks down on Mimi's king-sized bed. "You have to understand. Mimi and I never meant to hurt you. You were so young when it happened, Lily. Then, as you got older, we decided it was better if you didn't know."

Mimi nods. "B...better."

"But this doesn't make sense." The blood drains from my face, and I sink down beside Francesca. "Who was murdered?"

Mimi and Francesca exchange glances.

"Tell me," I demand.

Francesca hesitates. "Big Mike," she finally says.

Mimi's second husband? My eyes widen. "I

don't understand."

"It was my fault," Francesca says. "Mimi was only trying to protect me."

"No," Mimi grunts. "*His* fault."

Francesca lifts her shoulders in a helpless shrug. "I doubt the police will believe that when they find out what I did."

Am I losing my mind? It feels like it, sitting here listening to the two of them babble on about a murder. I was two years old when Mimi married Big Mike, Husband Number Two. Mimi has always referred to the time they were married as *the terrible twos*. I always attributed it to my age and the terrible toddler Mimi says I was, plus the gruesome circumstances surrounding Big Mike's death that same year. I don't remember Big Mike at all. Mimi inherited the chapel following his death. She never talks about their brief marriage, except to say that the best thing that came out of the *terrible twos* was Francesca, who moved into the villa with Mimi and me behind the Royal Wedding Chapel.

"It all happened long ago," Francesca says. "I had just started working at the chapel. It wasn't the Royal Wedding Chapel back then. Big Mike called it the Cherished Love Chapel." Her face darkens in a red stain. "I hadn't been there long, but I already hated it. Big Mike wasn't exactly a nice man to work for."

"Ha!" Mimi grunts with a violent nod. "Horrible."

"Big Mike and Mimi hadn't been married very long. Just a few months?" She looks to Mimi for confirmation.

"Yes." Her hands curl in tight fists. "Met him at... casino." She shakes her head as frustration covers her face. It's obvious she wants to tell the story but she can't form the words, and Francesca isn't talking fast enough to suit her.

"Mimi was a cocktail waitress at one of the casinos on the Strip—I think it was the Flamingo—when the two of them met. He was immediately taken with her, and I can't say I was surprised. You should have seen your mother back then, Lily. She was so beautiful. Not that you aren't still," she hastily adds with a fast look at Mimi, who impatiently rolls her eyes and waves for her to continue.

"I'd had the job at the chapel less than a year when the two of them got married. I loved the chapel, but I hated Big Mike—especially when he'd been drinking. I can't tell you how happy I was when I found out he was marrying Mimi. I thought once they married, surely things would change, that he would change. At least, that's what I hoped would happen. They got married, and they brought you home. That was the first time I met you, Lily.

"You were just a little thing. You'd just started walking and you were into everything. Mimi used to bring you over to visit me at the chapel." Francesca's face brightens as she glances at Mimi. "Remember how Lily used to tear around the rooms, touching everything and crawling around on the altar risers? She was a regular little spitfire."

Mimi nods and a soft, crooked smile slowly covers her face. If I didn't know better, I might think she was experiencing a maternal moment.

"But you weren't there often. Big Mike didn't like having you around." Francesca's eyes narrow. "He said the chapel was no place for kids. That's all you were to him... a kid. He especially didn't want you underfoot when he'd been drinking. He used to scream and curse at Mimi when he'd catch her with you at the chapel. I suppose nowadays they would call it verbal abuse, but back then, we didn't know any different. We just thought he was a mean drunk."

Mimi's face hardens in a scowl. "Mean drunk."

"The chapel business wasn't doing well. Big Mike was drinking a lot. Often I'd find him in his office, passed out on the couch. Mimi began bringing you over more often, and the two of us would play with ideas on how to build the business and how to bring in more brides. But Big Mike didn't like hearing about any of that. He didn't want Mimi anywhere near the chapel. He said she belonged at home, in the villa."

"He was... a shithead," Mimi mutters.

I stare wordlessly at my mother. Always so particular about her choice of words, she's swearing like a sailor.

"You're right." Francesca agrees. "Big Mike *was* a shithead."

"Finish," Mimi urges.

A solemn look descends upon Francesca's face. "The night it happened, Big Mike was in a foul mood. He'd caught Mimi and you over at the chapel again. We were all together, the three of us, in the King Edward's Chapel— back then we called it Cupid's Love Bower. You were there, Lily, toddling around the room, playing in the pews. Mimi and I were going over some ideas we had when Big Mike got back from a meeting downtown and found us.

"He was drunk as a skunk." Her face darkens. "He yanked Mimi up by the arm and dragged her out of the chapel and out the door to the villa." Francesca shudders. "It was horrible. I could hear them all the way across the courtyard. He was screaming at Mimi for having disobeyed him, and she was yelling at him to let her go. I had to do something. I scooped you up in my arms and rushed out of the chapel. When I got to the villa, I found Big Mike with Mimi in his office. He had her pinned against the desk, threatening her. I screamed at him to let her go. He turned and saw me standing there with you in my arms. 'Get that goddamned kid out of my sight or I'll kill her, too,' he swore. Then he dropped his hold on Mimi and started for you and me."

Her face blanches. "I pushed you out of my arms and out the door. Then I slammed it behind me so he couldn't get at you. He grabbed me and shook me so hard I thought my neck would snap. I was so scared. He was like a madman. His face was nearly purple, and I could see the veins bulging in his neck. I couldn't get away from him. I remember thinking that he was going to choke me and I would end up dead. Then suddenly, Mimi rushed him from behind. She beat him with her fists and screamed at him to leave me alone. Finally he let go of me and grabbed Mimi and dragged her back across the room. He threw her against the desk, and she fell to the floor on her hands and knees. He stood there, laughing. He called her horrible names."

"Bitches," Mimi grunts, her face a contorted mask of fury. "He... called us two bitches."

Francesca's head bobs in agreement. "He bent over Mimi with his fists in her hair, and he slammed her head into the floor. Then he started kicking her. I knew if I didn't do something, he'd end up killing her. I was so scared. Big Mike was so big, and he was in a rage... but I knew I didn't have a choice. I could hear you screaming on the other side of the door, crying and pounding on it.

"I couldn't let him hurt either of you. He had his back to me and was just about to kick Mimi again when I rushed him. He must have heard me coming because he turned and lunged for me. I don't know how I managed to duck away, but somehow I did. Knowing he had missed made him even madder. He started for me again with the meanest look I've ever seen in anyone's eyes. That's when I knew for certain he meant to kill me—kill us all—and that's when I saw my chance.

"I threw myself against him as hard as I could and caught him off guard. He staggered backward and tried to catch his balance, but he was too big and too drunk. He went down hard and fast and as he fell, he cracked his skull on a corner of the desk." She grimaces. "I'll never forget the sound of his head hitting that desk."

I stare at her in horror as the implication of what happened that night so long ago hits me full force. "My God, Francesca. Was he dead?"

"We didn't know," she says slowly. "At first we thought he might be. There was lots of blood pooling around his head and he wasn't moving. I couldn't move, either. I stood there, staring at him on the floor. It felt like something out of a dream, like breathing underwater. Mimi crawled over and put her ear against his chest. She thought he was still breathing, but she wasn't sure. He'd slammed her around so much, her ear was bleeding and she was in a lot of pain. She wanted me to listen and see if I could hear a heartbeat, but I couldn't move. Just seeing him there on the floor, and all that blood—I remember I was shaking. I must have been in shock. I couldn't force myself to go near him."

"What did you do then?" My voice is barely a whisper. "Did you call the police?"

Francesca shakes her head. "I'm afraid not, honey."

"So what did you do? Didn't you try and help him? If he was still alive, didn't you get him medical attention?"

She hesitates and throws Mimi a quick glance.

"You must have done *something*," I press.

Her head bobs up and down. "I helped Mimi get back on her feet."

"And..." I prompt.

She bites her lip and finally meets my eyes. "And then we got out of that room and locked the door behind us."

"Deep breaths, Lily. That's right, just keep taking deep breaths." Francesca's voice floats next to me as I sit on Mimi's bed, head between my knees. "Oh, Mimi, I was afraid this would happen. Maybe we shouldn't have told her."

I shake my head and open my eyes, grateful to see that the room has stopped spinning. Slowly I bring myself upright. "No, I'm glad you did."

Francesca pats her pocket for a tissue. "I'm so sorry. We always swore we wouldn't tell you. How I wish none of this had happened. But don't you see, I had to do it. I couldn't let him hurt Mimi or you. You were our baby, and so precious to us. No matter what, we had to protect you. That night, after it happened, we locked ourselves in this very bedroom with you until it was finally dawn. Then I stayed here with you while Mimi went back to Big Mike's office. She checked on him and when she came back, she told me..." Francesca blanches.

"Dead drunk," Mimi grunts and nods. "...and dead."

I shudder, imagining how she would have unlocked the office door, discovered Big Mike's body on the floor exactly where they had left it, bent over to check for a pulse. How did Mimi find the nerve? I never could have done that.

"We called the police once we knew for sure he was dead," Francesca says. "I wanted to turn myself in, but Mimi refused to allow me to do it. She said I had to keep quiet about what had happened, that if I told them the truth, the police would arrest me. I'd be arrested for Big Mike's murder and end up in prison."

"Francesca, don't be silly. Clearly it was self-defense," I argue, though I have no idea if that's the case. I am not a lawyer. And while it's true she'd acted to save us all, *if*—and this is a big *if*—Big Mike was still alive when they locked him in the office, then they deliberately left him without medical attention in the hope that he would die. He could already have been dead... but what if he wasn't? That definitely must qualify for some type of criminal liability. I shudder just thinking of Big Mike that night, alone in his office on the floor, the life slowly draining out of him. If Francesca and Mimi had called the authorities sooner, someone might have been able to save him.

Save him so he could do what? Eventually recover and return home, only to make their lives more miserable? Make them suffer more mistreatment and abuse?

"The police never questioned our story," Francesca continues. "We said we didn't know when Big Mike had come home. We told them we were all asleep and that when we woke up in the morning, we found him in his office, dead. They had no reason not to believe us. An autopsy revealed his blood-alcohol level to be twice the legal limit. A few weeks later, they pronounced his death to be accidental due to a self-inflicted blow to the head. I suppose it was an easy assumption to make. The official ruling was that he must have come home late that night, extremely drunk, gone into his office, and at some point staggered and fell against his desk. That's when he hit his head, causing the fatal blow." She folds her hands in her lap. "Case closed."

I stare back and forth between Francesca and Mimi. Two cohorts, complicit in crime. All these years, they kept the facts surrounding his death a secret. I never had a clue. Suddenly I realize why the large room down the hall off the kitchen was always empty when I was growing up. The room that Mimi refused to work in. The room I've turned into my own personal office, where my laptop and briefcase now rest. The room I've chosen as my office space was the scene of Big Mike's murder.

"Please don't hate us, honey," Francesca pleads. "We never meant to hurt him."

It takes some minutes before I can finally speak.

"I realize that." My voice sounds tinny and hollow, like someone else is talking. The past few hours have morphed into a nightmare, and I'm not sure how many more truths my head and heart can handle. First, I discover they lied to me about my father. Now I find out the two of them are involved in a murder.

All these years. All these secrets. All these lies. But we can't keep the secret any longer.

"You can't leave it like this."

"What do you mean?" Francesca's eyes widen with fear. "You won't tell anyone, will you, Lily?"

"I don't know." I close my eyes, try to muddle through my thoughts. What would be the best thing? The right thing? The ethical thing? "Maybe we should tell Ed. He deals with criminal matters every day."

"No." Mimi's head swings violently back and forth like a pendulum on a clock that's been wound too tight and has suddenly gone off-balance. "No."

"But we're talking about murder," I remind her. The more I think about it, the more I'm convinced telling Ed is the right thing to do. "He'll know how to handle this."

"What if they decide to prosecute me?" Francesca whispers. Her eyes are growing wider and more panicked by the second. "There's no statute of limitations on murder. I don't want to go to jail."

Dear Francesca. She looks so scared. I'm scared, too. There's no doubt in my mind that a crime was committed. Was it self-defense when Francesca pushed him? Absolutely a valid argument. But if they admit to the police that they didn't help Big Mike, that he might have been alive when they locked the door behind them, most likely they'll both be found complicit in his death. Once the police hear the story, they'll have no choice but to arrest Francesca, and Mimi, too. I close my eyes and try to block out the image of the two of them huddled together in a prison cell.

"Ed will know—"

"No Ed!" A violent bang, a loud crash, and my eyes snap open. Mimi's makeup, perfume bottles, and anything else that was on her dressing table now litters the floor.

She pounds her fist against the empty table, glaring at me. "No! No! No!"

I swallow down the rage churning through my stomach. Why is she so insistent about not asking him for help? No wonder the two of them ended up divorced. Both of them are just as stubborn as the other. Neither gives an inch. But if she went to Ed, if she let down her defenses, I know he would help her. Ed would drop everything for her in a heartbeat. He might not love her anymore, but he still cares for Mimi. I saw the way he looked at her in the hospital that first night when he thought no one was looking. There's still something between them. There always has been and there always will be.

"Who else knows about this?"

Francesca and Mimi exchange glances, then Mimi quickly shakes her head. But something in her eyes gives the secret away. They've told someone else. I'm certain of it.

"Who?" I demand. "Who is it?"

"No one, honey." Francesca fingers her ring, twists it round and round on her finger. "You're the only one."

I whirl and face Mimi. "You told Jack, didn't you?"

"Of course she didn't." Francesca's hand trembles as she clutches my arm. "Mimi would have told me. She would have told you."

But the triumphant, twisted smile on Mimi's face tells a different story. Poor Francesca. She thinks she knows my mother, but she doesn't have a clue about the kind of woman she's been dealing with all these years. Mimi's blue eyes glisten, hard and cold as ice. I swallow over the fury in the back of my throat. Betrayed again, by the woman who gave birth to me—*and* the man responsible for my daughter's birth.

"How much does Jack know?" I ask.

Mimi lifts one shoulder and shrugs.

I'd like nothing better than to wrap my fingers around her neck and choke the truth out of her. "How much?" I demand.

She turns her head away.

"The money came from Jack," I suddenly guess. "He's the one who's been helping you keep the chapel open."

"Oh, dear." Francesca worriedly glances back and forth between the two of us.

"You told him everything, didn't you?" I demand. "You told him about the murder, about Big Mike..."

Francesca gasps.

"Jack knows everything, including how you made up the whole story about your connection to the British royal family." My heart is beating so fast I'm afraid it will fly right out of my chest. "He knows the truth about my father, too... doesn't he? Jack knows he's still alive."

Mimi's silence says it all. Jack knows everything. All this time, all these years, and he never told me. He knew about the chapel; he knew about Big Mike. He knew about my father. I could forgive him some things, but this betrayal, not telling me my father is still alive, is beyond forgiveness. I feel myself grow cold, a distant throbbing in my temple pounding out the cacophony. *Never. Never. Never.* I will never forgive him. *Never.*

I rise from the bed and start for the door.

"Wait, Lily, don't go," Francesca pleads.

My hand is on the doorknob as I turn to face them. Two

old women, hiding secrets all these years. What do they want from me? Forgiveness? Redemption? If they think I'm going to cover things up like they've been doing, hiding the past and all its dark, dirty secrets, they have another think coming. Big Mike's murder is not my secret to divulge, but the other one is. Especially since I have a personal stake in the matter.

My father is still alive, and I intend to see him. But not yet. There's a party tonight, and I've got some unfinished business to attend to.

The birthday boy had better watch out. I bought a killer dress a few weeks ago, and the way I feel right now, I'm in the mood for it.

I just might murder Jack.

Chapter Seventeen

C AESAR'S PALACE IS RENOWNED FOR world-class service, lavish décor, and luxurious events, so it comes as no surprise that Ed's fiftieth birthday bash for Jack is over-the-top. When Francesca, Mimi, and I finally arrive, we're escorted by Roman guards to one of Caesar's premiere ballrooms, which is easily filled with what appears to be at least two hundred guests. I spot plenty of familiar faces, the movers and shakers of the Las Vegas business community—even the mayor is in attendance. People greet us as we slowly wind our way between tables gowned in virgin white and decadent gold. Champagne bottles grace every table. Front and center, a jazz combo—Jack's favorite music—has people swaying on the dance floor. Ed must have dropped a bundle on this party.

"You finally made it." He bustles up to meet us as we're halfway into the room and greets each of us—including Mimi—with hugs and kisses. Normally Ed's a bourbon man. For him to be in these kind of spirits—plus wearing a tux—I'll wager he's been swigging champagne. "You missed the big entrance. Boy, was Jack surprised."

"Speaking of Jack, where is the birthday boy?" I lift my voice over the music as a waiter approaches, balancing a tray filled with flutes of champagne. I'm not much of a drinker, but I don't even think twice at seizing the moment and some of the bubbly.

"He's around somewhere," Ed says with a shrug. "You know Jack, always working the crowd. I sure am glad to see you all. You doing okay, sweetheart?" He tucks his hand under Mimi's elbow. She grunts a little and shuffles her walker away from him, but Ed merely laughs and holds on tighter. "Come on, I'll show you where you're sitting. We put you at the head table with us."

Head table? I down my champagne in one long swallow. I hadn't counted on being anywhere near Jack. God help him if we're seated next to each other. Right now, I don't trust myself anywhere near that man... especially if I'm within reach of a nice sharp steak knife.

The center of the room boasts an elegant table with a gleaming gold candelabra surrounded by a fragrant swirl of orchids and white roses. Hand-engraved place cards grace each table setting. A table for six. I skirt the table and sure enough find my name next to Jack's. I switch the cards around as Ed and Francesca help Mimi into her chair. No one notices as I place the birthday boy between his daughter and his father. *Boy, girl, boy, girl, girl, girl.* Works for me.

"You finally made it." Tori rushes over to us as I snatch another glass of champagne from a passing waiter and sink into my own chair. "Isn't the party fantastic? Isn't the room beautiful?"

Speechless, I take in the sight of my seventeen-year-old daughter, complete with a glass of champagne in hand. With her hair up, wearing ridiculously high heels and a dangerously short ice-blue dress that molds her body, Tori could easily be mistaken for someone in her early twenties. Obviously, the young man hovering close behind her has already made that mistake.

Tori pulls him forward. "This is Steve."

I force a tight smile for the handsome young man who looks much too old to be escorting my daughter.

"It's a pleasure to meet you, Mrs. Alexander," he says in a smooth voice. "Your husband is a great guy."

Oh good God, he thinks I'm married to Jack. I grab my champagne and inhale half the glass.

Tori doesn't bother to correct him about the family faux pas. "Steve just graduated from UNLV. He's been telling me all about the university." She beams at him over the rim of her glass as she sips more champagne. "It sounds absolutely wonderful."

"You'll love it," he assures her.

She nods and throws me a bright smile. "I've decided that's where I'm going to college."

Over my dead body.

I throw Steve a bright smile of my own. "Has Tori happened to mention that she's still in high school? And that she's only seventeen?" I reach over and remove the champagne flute from her hand, placing it on the table. "Sorry, my dear, but you still have a few years to go before you're legal."

"Mother!" Tori's face reddens. She makes a grab for her glass. "I can't believe you did that."

"Believe it," I say, smiling sweetly and with a firm

hold on the stemware so she can't retrieve it. Don't they have anyone checking IDs at the bar?

"Uh, nice meeting you, ma'am." Steve backs up several steps and crooks a finger at Tori over his own glass. "Catch you later."

Tori folds her arms across her chest and eyes me with a malevolent look that tells me I just shot to the top of her list of ten-most-hated-females in the world. "I cannot believe you embarrassed me like that."

"And I can't believe you are drinking champagne."

"Why shouldn't I?" Her eyes blaze electric blue, just like Mimi's. "You always let me drink wine at home when we're having a party."

"That's different and you know it," I say, wishing I'd never allowed her to drink in the first place. "First of all, we are not at home. This is a public place. If anyone found out, Caesar's could lose their license."

"That's ridiculous. Nobody's watching, and nobody cares." She shoots me a smoldering pout that only teenage girls can manage to pull off. "Besides," she adds, "Dad said I could."

I roll my eyes. Why am I not surprised? Jack has never been able to say *no* to Tori. Anything to keep his baby happy.

"Yes, well, your dad doesn't always think straight. I suppose he picked out that dress for you, too."

"There is nothing the matter with my dress. I happen to like it," Tori says hotly. "And for your information, Dad didn't buy it. Grandpa Ed did. He gave me some money and told me to get myself something pretty for the party tonight."

Panic builds in Ed's eyes as I turn to confront him.

"Now, wait just a minute, Lily, before you go getting all mad at me. I'll admit I gave her the money, but I didn't help her pick it out." He clears his throat and eyeballs Tori. "And just for the record, sweetheart: I think your mom is right. The dress is a little short."

"Why is everyone ganging up on me?" Tori grumbles. "None of you know anything about fashion or having fun."

"Don't worry, she'll grow out of it," Francesca predicts as Tori stomps off in the opposite direction.

"Actually, I'm more afraid that she'll pop out of it," I say, watching as she winds her way through the crowd, ending up near the jazz combo—and the birthday boy himself. Jack leans in close, listening carefully as Tori's mouth runs nonstop. She talks with her hands, gesturing wildly in my direction. I finish off the rest of my champagne, imagining the torrent of complaints against me she's lodging with her dad. She ends with a pretty pout and searches his face for approval, but Jack merely laughs and brushes her cheek with a kiss. Then, taking her in his arms, he whirls her onto the dance floor.

The crowd parts and suddenly the two of them—father and daughter—are alone in the spotlight as the combo starts up in a familiar soft jazz song. Jack is an excellent dancer, and even in her high heels, Tori never loses the beat as he swings her around the room and they sway to the music. By the time the song finishes, Jack's face is a ruddy red and the pins are tumbling from Tori's hair. She throws back her head with a throaty laugh as the crowd bursts out in spontaneous applause.

"They look good together, don't they?" Ed pops an

appetizer in his mouth, folds his arms across his chest, and watches them with a satisfied smile that covers his entire face.

"Mmm." I finger my empty glass. The champagne has blurred my thinking, and my mind nibbles around the edges of Steve's recent comment. How many others in this room have mistaken me for Jack's wife? If someone didn't know us, it would make perfect sense. I'm seated at the head table with his father, and Jack is on the dance floor with our daughter. The two of them laugh and hug as the music winds down, then clap and begin dancing again as the band breaks out in a jazzed up version of *Happy Birthday*.

What if things had turned out differently? What if the man I hero-worshipped all those years had found me attractive when I finally grew up? *What if...?*

I slap my hand against my forehead. Am I insane? How could I have ever looked up to this man? After what I discovered today, Jack Alexander isn't the hero. He could never be the hero. He is now my sworn enemy.

And the enemy has just led our daughter back to the table.

"Happy birthday." Somehow I manage the words as Jack sinks into the vacant seat beside me. He doesn't intend to sit there during dinner, does he? I switched those name cards for a reason.

"Thanks," he says as a young man approaches and claims Tori for a dance. Together we watch him lead our daughter back to the dance floor where they launch into a fast version of a jazz classic.

"Where do kids find the energy?" Jack rakes a hand

through black hair streaked with the perfect amount of gray. If I didn't know better, I might guess he had it professionally done. Nothing that happens in this town surprises me. But even Jack isn't that vain. "After dancing like that, I feel every one of my fifty years."

I eye him as he swigs down some champagne. "Yes, well, perhaps you should do it more often."

He eyes me with one of those grins that melts me right down to the tip of my toes. "To tell you the truth, I would spend more time dancing, if I had the right partner." His gaze moves slowly down my body. "By the way, I like the dress. Very nice."

"Thanks." I slouch in my chair, regretting my fashion decision. Too short. Too revealing. The last thing I want is a compliment from Jack. Or him anywhere near me.

He leans in close, near enough that I'm surrounded by a smoky mix of the signature cologne he's worn since college, the fresh scent of soap, and the musky fragrance that is all male and pure Jack. I swallow hard, force myself to concentrate. I don't care if it is his birthday. I don't care if we are at Caesar's. He is not going to get the best of me. Not this time. Never again.

"What's wrong, Lily? Come on, it's a party."

"I'm not exactly in a party mood." I pull away from the touch of his arm draped against the back of my chair.

"Know what your problem is? You need to learn how to relax. Come on, dance with me."

"I don't want—" But before I know it, he has me on my feet and in his arms. He sweeps me onto the nearly empty dance floor as the band breaks into a jazz classic. The slow, slumbering number with a saxophone wailing a deep, throaty bass throws a shiver down my spine... or perhaps it's the feel of Jack's arms around me as he pulls me close.

"Now, isn't that better?" he whispers in my ear. "We have the whole dance floor to ourselves. Nice and private."

I peek over his shoulder as the room spins by. "Not exactly private. Everyone is watching."

"Good. Let them." His breath is warm against my neck. "Have I told you how beautiful you look tonight?"

I pull back slightly and eye him. "How much have you had to drink?"

"Not near enough." He chuckles softly. "Dear sweet Lily, ever the cynic. What can I do to melt that heart of yours?"

It's melting faster than he realizes. What is the matter with me? This isn't what I want. He isn't what I want. I struggle in his arms. "We're done here, Jack. Let me go."

"Come on, indulge me. It's my birthday." He pulls a glass from a passing waiter and offers it to me. "Have some more champagne."

"I don't want any champagne. I've had enough champagne." I stagger slightly, halting in the middle of the dance floor. "The only problem I have is *you*."

"Me?" He leans back on his heels and blinks. "What did I do?"

"Plenty." Silently I curse those three glasses of champagne. I know better than to drink on an empty stomach. Still, I'm sober enough to handle Jack. "You and I are going to have a little chat."

"What about dinner?" he protests as a waiter passes us with plated salads.

"This will only take five minutes. They can start without us."

Plus, I doubt we'll be missed. Last I noticed, Tori was AWOL, too. I snatch Jack's hand and pull him through the crowd and out the door into a wide, carpeted hallway.

"What's this all about?" he asks.

"You." I push him up against the wall, stabbing him in the chest with a finger. "You. Mister. Are. In. Deep. Trouble." I poke him hard, emphasizing each word. "And I don't care if it is your birthday."

He grabs my finger and brings it to his lips, brushing it with a kiss. "Have I ever told you how sexy you look when you're mad?"

"Cut the crap, Jack," I hiss. "I want the truth."

"Truth about what?" His eyes cloud as his smile fades. "What are you talking about?"

"Don't try to deny it. I know you're the one who's been giving her money." If I weren't a lady, I'd spit in his face.

He frowns. "Well, I'll admit that Tori hit me up for some extra cash, but you know I'd give her—"

"Forget Tori," I say, shrugging off his protest. "You know exactly what I'm talking about. Those secret cash deposits you've been funneling to Mimi."

His eyes narrow. "I don't know if I'd call them *secret*. It was business, Lily, nothing more. She needed money and I wrote her a check."

I scoff. "That's all you have to say for yourself? *I wrote her a check*?"

"Okay, maybe several checks," he admits. "What about it? They were merely loans. Business loans."

"And I suppose you're going to tell me that you had no

idea what she did with them."

He blinks. "It sounds like you're going to tell me."

I roll my eyes. "Sorry, I'm not buying. You'll have to do better than that."

He shoots me a dark look. "What the hell are you talking about?"

"You know exactly what I mean." I fold my arms against my chest. Inside it feels like someone turned off a switch, and I've shut down, cold and dead. The blast of frigid air from the ceiling air-conditioning doesn't help. "I can't believe I was so stupid. You actually had me starting to believe that you were one of the good guys."

"I already said I didn't —"

"Why didn't you tell me you gave her the money?" I demand. "You should have told me weeks ago, but you never did. Why keep it a secret?"

"Do you think I'm nuts? You've made it perfectly clear how you feel about the chapel. If I'd told you I'd given Mimi money to keep the place going, you never would have talked to me again."

"You've got that right," I mutter. "So, you admit you've been bailing her out financially. What about the rest of it?"

"The rest of what?" He eyes me warily. "What are you talking about?"

"Don't act so innocent. You know perfectly well that she never put the checks in the chapel account. She ran them through her personal checking account. She deposited cash into the business, and she never reported it to the IRS."

His eyes narrow and he grabs my arm. "What are you saying?"

I shrug from his grasp. "Mimi is in trouble. Big trouble. The IRS is auditing the chapel, and Mimi never reported the money you loaned her."

"Christ Almighty." He rakes a hand through his hair. "The IRS? What in God's name was she thinking?"

"That's the problem. She wasn't thinking." I think of the IRS agent's phone call, the ultimatum in his voice.

Jack jams his hands in his pockets and stares at me. "How bad is it?"

"Bad." I dance around the edges of exactly how bad. I don't know for sure, but we'll discover it soon enough.

"Goddammit. I should have paid more attention to what she was doing." Jack hangs his head and stares at the plush carpet beneath our feet. Far in the distance, I hear the noisy *ding-ding-ding*! of slot machines. The doors to another ballroom open and guests empty out, strolling past us with curious glances.

"Don't try and pretend you didn't know," I say.

"Of course I didn't," he says sharply. "Do you think if I had I would have stood by and let her do something as stupid as that?"

"We need to find someplace more private." I grab his arm and pull him down the hall toward the closest door. The one marked *Ladies*.

He slides back on his heels and balks. "Are you crazy? I can't go in—"

"I'm not crazy, and yes, you can." I haul him through the door before he can sputter another word. The ladies' room is one of those elegant lounges found in high-class establishments with a small, separate salon from the actual do-your-business area. The lounge is small and airy, with walls done up in beautiful striped wallpaper of creamy silk and elegant gold, a plush settee near the door, and two dainty chairs in front of a large mirror to help with makeup repairs.

Jack gawks as his head swings in a double-take. "No wonder women spend so much time in the bathroom. The only thing missing is a big-screen TV."

"Oh, for heaven's sake," I mutter and jerk my thumb over my shoulder at the creamy white door behind us. "The bathroom's in there."

The door swings open and an older woman in a rhinestone-encrusted dress covering a large chest that looks like it's caught a full wind sails out of the bathroom, only to halt dead in the water. She gives Jack a boggle-eyed stare. "Well! In all my life, I never!"

He snaps off a smart salute. "That makes two of us."

"This is a private conversation," I tell her, stepping before him and into the line of fire.

Her chin and chest rise imperiously. "I don't know what the two of you are up to, but I suggest you both leave before I report you to the authorities. You, young man, have no business in here. And as for you..." She points at me in a perfect Mimi-imitation. "You would do well to remember that rudeness in life will get you nowhere." With a huff, she whirls around and sails out the door.

Jack leans against the makeup mirror and folds his arms across his chest. "Guess she told you," he says drily.

"Oh, shut up," I mutter. Grabbing his arm, I haul him through the swinging door and into the sacrosanct ladies' room.

"Hey, watch the shirt!" he protests. "It's custom-made."

"Swear to God, Jack, you are fussier than a woman." Relieved to find no attendant on duty, I release him. The bathroom is large and airy with a glistening tiled floor, a bank of gleaming stalls, and a plush, cushioned bench near one wall.

"Not as fancy as the other room, but it's still better than a bunch of urinals." He glances around with interest, taking in the beribboned baskets of fancy soaps, scented hand lotions, mouthwash, and other sundries.

"This isn't a private tour. Let's make it quick. I want the truth."

He takes a stance in the middle of the floor and crosses his arms against his chest. "I'll admit I gave Mimi some money. She came to me about six months ago, asking for a loan. Sure, I gave her the money. I assumed it was for the chapel. Why else would she need it? But frankly, Lily, what the hell did you expect me to do? I couldn't watch her go under. I handled her fourth divorce and she came out of it flat-ass broke. That creep took her for everything she had."

He halts suddenly, yanks at his tie as if it's about to strangle him. "That was confidential information, by the way. I just breached an attorney-client privilege. I could be disbarred for what I just told you." He shakes his head slowly. "Why she married the guy in the first place is beyond me. Mimi's been around. She should have known he was a player. Well, he played her all right. Took her for everything she had and then some. She mortgaged the chapel and she couldn't make the payments. When she turned to me, I helped her out."

"So it's true." Hearing him confirm my fears feels like

a punch in the stomach. I sink against the counter. "And the IRS?"

Jack shakes his head. "I don't know about that."

"You're sure? Swear on your mother's grave? Swear on Tori's head?"

He huffs a deep sigh. "Lily, when have I ever lied to you?"

I love you, Lily. You and only you. I'll love you forever. Jack has quite a selective memory. I've never forgotten the words he whispered in my ear that night... but he has. Jack will say anything to get what he wants. That night at Caesar's Palace, he told me exactly what I wanted to hear.

And here we are again. Right back at Caesar's. Right back where we started.

"You know what, Jack? Forget it." I whirl away, turn toward the door. "It doesn't matter. Nothing matters anymore. I'll handle it myself."

He nails me in his arms before I can move. "Not so fast. You started this and now you're going to finish it." He chews out the words. "Are you positively sure that the IRS is involved?"

"I have the agent's name and business card in Mimi's office."

His grip on my shoulders tightens. "Look, Lily, I know you think I'm not such a great guy. And I'll admit I've made mistakes. Mistakes I truly regret. But can't you cut me a break?" His eyes search my face. "Both of us know how Tori feels about the chapel. Seeing it go under would break her heart. If nothing else, I did it for her. But if I had known Mimi intended not to report the money, you can be damn sure I never would have given it to her." He shakes his head. "I don't understand what she was thinking. You don't mess with the IRS."

"You should have told me, Jack. I deserved to know. I'm her daughter. Maybe I could have helped." A surge of fresh anger rushes through me, washing over the sadness and self-pity. "Instead, she's going to lose it all."

"We don't know that."

"Yes, we do. Let's be realistic. We both know that Mimi will never be the same. She'll never be able to run the chapel the way she used to. She'll never be able to perform weddings like she did in the past. It's been nearly two months and her mouth still droops. She can barely walk. She can barely speak."

"We'll hire somebody," he says. "I've got money. I've made some good investments. We'll work things out."

"The man from the IRS didn't sound very interested in working things out."

"Let me deal with the IRS. I'm an attorney, remember? We can get this all figured out. We'll get through it, Lily. Together."

He pulls me into his arms, brushes the hair from my face, gazing at me with one of those tender looks that makes me remember why I fell in love with him in the first place. Crazy, head-over-heels in love. And suddenly, I want to believe him. More than anything else in the world, I want to believe him and every word coming out of his mouth. I want so much to believe that for a quick second, I forget everything that's gone wrong between us. I believe that Jack Alexander is back in my life. I believe he's the man I always thought he was.

And then, without warning, an image of Rita pops in

my head and the time we spent together in the chapel this afternoon. How devastated and dazed I was at hearing her story. How I devoured the photos of a man she claimed is my father. How she told me of his diagnosis, how the rages of Alzheimer's had already claimed his mind. I think of all the years wasted, all that time we could have spent time together... except neither of us knew. Mimi left without telling my father she was pregnant, and she never told me he was still alive and well, living in Detroit. Mimi shared her secret with two people: Francesca and Jack. Francesca has already expressed her remorse and regret. But Jack hasn't admitted anything. He knew all along and he never said a word.

How I wish it would have been you.

I yank away from him and stagger backward. "It won't work, Jack." *Fool me once, shame on you. Fool me twice, shame on me.* "I will never forgive you for not telling me the truth. I hate you, Jack Alexander. I hate you."

"What the hell are you talking about?" He looks at me like I'm babbling nonsense. "I already told you I gave her the money. But I didn't know about the IRS—"

"The money I can forgive," I say. "But what about my father? What about the murder? You're a lawyer. You could have prevented this and you did nothing. Maybe if you hadn't given her the money, Mimi wouldn't have done what she did and the IRS wouldn't be involved. There wouldn't be an investigation. But it's too late now. Once they find out about my father and Big Mike's murder, Mimi and Francesca will probably both end up in jail."

"Murder?" His eyes narrow as he grabs my arm. "What murder?"

"Don't you touch me," I whisper, breaking away from him. "Don't you ever dare touch me again." I catch a glimpse of my face in the mirror and I barely recognize myself. My hair is disheveled, and there's a wildness in my eyes that reminds me of a mad woman.

"Lily, you're not making sense. All this talk about your father... and what's this about a murder? I don't know anything about a murder."

"You knew my father is still alive. You kept it from me. Just like you kept the murder from me, too. No more lies, Jack. I don't want to hear them." But even as the words slide out of my mouth, something I read on his face, something I see in his eyes, makes me hesitate. What if Jack is telling the truth? What if he doesn't know?

What if he never knew?

Then I remember everything Francesca and Mimi told me. There's no way the two of them could have handled this on their own. Of course Jack knows. He's always known. How could he not?

And the tiny crack in the door that is my heart slams shut, locking him out forever.

"Lily, you've got it all wrong."

"Oh, really?" I yank away from his touch. "They're two old women, Jack. This could very well kill them. I'm warning you now: if anything happens to either of them, it will be on your head. You tried to ruin my life when Tori was born, but I refuse to simply stand here and let you destroy them, and Tori, too. As far as I'm concerned, Jack Alexander, you can go to hell."

Suddenly there is a soft scuffle and a muffled gasp behind us. That's when I realize we are not alone. Someone is with us in the ladies' room. Someone has been here the entire time. Someone has heard everything we said.

Jack presses a finger against his lips. We lock eyes, listening for what comes next.

It is not a long wait.

The door of a metal stall crashes open and a flash of ice-blue dress and flying blond hair streaks past us and out the door.

"Oh, my God." My heart pounds in my chest.

"Tori! Stop!" Jack dashes out the door after her, leaving me perched alone against the bathroom sink. I grip the edge of the cold counter, thinking of everything Tori must have overheard. The IRS audit. The chapel closing. Big Mike's murder. Mimi and Francesca in jail. And the terrible things I shouted at Jack. Things a child should never hear spoken between her parents. That he lied to me. That I hated him. That he could go to hell.

I stagger into one of the open stalls and barely reach the toilet before the retching starts. I sink to my knees and hug the toilet. The nausea comes in waves, over and over, and everything comes up... the champagne, the hors d'oeuvres. I heave and cough, gagging through my tears.

Please, God, help him find her.

Chapter Eighteen

JACK IS ALONE WHEN HE finally returns to join us. We lock eyes as he approaches the table. He shakes his head slightly as he sinks into the chair beside me. He gropes under the tablecloth, finds my hand, gives my fingers a tight squeeze.

I'm sorry.

I'm sorry, too. I'll forgive him anything if only we find Tori.

"Where the hell have you been?" Ed stabs his fork in Jack's direction. "This happens to be your party, you know. And where the hell is Tori?"

Jack casts me a pointed look, but I'm no help. All this time I've been hoping and praying that he would find her, that it wouldn't be necessary to confess to everyone what has happened.

He grabs his glass from the table and downs the bourbon in one gulp. When he looks up, it's with bleary eyes. "I don't know," he says. "She took off."

"What do you mean, *she took off*?" Ed demands. "Took off *where*? What's the matter with you people? We're in the middle of dinner."

Jack grows silent and stares at me with hollow eyes.

Ed glances back and forth between the two of us, his face redder than the cherry tomatoes in his salad. "What the hell is going on? Something's up, and you two know it."

I pull in a deep breath. "Jack and I had an argument. We said... some things, and unfortunately, Tori overheard us." I feel Jack's fingers gripping mine tighter. It helps me find the courage to go on. "She got upset and ran off."

"But where is she?" Francesca gasps.

"We don't know," he admits.

"Oh, for Christ's sake." Ed's voice chews the air. His face is a mottled purple. "Haven't we had enough of this? The two of you are adults. Time you both started acting like it."

Ed doesn't know the half of it.

"I knew something was wrong." Francesca pushes away her plate.

I turn to Jack. "Have you checked the casino floor?"

He nods. "I couldn't spot her. But if she was on the floor, she couldn't have been there long. They would have asked for ID and told her to move along."

Mimi's face contorts in a grotesque mixture of outrage and concern. "Phone," she mouths the word.

"I've been trying, but she isn't picking up." Jack throws his cell on the table.

"Let me try." I fish my own cell from my bag and try Tori's number, but it goes to voicemail, just like the last three times I've tried. The jazz quartet keeps playing, but the music no longer stirs my soul. After everything that's happened today, I'm in no mood to celebrate. I can't just sit here. What if Tori has already left Caesar's? What if she's long gone? She took off once without telling me and drove across the desert. What if...

I grab my clutch, push back my chair, and stand. "I'm going home. Maybe she's there." I say it, but I don't believe it.

Francesca puts down her fork. "Maybe we should all go."

"No, stay and finish your dinner." There's no use in ruining everyone's evening. "I'll phone once I get home and let you know if I've found her."

Jack throws down his napkin. "I'm going with you."

"You can't," I say quickly, though I'd give anything if he *was* going with me. Jack looks just as scared as I feel, and I wouldn't mind the company. Plus, I can't blame all of this on him. It takes two to tango, two to argue, and two parents to love a child. Tori is Jack's daughter, too, and I know how much he loves her. "It's your birthday, remember? This is your party. You can't leave your guests."

"But how will you get home? Jaabir dropped us off," Francesca reminds me. "You don't have a car."

"I'll grab a taxi. I promise I'll phone as soon as I get home." I throw my napkin on the table and weave my way to the door. If Tori is still at Caesar's—which I highly doubt—she might just have a change of heart and return to the party. But if she's already left the casino property, she has a good half-hour start on me. She has her own car. She could be anywhere. But my hope and my prayer is that she's at home.

My thoughts spiral downward as the minutes pass and I'm forced to wait in a long line of chatting tourists for a taxi. A traffic accident on Las Vegas Boulevard snarls traffic for nearly twenty minutes, further darkening my mood. It's positively black by the time I reach the villa, only to find it bathed in darkness. Tori's car isn't in the garage. I check the villa, open every door, check every room.

No Tori.

I end up in the kitchen where I sink into a chair, kick off my shoes, and fish out my cell. I stare at it bleakly, imagining all of them at Caesar's, waiting for my call. My stomach knots as I think of Jack, and how hard this will be on him. Once I make the call, I take away his hope. He never meant to hurt her. Neither of us did. I sit there another moment, remembering how he caught my hand, how he held it tight. Until now I've managed to hold it together, but I'm not sure what will happen if I hear Jack's voice. I might crumble for good.

I close my eyes and squeeze out a few tears, brush them away with the tip of a finger. Then, taking a deep breath, I pick up the phone, punch in Ed's number, and relay the news.

"We just finished dinner," he says. "We'll be there as soon as Jack cuts the cake."

I head for my bedroom, shrug out of my dress and pull on a pair of worn jeans and a faded *I Got Married at The Royal Chapel!* T-shirt. I pull my hair up in a quick ponytail, grimacing in the mirror. My makeup is smeary and I look a wreck, which is exactly how I feel inside—a total wreck. I wander through the house, checking every room one more time, just in case. But I already know it's a futile search. Tori isn't here.

Some minutes later, I hear the front door open, then voices rumbling in the kitchen. Ed has Mimi and Francesca in tow.

"Jack will be here as soon as the party is over," Ed says.

I make tea for us all, but Ed pours himself a tumbler of bourbon. Mimi pushes her cup toward the bottle, and Ed splashes a generous dollop in her cup, plus Francesca's. I give in and join them. Two hours later, the party over and his guests departed, Jack stumbles in the door. His tux is rumpled, his tie undone. Deep furrows etch the dark stubble on his face.

"Is she home?" he asks hopefully. One look at our faces and the half-empty bottle in the middle of the table and his face drops. He sinks down and pours himself a double shot.

"We have to think positive. She couldn't have gone far," Ed mutters.

"She could be in San Diego or halfway across the country by now," I say. "She has a car, remember?"

"You don't think she would leave town, do you?" Francesca whispers.

"No... way," Mimi grunts. She stabs each word with a finger against the table. "No. Way."

Mimi is right. Tori would never leave this town. She loves the city too much. She loves Mimi, and she loves the chapel.

And suddenly, in the midst of the void, an idea blossoms in my heart. Would she? Is it possible? I spring to my feet. "I'll be right back."

Jack stares at me through bleary eyes. "Where are you going?"

I shake my head. I have no idea if I'm right or not. I don't want to give false hope.

Standing, he shoves in his chair. "I'm coming with you."

I race out the kitchen door with Jack hot on my heels. We fly across the courtyard, through the chapel Court Garden, past the wedding gazebo, and cross the cobblestones to the chapel's entrance. As usual, the outside of the building is lit up as brilliantly as Buckingham Palace, but the chapel windows are shrouded in darkness. My hands shake as I fumble with the lock.

"Let me do it." Jack gently pushes me aside. Within seconds, the lock tumbles open and the door swings wide.

"Tori!" he shouts into the murky darkness of the Royal Reception Room. "Tori, are you here?"

I follow him in, snap on the lights. The chandeliers bring the room to blazing life. I glance around, then gasp. My hunch was right. Tori *was* here... but she's long gone.

"Jack, look." My finger trembles as I point to the showcase with its bulletproof glass where the heirloom diamond tiara always rests, safely nestled on its blue velvet pillow.

The cabinet is open. The pillow is empty.

"She took the tiara." My legs start to crumble. He catches me in his arms, cradles me close. I don't fight him. There is no fight left in me. Finding Tori is the only thing that's important.

"We have to find her." I struggle against the thought of doing nothing. "She's out there all alone."

His grip on my shoulders tightens. "Do you think she might have gone back to San Diego?"

"No, I think she's still in town. And she has the tiara." I

Royal Secrets

nod toward the empty cabinet. "I think she'll try to sell it."

He releases a hard breath. "All right, then that's where we'll start... even if it means visiting every pawn shop in town."

"Sweet Jesus." My stomach lurches at the thought of how she'll react. "Tori will be devastated when she learns the truth."

His eyes narrow. "Truth about what?"

"The tiara, naturally. No one will want to buy it."

"What the hell are you talking about? The thing has to be worth a small fortune. It's been in your family for generations, not to mention its ties to the Vegas community. Any pawn-shop dealer in the city would empty out his safe to get his hands on a piece of history like that."

No, they wouldn't. The tiara is worthless. I know that, and so does Jack. So why is he talking like he believes otherwise?

Then suddenly my heart leaps into overdrive, taking up all the room in my chest, squeezing out my breath as the enormity behind the truth he is saying kicks in. Jack believes what he's saying because he thinks it's the truth. All this time, he never lied to me. When we argued tonight, he was being honest. He doesn't know about my father. He doesn't know about the murder. And he doesn't know the secret Mimi and Francesca kept all these years.

The secret about the Royal Wedding Chapel and Big Mike's murder. The secret about my father. The secret about our family ties to the British aristocracy. Long ago, two women shared a secret and dreamed up a story to go along with it. But that's all it is... a story fashioned out of imagination and desperation.

253

The tiara isn't real. It can't be real. How can there be a family heirloom if the family never existed?

"Listen!" Suddenly Jack stiffens, puts a finger to his lips, cocks his head. "Did you hear that?" he whispers.

"Hear what?" I whisper back.

"Shhhh," he cautions.

I strain to hear a sound, any sound, but it's useless. The central air kicks in with a soft whoosh after a moment. I shake my head. "I didn't hear anything."

His shoulders sag as he gazes down at me. Suddenly I remember that today is his birthday—no, that was yesterday. It's well after midnight, and Jack is fifty now. Tonight he looks every one of those years that were blazing as candles on his birthday cake. And all the anger and resentment, all the frustration and fears I've felt and held against him, melt away at the sight of a man in defeat. Have I done this to him? Is this what happens when you fight all the time? When you hurt each other with words and actions? When you lash out, despite the love?

I lift my hand and touch his cheek. "You okay?"

He doesn't speak a word, simply reaches up and squeezes my fingers, pressing them to his lips. Then, before either of us realize what is happening, I'm in his arms again, and Jack is no longer kissing my hand, but kissing me. His mouth presses against my own, and our breath mingles, hot and heavy. Everything starts to tumble away. My heart is in free fall, and at the moment, there is nothing I want more in the world than exactly this.

This, and Tori.

"No." I break out of his arms. "No, Jack, we can't. Not like this. Not now. This isn't the time."

His eyes search my face. "There'll never be a better time, Lily. You need to hear exactly how I feel."

But I already know. He's made it perfectly clear. Jack is an independent man who loves women... all kinds of women. He's not interested in the clingy, emotional sort. And right now, that's exactly what I am. An emotional mess.

"When are you going to quit running away? What's got you so scared?"

I blink. "What?"

"Running away," he says. "You do it all the time."

"I never—"

"Yes, you do. You've done it since you were a little girl," he counters. "Back then, it was easy to find you. You were always in the chapel, hiding in one of the pews."

I do remember. This chapel was my sanctuary.

"But then you grew up. And when Tori came along, you ran away for good."

"That's not true," I whisper. "I didn't run away." I know the difference between running and leaving. It's called self-preservation. "I had a job. I had responsibilities. I had a child to take care of."

"Our child," he reminds me.

"Yes, our child," I say softly, "but you didn't want her." But what I really mean is you didn't want *me*.

His eyes narrow. "I never said that."

"You didn't have to. You made it pretty obvious." That he loved Tori? Yes. That he loved me? He said he did, but I didn't believe him.

"Let's be honest, Jack. My way was better. If I had stayed, you would have felt trapped. Neither of us would have been happy, and eventually you would have ended up hating me. That's not the kind of life I wanted for us."

But isn't that exactly what Mimi did to my father? She ran away because she felt trapped. She ran away because she was unhappy. She ran away without giving their marriage a chance.

"So instead, you decided to play it safe." His voice is low and rough. "Don't you get it, Lily? That's all I'm looking for. It's all I've ever wanted. When are you going to quit running and give a guy a chance?"

"A chance for what? For you to break my heart? I know you, Jack, and I know what you're like. You're not a one-woman man. You never have been. I never would have been enough for you. There would have been other women. Did you really expect I could put up with that?"

"I'll admit I'm not a monk. There have been women in my life. Plenty of women." His eyes soften, questioning. "Didn't you ever wonder why I never married?"

Because he couldn't be faithful to one woman? No matter what else he might be, Jack is an honorable man. He would never commit to vows he knew he couldn't keep.

"It's because I've been waiting for you."

My breath catches as he reaches out to pull me to him, and tugs me into his arms. Can I trust this is happening? Can I trust that this is real, that he's telling the truth? Pulling back slightly, I search his eyes. He looks tired and haggard, every one of his fifty years written across his face. But there's something else, too. A sadness and a longing for something that could have been, mingled with a tiny flicker of hope for something that might still be.

"Don't go," he whispers in my ear. His hand caresses my cheek. "Don't run away again. Not when we've finally found each other." His voice catches with emotion. "If I hadn't been such a jerk, maybe things would have been different. Maybe—"

I shush him with one finger pressed against his lips. "Don't go down that road. We're way past *maybe*."

"Maybe not," he whispers. "Maybe there's still a chance we can make things right. Maybe tonight was meant as a second chance."

"Do you believe in second chances?" I search his eyes.

He grips me tighter. "Maybe I can make you believe."

We lock eyes and stand there some seconds. In his eyes, I read patience, kindness, tolerance... and something else. Could it be *love*? Can I believe him? Do I dare believe him? "Second chances come with a high price tag."

He grasps my shoulders, stares into my eyes. "I'd give everything I own if it meant a second chance with you." He pulls me close again, sealing the promise with a kiss. The wild burning desire I taste on his lips leaves no doubt in my mind that he's telling the truth. Maybe there's a chance for us after all. Maybe I can allow myself to believe that dreams can come true. That happily ever after isn't something you read about in a fairy tale, but something that happens in real life, too.

My life.

Our lives.

He catches my hand. "We should go back. They're probably wondering where we are."

I nod and he snaps off the lights, leaving us in sudden darkness. Moonlight filters through the stained-glass window. He starts for the door, pulling me after him, but I don't move.

"Wait," I whisper. "Look."

I point to the sliver of light sliding out beneath the door of the King Edward's Chapel.

His fingers curl around mine and we steal across the reception room floor. He puts an ear against the chapel door, then steps aside, making room for me. I grab the handle and slowly, silently, open the door.

King Edward's Chapel, our largest room, is filled with pews that can easily accommodate one hundred guests. But tonight, the only guest is the little blonde in the icy-blue dress doubled over on the step in front of the altar. At her feet, tossed aside, rests the royal tiara.

"Tori?" Jack moves quick as a cat, stealthy and sleek. In seconds, he is at her side, crouching before her. Something inside me shifts as I watch him reach out and gently touch her arm. "Sweetheart?"

Finally she lifts her head. My wild, passionate girl has disappeared, smeared away in a tangle of trauma and tears. I sink down beside her, gather her in my arms.

"Oh, Tori. We've been so worried about you." I smooth her hair, brush her forehead with a kiss. "I love you, sweetie. Your dad and I both love you."

"I only wanted to help." Her eyes pool with more tears. "I thought if I took the tiara, maybe I could get some money to save the chapel. But the man at the pawn shop said it was junk." She nudges the edge of the tiara with one toe. "He offered me five hundred dollars, but only because it's been at the chapel so many years.

"Why did she lie?" She turns to me. "Why did Mimi lie to us?"

It has finally happened. The one thing I've never

wanted, the thing I've always dreaded, the thing I've spent my entire life—Tori's life—trying to protect her from. Her hopes are crushed and her dreams destroyed.

"I'm sure she had her reasons," I swallow over the surprise of hearing myself defending Mimi.

"To lie to your family?" Tori pulls away, swiping fresh tears. Her eyes blaze and her face contorts with the kind of outraged passion and fury found only in teenagers who are still young enough to believe that the world exists in black and white. "How does lying help anyone?"

Jack sinks down on the step and drapes an arm around her. "I'm sure whatever reasons she had, they were important."

Do I tell them? Neither of them know the truth. They don't know about my father or the tiara's secret. They don't know about Big Mike. They don't know about the murder.

A scuffle in the back of the room and the three of us glance up in unison.

"Sorry... sorry." Mimi shuffles down the aisle, gripping her walker, with Francesca and Ed close behind. Her eyes glisten, but there are no tears. "My fault," she says as she nears us. "All my fault. Rr-ruined."

"It's not your fault." Francesca bustles past her as they reach the front pew. "It just happened. Lily knows the truth, and it's time everyone else did, too."

"Does this involve the murder?" Jack asks.

"Murder?" Ed hustles forward with a deep frown. "What murder?"

Francesca glances at Mimi. "Do you want to tell them, or shall I?"

Mimi shoves her walker aside, sinks into the front pew,

and waves her hand in a go-ahead motion.

"I think it might be better if you sat down, too." Taking Ed's arm, Francesca leads him toward Mimi.

He shoots me a bewildered look as he grabs the front of the pew and lowers himself down next to Mimi. Then all of us listen as Francesca slowly begins reciting the story. Most of it I have already heard; some from Rita earlier this afternoon and some from Francesca while we were in Mimi's bedroom. Some of it, I deduced on my own. Everyone sits transfixed, listening to the story... especially when Francesca gets to the part about Big Mike's murder.

"She wouldn't allow me to turn myself in. We closed the chapel and held our breath, waiting for the police to finish their investigation. Once his death was ruled as accidental, we decided it was time for a fresh start. He didn't leave much money, but the one thing Mimi did inherit was the chapel. We talked for weeks, planning on how to market it. Remember, this was the late sixties, and the wedding business was booming. Everyone wanted to come to Las Vegas and be married like Elvis and Priscilla. But Mimi was convinced we needed something different, something that would make us stand out from all the other chapels. We scoured the newspapers and the public library for ideas.

"Then one day, Mimi stumbled across an old news item about the death of the last remaining heir of a family in England. A family with distant ties to the British throne. A family with the same last name of Lavender. She came home all excited and told me about it. That was the beginning. We were up all night, making plans. By morning, the Royal Wedding Chapel and Mimi's new identity as the grieving widow of Lawrence Lavender, British noble, was born.

"And that, Lily, is why she made up the story about your father." Francesca turns to me with eyes that are weary and careworn. "That is also why Ed walked out."

"What?" Jack and I utter in unison, exchanging stunned glances. We stare at Ed, doubled over in the pew, head bowed. Mimi's hand rests lightly on his back.

"Ed handled setting up the business for Mimi," Francesca explains. "That's how they met. He took care of her legal work and the two of them began seeing each other. It wasn't long—maybe a year, a little less—before Ed began pressing her to marry him. But Mimi refused. She'd never told him the truth about her first marriage. She was afraid he would discover that she'd been married and divorced, and that her first husband—Lily's father— was still alive. The years passed, but Ed never gave up. Finally—Lily, I think you were about ten years old—Mimi accepted his proposal and the two of them were married. For years, she managed to keep the truth from him. But eventually he discovered her secret."

She turns to me. "Once he learned your father was still alive and that Mimi had concocted the story about the British royalty and the tie-in to the Royal Wedding Chapel, he insisted she tell you the truth. He said that you were old enough and had a right to know that your father was still alive. But Mimi wouldn't do it. She was afraid. Ed knew about your father, but he didn't know why we'd invented the story. He didn't know the truth about how Big Mike had died, and Mimi insisted that we didn't dare tell him. She was certain if Ed found out what had really happened the night of Big Mike's death, he would insist that I turn myself in to the police. She was only trying to protect me, you see. We knew that I would be arrested for his murder. So she put Ed off. They argued for days, and finally he gave her an ultimatum: *tell Lily the truth about her father.* Instead, she told Ed it was none of his business. And he walked out."

I sit, stunned by the story I've heard. In some ways it's unimaginable, but I have no doubt it's the truth. One look at Ed's bent form, the tired way he rubs his forehead, shakes his head, and I know. One look in Mimi's eyes, the bleak sadness I find there, the *"sorry,"* she mouths in my direction, confirms it. And if that wasn't enough, there is one final truth laid out before me. It is in the tender touch as Mimi reaches for him, and the tight hold Ed has as he takes her hand and clasps it against his lips.

All these years, listening as they bickered, I assumed it was because of their bitter divorce. They always acted like they hated being in the same room with each other. But that wasn't the case. Now I realize that their quarreling was like that of an old married couple who love each other but can't find a way through the mess to resolve their differences. Neither of them refused to capitulate.

And when Ed walked away, so did Mimi's heart.

My mother is a strong woman. A woman who refuses to allow adversity to stop her. A woman in charge of her own life. The only way she managed to survive Ed's leaving was to hold her head high, pretend it didn't matter, and walk away, just like he did. But the truth is, she still loves him. She never stopped.

I drag in a ragged breath, shuddering as the enormity of my own guilt weighs upon my heart. *Sins of the mother.*

Is that what I've done? Mimi ran away from my father, and I ran away from Jack. She left Detroit, and I left Las Vegas and my family behind. She made a life for Francesca and me, just as I tried to make a life for myself and Tori.

A life where I could make my own rules and do as I please.

Exactly like Mimi did herself, so many years ago.

Who am I to judge her? I have no right to do so. I am just like my mother.

Jack quietly fills us in on the details he learned while handling Mimi's recent divorce. How Husband Number Four stole money from her for his gambling habit. How she was too ashamed to let anyone know.

And finally, when Jack is finished, Mimi herself begins to speak. In garbled, halting words, we hear her admit how the IRS came calling with an audit. How it was discovered she hadn't paid the taxes. How she was informed a tax lien would be placed on the property. How, if she didn't come up with the money, they would close down the chapel and put it up for public auction.

Her story is a mixture of drama and intrigue, of subterfuge and secrecy that would put the best royal courtier to shame. She did what she felt she had to do in order to save the chapel and Francesca. Instead of trying to save herself, Mimi tried to save someone she loved.

Tori struggles to her feet and crosses the few feet separating her from Mimi. She sinks to her knees and buries her head in her grandmother's lap. Mimi clumsily strokes her hair as Tori silently weeps. I feel like weeping, too. My daughter has just taken a giant step out of her childish world of black and white, into an adult world filled with forgiving shades of gray.

"Pop?" Jack's low voice rumbles through the chapel. "Got any idea on what we do now?

Ed lifts his head. His eyes are bleary. "That's up to Mimi and Francesca."

"I don't want to hide anymore," Francesca says in a firm quiet voice. "I think we should let the authorities handle things from here." She glances at Ed. "Would you represent me?"

"Jack would be best at handling your defense," he says carefully. "He has more experience in criminal matters."

"All right." Her voice quivers slightly. "But what about Mimi?"

Ed's fingers tighten around my mother's hand. "If that's what she wants."

Mimi stares at him a long moment. Then, without a word, she leans into Ed, tucks his hand close against her heart and, closing her eyes, nods.

"That settles it," Jack murmurs to me in a quiet aside. "We'll go to the police tomorrow."

I feel spent and sick, thinking about the *what-if's*? What if Mimi and Francesca are both arrested? There is no statute of limitations on murder. What if they are charged on open murder? They'll be fingerprinted and booked. They'll be put in a jail cell until we can make bail. The thought of the two of them behind bars, even if only for a few hours, is inconceivable.

"I know it seems bad, but we'll get through this." Jack takes my hand and presses it. "We'll make things right. I promise."

He's made plenty of promises in the past, but this time

I believe him. More important, I trust him.

Jack will make things right.

When I finally tumble into bed, sleep refuses to come. My thoughts march back and forth, tramping through my brain like an army of foot soldiers refusing to capitulate and lay down their weapons. The war is over. Don't they realize they can't win? Yet, isn't that what I've been doing all these years?

I've spent my life fighting things over which I have no control. Armed with an arsenal of fierce independence and stubborn insistence, I continued to assert that I knew best. I ran away when the going got tough. I'm good at standing on my own two feet, but I'm not so great when it comes to turning things over, leaning on others, allowing them to help me, to love me.

Trust your head, not your heart. Take charge of your own life. Be in control. Lessons my mother taught me. Yet Mimi never meant to hurt me. She did what she thought was best in order to protect the people she loved. But instead, I took away the wrong message. I hardened my heart, turned away from my family, stepped up and made my place in the world. I'm a successful career woman. Tori is in private school. I've made us a comfortable home with a gardener who cares for the flowers and a housekeeper who keeps things tidy and clean. Yet where has it gotten me? I'm barely home enough to enjoy the quiet luxury of my own living room or relaxing in the garden. My daughter doesn't trust me enough to share her secrets and dreams. My mother and I barely speak. How did all this happen?

More important, how do I fix it?

When do I quit running away and stand up for those I love? When do I quit running away and stand up for me? Once upon a time, I did what I wanted—or what I thought I wanted. I allowed those soldiers of selfishness and grandiosity living in my head to take the charge, and I blindly followed their command. If only I had known. How much of what we don't know lies hidden in people's hearts? How much could be resolved—so many fears and misunderstandings—if people had the courage to face their fears and admit the truth?

What is my truth? What have I learned?

That I can't control people. Tori's running away this summer is all the proof I need.

That I can't control my own emotions. My tear-stained pillow is evidence of that.

That I'm tired of running away. Tired of pretending to be someone I'm not. Tired and wishing I had a safe place to rest my head... and someone's arms to hold me close.

Maybe I'm not as resilient as I thought. Maybe I no longer want to be.

Maybe it is time to finally give up the fight.

Chapter Nineteen

B RIDES, BRIDES, AND MORE BRIDES. The chapel is fully
booked, giving us no time to think or talk. But after
living through the past twenty-four hours, with all the sins
and secrets finally revealed, immersing ourselves in the
world of weddings feels more like a blessing rather than
a curse. Tori, Francesca, and I bustle through the chapel,
barely speaking except about the current ceremony or the
next to start. The day is a blur of silk and taffeta, ruching
and veils, tears and tiaras.

Jack shows up just after the last ceremony finishes. He
strolls over to join me outside in the courtyard as Jaabir
assists the bride and groom, an elderly couple in their
seventies, into the white stretch limo.

"Childhood sweethearts?" Jack asks with a faint smile
as we watch them depart.

"Yes, believe it or not," I say as the limo merges into
traffic on Las Vegas Boulevard. "Only he married someone
else, and she never married. Fifty years later, long after
his first wife died, they met up at a high school reunion
and fell in love all over again."

"She never married?" One eyebrow lifts. "That's going to be quite the honeymoon."

"I think it's sweet."

"You?" Mild surprise lights his face. "Lily, the Queen of *don't-bother-telling-me-about-romance-because-it-doesn't-exist*? What happened to that jaded girl I used to know?"

I think about the wild passionate kisses we shared last night and suddenly my heart is racing. A swift rush of color burns my cheeks. "Maybe she finally wised up."

"Maybe she did," he says, considering me with a thoughtful look as Francesca and Tori join us.

"Mimi's waiting in the villa," Francesca says. Her voice rings out strong, but her eyes are apprehensive, filled with fear.

"We might as well get this over with." Jack's face dissolves in a grim expression as he takes her arm.

Despite the oppressive desert heat, a cold shiver of dread snakes it way up my spine. Jack is here to advise them of their rights and responsibilities under the law. But after hearing the passionate way Francesca spoke last night and seeing the determined look in Mimi's eyes, there's no doubt in my mind how all this will be resolved. No matter what type of advice Jack gives them as legal counsel, Mimi and Francesca intend to turn themselves in to the police.

"I assume you're meeting in the villa?" Somehow I manage to get out the words.

Francesca nods. "Call if you need anything."

What I need is for my family to be safe. For Francesca not to have to confess to committing a murder. For Mimi not to have to admit her role in the sordid mess. For there to be no reason for Jack's presence here today... except for him to want to be here.

"Do you think he'll be able to keep Francesca out of jail?" Tori asks as we watch them head toward the villa.

"Your father is a very good attorney." I decide it's better not to share my fears that Mimi will join Francesca in confessing to the crime. "I'm sure he'll do his best to make things right and help them decide what to do."

"What about you?" Tori trails close behind as I enter the chapel. "What are you going to do?"

"The same thing I've been doing every day, I suppose." I drop into the chair behind the reception counter and attempt a smile. It's been a long and difficult day, but nothing compared to what lies ahead. I dread the thought of what the future holds for our family. "Try to get through whatever happens. Help however I can.

"That's not what I meant." Tori plants herself in front of the counter.

For the first time today, I take a good look at my daughter. With eight weddings back to back, there's been no time for us to talk. Taking in her troubled eyes, the pinched look on her forehead, I realize I should have made time.

"Why don't you tell me what you *do* mean," I suggest.

"All of this. The chapel. Everything." She waves a hand around the room. "Everything I thought was real in my life, everything I cared about..." She drops her head, long blond hair swinging in her face, but not quick enough to hide the disappointment in her eyes, the reality of romance destroyed. Last night caused a deep crack in the façade of the Royal Wedding Chapel. "None of it is real. It's all just a lie." Her voice is quiet and flat. "A big fat lie."

I never imagined I would feel so sad, seeing her passion for the chapel disappeared like waking up from a dream. My brave, beautiful girl. Where has she gone? "Is that what you think?"

Tori reaches across the counter and fingers the tiara resting beside the computer. After last night's revelations, no one has bothered to return it to its velvet pillow behind the bulletproof glass. She plucks it from the counter, gingerly placing the tiara atop her head.

"I've always loved this," she says in a halting voice. "Each year on my birthday, it felt as if I were wearing a magical crown. It made me feel like I was a princess, and that I could do anything. It made me feel bigger than myself. It made me feel like I was part of something special... something that other people didn't have."

My heart aches as I take in the sight of her somber face, the tiara sparkling atop her head. "But you are part of something special, Tori."

"No, I'm not."

"Yes, you are," I insist. "You're a part of us. All of us. Your dad, Grandpa Ed, Mimi, and Francesca. No matter what happens, that will never change."

"But maybe I don't want that anymore." Her blue eyes blaze to life. "They lied to you, Mom. They lied to us. They lied to everyone. Our whole lives are built on a lie. How can you live with that? Doesn't it bother you?"

"Of course it does." Less than three hours sleep last night is proof of that. I rub my forehead, pondering all that has happened. Yesterday I woke up assuming my birthright included a distant tie to the British throne. Today, that legacy has disappeared. But somehow, it doesn't matter, for I've gained something infinitely more valuable. The man I always believed to be lost to me is alive and living in Detroit. Yesterday, my father, Lawrence Lavender, was resurrected from the dead.

"We might as well lock the doors right now and keep them locked forever. No bride will want to be married here when the news breaks and they learn the truth." Tori yanks the tiara from her hair. "The Royal Wedding Chapel? We're not even related to the royal family." She tosses the tiara on the counter.

"Be careful. You'll scratch it."

She shrugs. "Who cares? It's just a piece of junk."

"But it's not. It's valuable to us. It's a part of our family history." I can't believe I'm saying the words. I try to remember how I felt when I was seventeen and butted heads with Mimi. It's not easy being a teenager, but being an adult complicates life even more. I always assumed once I grew up and had control over my life, things would be simple. But that's not the way it worked out. And perhaps that's the way things are meant to be. The older I get, the more I realize the less control I have over things—and people—in my life.

"Sometimes people do things because they don't know what else to do... because it seems like a good idea at the time. Just like when you ran away last month," I add gently. "I'm sure you had your reasons—"

"Get real, Mom. What else was I supposed to do? You never would have let me come."

"How did you know that? You never even asked,"

I remind her. "Instead, you took off and had me scared to death."

"I'll be eighteen in a couple of months. I can take care of myself."

"That is beside the point," I say. I'm not going to play semantics. This is beyond someone's date of birth. This is about caring for someone. This is about concern. This is about love.

"What you did was unreasonable and dangerous," I say. "No one knew where you were. What if something had happened? What if the car had broken down halfway across the desert?"

"It didn't."

"But it could have," I counter, determined not to give up.

"You are such a *mom*," she says with a practiced roll of her eyes.

"Sorry, but it comes with the territory." I don't care if she wants to hear it or not. It's time everything came out. "You're old enough to understand what it's like when you love someone. I was worried about you because I love you. I wanted to make sure you were safe. You're my daughter. I don't know what I would have done if something had happened to you. And if someone tried to hurt you, if someone..."

My voice wavers as Mimi suddenly comes to mind. Didn't she do the same thing for me? For Francesca? Her decisions, her sacrifices throughout the years; Mimi was only trying to protect us. I think of how last night ended, Mimi's one good arm pulling me close in an embrace, her eyes glimmering with tears, her voice contrite. "Sorry," she whispered. "So sorry."

And I was sorry, too. Sorry for all the mistakes I had made, the things I had done, for everything that had gone between us throughout the years. But all of that is finished now. The only thing to do is move on.

When Mimi and I left the chapel together last night, the only thing between us was the shiny metal of her walker.

"That's what happens when you love someone." My voice lifts, stronger, heated. "That's what love is all about. You care what happens when you love someone. You can't help it. I was worried about you. Just like I'm worried about Mimi and Francesca. Yes, they did things they shouldn't have. Yes, I'm angry and upset. But we can't turn our backs on them. They need us, Tori. They need us now more than ever."

And suddenly, everything I worried over last night, all my cares and concerns, dissolve as in a mist. The answer is so simple, I can't believe it didn't occur to me before. And before I realize it, I am on my feet.

"We stand together as a family." My voice is firm. "We do not run and hide. You say you're old enough to make decisions on your own? Fine. Go ahead. Decide for yourself. But remember this: whatever you decide, you will have to live with it for the rest of your life. I made some bad decisions a long time ago. I did what I thought was best at the time—and I've lived with plenty of doubts and regrets for many years. But not anymore. I intend to make things right. As for Mimi and Francesca, I am going to stand beside them and see this through. I can't do anything else, Tori. I love them. It's as simple as that."

My heart gallops in my chest as I watch her face pale

and her eyes narrow. My sharing hasn't touched her. She is beyond reaching. She is going to bolt. But I have no choice but to let her go. Everyone needs to learn to live with their own choices. Mimi chose her own path in life and so did I. Now the best thing I can do as a mother is allow my daughter to choose her path, too.

Tori shifts on her feet and draws in a deep breath.

I wait and I hope.

"You're right, Mom," she finally says in a small voice. "I can't leave. I love them, too."

"Oh, Tori." My heart melts and I cross the distance between us, take her in my arms. She buries her face in my shoulder as I stroke her hair and hug her close.

"I'm sorry," she murmurs.

"I'm sorry, too," I whisper. "For everything."

We stand there a moment, allowing both the apologies to settle in our hearts. Finally she lifts a tear-stained face. "What do you think will happen to Mimi and Francesca?"

"I don't know." I have to be honest. Tori is old enough to hear the truth. "But whatever happens, we'll get through it together. We can do anything as long as we're together."

And as I say the words, I realize my life—our lives—contain no greater truth. No hurt can touch us, no words can harm us. You can get through anything when you are surrounded by the people you love.

She pulls back slightly and dabs her eyes with a tissue. "Sorry I've been such a brat."

I laugh softly, kiss her forehead. "I'm sorry, too. I didn't mean to be overbearing."

"You're just doing your job, being a mom," she says with a flash of the magical smile that is pure Tori.

I give her one last hug. She is home, right where she belongs.

"How many weddings booked for tomorrow?" she asks.

"Six." I glance around the reception room. Things need to be restocked, plus I still need to close out today's accounts and ready the bank deposit. "I suppose I should get to work."

"I'll take care of things in the Queen Elizabeth Chapel," Tori says, "but first, there's something I need to do."

Reaching over, she gently lifts the royal tiara from where she tossed it on the counter. Cradling it as if it were indeed fashioned from glittering diamonds and precious gems, she crosses the room, opens the display case, and places the tiara back on the velvet pillow. She closes the glass door, snaps the lock, and turns to face me. It is a quiet moment, filled with reverence, and there is no need for words. Our hearts are together in complete understanding.

The tiara is exactly where it needs to be.

Home.

Epilogue

NEVER IN MY WILDEST DREAMS did I imagine that someday Mimi and Ed would end up together again. I felt like pinching myself a few weeks ago as all of us gathered to celebrate the first anniversary of their second marriage. Mimi glowed and Ed beamed as we lifted our glasses and toasted the second-time-around bride and groom. Life has a strange way of smoothing things out. Mimi and Ed have found each other again. Life is good.

Things turned out good for Francesca, as well. Just as I suspected she would, she turned herself over to the police and confessed to Big Mike's murder. But thanks to Jack's intervention, no charges were filed. As Jack reminded the prosecutor in a lengthy discussion, they were dealing with a defendant who had come forward of her own volition. With no eyewitnesses, only circumstantial evidence and a crime scene dating back more than forty years, the prosecutor quickly saw the wisdom in Jack's argument and dismissed the case before it began. Francesca was saved from the hint of scandal and the possibility of a trial and doing time in prison. When Jack brought her home, there were tears in her eyes and relief on her face. No more carrying around a load of guilt. No more angst about what she should have done or what might happen. No more fretting that someone might find out that the Royal Wedding Chapel was the stuff of nonsense, of which fairy tales are fractured.

There were smiles all around that night as we celebrated Francesca's freedom from the past. She'll never again need to worry about what might happen. She's free to do as she pleases. She's not even under house arrest. *Chapel arrest* would be the more appropriate term, I'm thinking. Francesca's heart will always be with the chapel and Mimi. As long as the chapel doors remain open, she will never leave. And now Mimi and the IRS have reached a settlement, courtesy of Jack, the chapel is safe.

Jaabir graduated with honors from UNLV this past summer. He turned in his keys to the white stretch limo in exchange for Mimi's computer password. She promoted Jaabir to General Manager the day after he received his business degree, and he now runs the chapel with Francesca's assistance. The two of them—with limited help from Mimi—make the perfect team. It's the ideal solution for now, but none of us can predict what the future holds. Life is all about change and how we cope with it.

None of us could have foretold Mimi's stroke, but all of us—Mimi included—have made our peace with the situation. It's been more than a year, and she's accepted the fact that she'll never make a full recovery. Mimi's dancing days are gone, but she's gotten very good at shuffling behind her walker. And while her body might not always cooperate, her mind remains as sharp as ever.

She still gets angry and slams her hand against the table when she drops a piece of food from her fork, when she can't move fast enough, when someone doesn't understand her garbled speech. But wouldn't any of us do the same? There but for the grace of God...

Through the drooling, the despair, and the day-to-day physical, mental, and emotional toll this cost her, Mimi has handled herself with grace and dignity.

I am forty years old, and I am still learning lessons from my mother.

And last October, I finally met my father. I flew out to Detroit at Rita's invitation for a visit with him. Any lingering doubts that he might not be who Rita said he was dissolved as I stood before his wheelchair and offered my hand. His smile was vacant, but his eyes were the same color as the ones staring back at me in the mirror each morning. Alzheimer's has claimed him, but I like to think there was a part of him that recognized me when Rita introduced us. As the warmth of his touch curled around my hand and settled in my heart, it felt like a piece of me had finally been returned and that I was whole again.

I visited with them at the nursing home for nearly two hours. I chatted with Rita and held my father's hand. At different moments as the conversation lagged, I found myself pondering what it would have been like if we'd had the chance to know each other. But *what-if* is a dangerous game, and there's no sense in bemoaning what can never be. The past is done and over, and for today, I'm grateful we have found each other. And I know I'll return to Detroit, even if it's only to sit by his side, hold his hand, and see him smile again. That smile made it all worthwhile.

It's been a lonely year without Tori. She made the decision at the end of the summer to stay in Las Vegas and finish out her senior year of high school. All of us took up nearly a row near the front of the packed auditorium as she graduated last month, magna cum laude. College is in her future, but she won't be attending one of the prestigious schools out East that I used to hope she would choose. Tori has been accepted into the Honors Program at UNLV. When the fall semester starts, she'll be working toward a degree in business and marketing with an emphasis on hospitality. Just as Mimi always planned, someday the Royal Wedding Chapel will belong to Tori. It's not something I would have ever wished or hoped for my daughter, but it's what Tori wants and I've made my peace with it. All of us have to choose our own path, and who am I to stand in her way? Tori is eighteen now. She's an adult and it's her life. All I can do is love her, support her, and hope she makes wise decisions.

At least I don't need to worry about her being lonesome or unsupervised. She has Jack around to keep an eye on her. After Ed married Mimi and moved into the villa, Tori moved into Jack's penthouse apartment. Father and daughter keep each other company. I stay with them whenever I'm in town. I'm flying in this weekend, at Jack's request, to interview new housekeepers. Their current one isn't very thorough. The last time I spent the night, I spied a fine layer of dust on the lampshade on my side of the bed before Jack snapped off the light.

As for me, I'm back again in San Diego and back at work. But with the word *retirement* now a part of Walt's daily vocabulary, I'm not sure I want to stay. Once upon a time, I believed his crown of succession would pass to me. And while the company seems to be grooming me for that scenario, I'm not sure I wish to inherit the throne. With Tori gone, San Diego no longer feels like home. While I still love the town, my house, and the ocean, I'm coming to realize that I love something—and someone—else a whole lot more.

Jack flies in regularly. He's waging a fierce battle to convince me to make the permanent move back to Nevada. I never dreamed I would ever consider returning to the city of a million lights and noisy slot machines, that I would seriously consider helping Tori run the chapel, or that I would someday eventually end up with Jack. But I've discovered that life has a funny way of surprising you. In the end, it's not about where you live or what you do or how much money you have. It's about being with the people you love. Safeguarding their happiness and sharing your own joy with them. That's the thing that truly counts. The longer I stay in San Diego, the more my heart tells me I'm in the wrong place.

I think I know where I belong.

Just like The Royal Tiara. It still remains where Tori placed it that night, safe behind bulletproof glass, nestled on the velvet pillow where it has reposed for nearly forty years. Brides entering the doors of the Royal Wedding Chapel still stop to admire. They ooh and ahhh, assuming that every glittering jewel is genuine, that the tiara is priceless. And they're right. It is priceless to those of us who know the secrets behind the glittering royal diadem.

Of a cold, lonely graveyard across the ocean. Of a wild, fiery night filled with mayhem and murder. Of a man with a vacant smile and eyes so like my own. Sins and secrets hidden for years. Sins and secrets that threatened to destroy us all. Sins and secrets finally exposed to the light of day. Yet our family survived, thanks to Mimi's sacrifice, Francesca's loyalty, Ed's love, Jack's fidelity, and Tori's passion. We are the stronger for it, and I can't imagine a better ending.

Sometimes, happily ever after really does come true.

About The Author

KATHLEEN IRENE PATERKA IS THE author of numerous novels which embrace universal themes of home, family life and love, including the acclaimed Women's Fiction series '*The James Bay Novels*': **Fatty Patty**, **Home Fires**, **Lotto Lucy**, and **For I Have Sinned.** Kathleen, an avid royal watcher, is the resident staff writer for Castle Farms, a world renowned castle listed on the National Historic Register, and co-author of the non-fiction book *For The Love of a Castle*. Having lived and studied abroad, Kathleen's educational background includes a Bachelor of Arts degree from Central Michigan University. She and her husband Steve live in the beautiful north country of Michigan's Lower Peninsula. Kathleen loves hearing from readers.

Visit her website at
http://www.kathleenirenepaterka.com
or follow her on Facebook at
http://www.facebook.com/KathleenIrenePaterka.

www.ingramcontent.com/pod-product-compliance
Lightning Source LLC
Chambersburg PA
CBHW050013180626
46810CB00002B/398